"I WANT TO KISS YOU, IVORY KEENE." CURRY SAID QUIETLY.

✚

"I shouldn't try, and you shouldn't let me."

"If you say so," she replied. "But it will be a great loss if you don't."

His chest rose and fell heavily. With his fingers he traced her lower lip. Some things were inevitable, he thought as his lips parted and pushed down on hers.

She tasted of rose petals. Her mouth was faintly tremulous, hesitant, unsure of itself.

Her body brushed against his and she shivered as his deep, soft laughter became husky.

"You're dangerous," she accused.

"Yes. I am."

✚

ALL THAT GLITTERS

✚

"Exciting, sensual, fast-paced . . . Susan Kyle at her best."
      —Jayne Ann Krentz on *Escapade*

Books by Susan Kyle

AFTER MIDNIGHT
ESCAPADE
NIGHT FEVER
TRUE COLORS
ALL THAT GLITTERS

Published by
WARNER BOOKS

ATTENTION: SCHOOLS AND CORPORATIONS

WARNER books are available at quantity discounts with bulk purchase for educational, business, or sales promotional use. For information, please write to: SPECIAL SALES DEPARTMENT, WARNER BOOKS, 1271 AVENUE OF THE AMERICAS, NEW YORK, N.Y. 10020

ARE THERE WARNER BOOKS
YOU WANT BUT CANNOT FIND IN YOUR LOCAL STORES?

You can get any WARNER BOOKS title in print. Simply send title and retail price, plus 95¢ per order and 95¢ per copy to cover mailing and handling costs for each book desired. New York State and California residents add applicable sales tax. Enclose check or money order only, no cash please, to: WARNER BOOKS, P.O. BOX 690, NEW YORK, N.Y. 10019

SUSAN KYLE
ALL THAT GLITTERS

WARNER BOOKS

A Time Warner Company

WARNER BOOKS EDITION

Cover design by Diane Luger
Cover photograph by Franco Accanero
Hand lettering by Carl Dellacroce

Warner Books, Inc.
1271 Avenue of the Americas
New York, NY 10020

Ⓦ A Time Warner Company

Printed in the United States of America

First Printing: May, 1995

10 9 8 7 6 5 4 3 2 1

PROLOGUE

THE bright Texas sun was hot on Ivory Keene's short, wavy blond hair. She'd only just had it cut. Its natural wave gave it golden highlights, adding to the soft radiance of her oval face with its creamy complexion and faintly tormented warm gray eyes.

Her youth made the woman standing on the porch, watching her, feel her age even more. It added to Marlene's resentment toward her only child. She took an impatient draw from her cigarette with her too-red lips, wrinkled a little around the edges from years of smoking. She used concealers, but they were cheap and didn't work. If Ivory had taken the modeling job Marlene had tried to push her into, she would have had money for expensive cosmetics. She'd coaxed and demanded and cried, but for once, she hadn't been able to move the silly girl. Instead Ivory had managed to get a scholarship to a fashion design school in Houston and now she was determined to go there.

"You've been out of high school for two years. You'll be older than most of the other students," Marlene argued from the porch, still hoping to keep Ivory from leaving. "Besides, you don't even know how to set a proper table or get along in polite society," she added meanly.

"I'll learn those things," Ivory replied in her quiet drawl. "I'm not stupid."

I'll have to learn everything you never taught me, Ivory thought as she stood in front of the house, watching for the neighbor who was giving her a lift to the bus station. Her mother had never been sober long enough to teach her much except how to fetch glasses and bottles and wait on her boyfriends. She felt a chill, even in the hot sun. Come on, she called silently to her neighbor, please come on, before she finds some way to stop me!

"You don't even own a decent dress," her mother scoffed. She herself was wearing a nice dress, a present from her last boyfriend. Ivory's was a homemade cotton one, an original design and nicely made, if cheap. The girl could sew, all right, but one needed more than a little talent to become a famous designer. It amused Marlene that Ivory thought she had the brains or the personality for such a career. Now, Marlene knew she could have done it herself when she was younger. Except that she'd never learned to sew, and she didn't want to spend every waking hour working.

Ivory's slender hands clenched the old suitcase. "I'll get a job. I know how to work," she added pointedly.

Her mother had always made sure that Ivory had had jobs since she had been old enough to be employed.

The sarcasm didn't faze Marlene, though. It was early morning, but she had already had her first drink of the day. She was moderately pleasant, for the moment. "Don't forget to send me some of your salary," she reminded Ivory. "You wouldn't want me to tell all the neighbors how you walked out and left me to starve, would you?"

Ivory wanted to ask her mother if she could possibly do any more damage to her reputation in the community than Marlene had already done, but there was no point in starting an argument now. She was so close to freedom that she could almost taste it!

"You'll be back," Marlene added smugly and took another puff on the cigarette. "Without me, you'll fall flat on your face."

Ivory gritted her teeth. She would not reply. She was twenty. She'd managed to finish high school in spite of having to work and in spite of her alcoholic mother. She'd tried to understand why Marlene was the way she was; she'd tried to encourage her mother to get help with her drinking problem. All her efforts had failed. There had been one or two incidents that would be hard to forgive, much less forget. In the end, she'd taken the advice of the family doctor. You can't help someone who doesn't think she has a problem, he told her. Get out, he said, before she destroys you, too. Ivory hadn't wanted to desert the only relative she had in the world.

On the other hand, her mother was more than she could handle. She had to leave while she still could. If she could manage to get through design school, her talent might help her rise above the poverty she'd endured all her life.

She looked down the road and thought back to her school days, to the children who had laughed at the way she lived, made fun of her clothes and her ramshackle house and her poor, sharecropper father's illiterate drawl. They had all heard that her mother had been forced to marry Ivory's father because she'd gotten pregnant when she was just fourteen, and that knowledge had damaged her own reputation in the community. Marlene had boyfriends, too. A little while after Ivory's father died, her mother had taken up with one of her lovers, the town's richest citizen, and painted her child as an immoral, ungrateful thief. Marlene had gained some respect because of her lover's financial power; but even so, little Ivory was never invited to other children's parties. She was the outsider. Always, it seemed, people here had laughed about her, gossiped about her. But she was young and strong. She had one chance to escape all of it and make a fresh start somewhere she wasn't known. She was going to take it.

"You'll be back," Marlene said again, with cruel satisfaction, as a car appeared on the horizon.

Ivory's heart leaped. Her hands were sweaty on the handle of the suitcase. She looked behind her at the dilapidated old house with its sagging porch and peeling paint, her mother in a fancy dress and high heels with too much makeup on her thin face and black color on her thin hair. Marlene had been pretty once, but now she looked like a caricature of her old self, and her blue eyes were glazed most of the time. Since her lover's death earlier in the year, she'd started to drink more heavily. The money he'd left her was running out, too. Soon, it would be gone and she'd want someone to support her, namely, her daughter.

Ivory was going to escape, though. She was going to get away from the smothering dependence of her mother and the contemptuous attitude of her community at last! She was going to make a name for herself. Then, one day, she'd come back here dressed in furs and glittering with diamonds, and then the people who'd made fun of her would see that she wasn't worthless!

The late-model Ford stopped at the front gate, raising a cloud of dust on the farm road. Their neighbor, a middle-aged man in a suit, leaned across and pushed the door open.

"Hop in, girl, I'm late for my flight already," he said kindly.

"Hello, Bartley," Marlene said sweetly, leaning in the window after Ivory had closed the door. "My, don't you look handsome today!"

Bartley smiled at her. "Hello, honey. You look pretty good yourself."

"Come over for a drink when you have a minute,"

she invited. "I'm going to be all alone now that my daughter's deserting me."

"Mother," Ivory protested miserably.

"She thinks she wants to be a fashion designer. It doesn't bother her in the least to leave me out here all alone with nobody to look after me if I get sick," Marlene said on a sigh.

"You have the Blakes and the Harrises," Ivory reminded her, "just up the road. And you're perfectly healthy."

"She likes to think so," Marlene told Bartley. "Children can be so ungrateful. Now you be sure to write, Ivory, and do try to stay out of trouble, because other people won't be as understanding as I am about . . . well, about money disappearing."

Ivory went red in the face. She'd never been in trouble, but her mother had most of the local people convinced that her daughter stole from her and attacked her. Ivory had never been able to contradict her successfully, because Marlene had a way of laughing and agreeing with her while her eyes made a lie of everything she said. At least she'd get a chance to start over in Houston.

"I don't steal, mother," Ivory declared tensely.

Marlene smiled sweetly at Bartley and rolled her eyes. "Of course you don't, darling!"

"We'd better go," Bartley said, uncomfortably restraining himself from checking to make sure his wallet was still in his hip pocket. "See you soon, Marlene."

"You do that, Bartley, honey," she drawled. She patted Ivory's arm. "Be good, dear."

Ivory didn't say a word. Her mouth was tightly closed as the car pulled away. Her last sight of her mother was bittersweet, as she thought of all the pain and humiliation she'd suffered and how different everything could have been if her mother had wanted a child in the first place.

Houston might not be perfect, but it would give Ivory a chance at a career and a brighter future. Her mother wouldn't be there to criticize and demean her. She would assume a life of class and style that would make her forget that she'd ever lived in Harmony, Texas. Once she made her way to the top, she thought, she'd never have to look back again.

CHAPTER
ONE

THE November air was brisk and cold. The stark streetlights of the Queens neighborhood wore halos of frosty mist. The young woman, warm in her faded tweed overcoat and a white beret, sat huddled beside a small boy on the narrow steps of an apartment house that had been converted into a shelter for the homeless. She looked past the dingy faces of the buildings and the oil-stained streets. Her soft gray eyes were on the stars she couldn't see. One day, she promised herself, she was going to reach right up through the hopelessness and grab one for herself. In fact, she was already on the way there. She'd won a national contest during her last month of design school in Houston, and first prize was a job with Kells-Meredith, Incorporated, a big clothing firm in New York City.

"What you thinking about, Ivory?"

She glanced down at the small, dark figure sitting at her side. His curly brown hair was barely visible under a moth-eaten gray stocking cap. His jacket was shabbier than her tweed coat and his shoes were stuffed with cardboard to cover the holes in the soles. A tooth was missing where his father had hit him in a drunken rage a year or so before the family had lost their apartment. It was a permanent tooth, and it wouldn't grow back. But there was no money for cosmetic dentistry. There wasn't even enough money to fill a cavity.

"I'm thinking about a nice, warm room, Tim," she said. She slid an affectionate arm around him and hugged him close for warmth. "Plenty of good food to eat. A car to drive. A new coat . . . a jacket for you," she teased, and hugged him closer.

"Aw, Ivory, I don't need a coat. This one's fine!" His black eyes twinkled as he smiled up at her.

She remembered that smile from her first day as a volunteer at the homeless shelter, because Tim had been the first person she'd seen when she came with her friend Dee, who already worked there. Ivory had not been eager to offer her services at first, because the place brought back memories of the poverty she'd endured as a child in rural Texas. But her prejudice hadn't lasted long. When she saw the people who were staying at the shelter, her compassion for them overcame her own bitterness.

Tim had been sitting on these same steps that first day. He and his mother had been staying at the homeless shelter along with his two sisters. It was a cold day and he wore only a torn jersey jacket. Ivory had sat down and talked with him while she waited for Dee. Afterward, when Dee had asked casually if Ivory would like to volunteer a day a week to work there with her, she had agreed. Now, she almost always found Tim waiting for her when she came on Saturdays. Sometimes she brought him candy, sometimes she had a more useful present, such as a pair of mittens or a cap.

Tim's mother loved him and did all she could for him; but she also had a toddler and a nursing baby, and her situation, like that of so many, was all but hopeless. She had a low-paying job and the shelter did, at least, provide a home.

"I would like a room," Tim mused, interrupting her thoughts. He'd propped his face in his hands and was dreaming. "And a cat. They don't let us have cats at the shelter, you know, Ivory."

"Yes, I know."

"I made a new friend today," he said after a companionable silence had passed.

"Did you?"

"He stays at the shelter sometimes. His name's Jake." He sighed. "He used to be a bundle boy in a manufacturing company. What's a bundle boy, Ivory?"

"Someone who carries bundles of cut cloth to be sewn," she explained. She worked in the fashion sector. It wasn't the job she'd dreamed of, but it paid her way.

"Well, the place he worked closed down and they moved his job to Mexico," Tim told Ivory. "He can't get another job on account of he can't read and write. He shoots up."

Her arm around him tightened. "I hope you don't think that's cool," she said.

He shook his head. "I wouldn't do that. My mama says it's nasty and you can get AIDS from dirty needles." He glanced at her with a worried look that she didn't see. "Is that true, Ivory?"

"Hmm? Oh, AIDS from needles? Well, if you used a dirty needle, maybe. That's something you shouldn't have to worry about," she added firmly, thinking how sad it was that an eight-year-old should know so much of the bad side of life.

He sighed. "Ivory, this is a real bad time to be poor."

She smoothed a wrinkle in his cap and wished for the hundredth time that she could do more for Tim and his family. After paying the rent and utilities for her own apartment and sending money home to Marlene, there wasn't a lot left. Even though she was comfortable now, she remembered the hopelessness of being poor, with nothing to look forward to except more deprivation.

"There's never a good time to be poor, I'm afraid, but, listen, Mrs. Horst down the hall from me gave me a plate full of gingerbread and I brought some today. Would you like a slice of it, and some milk?"

Tim's face brightened. "Ivory, that would be nice!"

Kells-Meredith Incorporated was on Seventh Avenue in the garment district. It was an old business that Curry Kells, the newest mover and shaker in the New York financial world, had bought out and redesigned. Ivory had never seen him in person, but the senior design staff held him in awe. He didn't have much to do with the day-to-day working of the company, spending most of his day at his corporate office on Wall Street. He looked in occasionally, to see that everything was in working order; but since Ivory had been working for the company, she hadn't been around during his rare visits.

She wondered what it would be like to ride around in stretch limousines and eat at the finest hotel restaurants. She had worked hard to improve her speech and her table manners, but she hadn't had much chance to test her new social graces in high society. Her dreams of becoming an overnight sensation in the New York world of fashion had gone awry from the day she arrived in town fresh out of design school. Winning first place in the design contest had, indeed, secured her a job as a sketcher-assistant to a designer at Kells-Meredith. It was a far cry from the junior design position she'd hoped for. She knew that years of hard work were required for even the smallest promotion, but she'd dared to hope that she was talented enough to go right to the top.

The big designs, the ones that would be shown in seasonal fashion shows, however, were those of the top in-house designers. Ivory wasn't permitted to submit designs of her own because the senior designer, Miss Virginia Raines, felt she hadn't enough experience to think up usable ones. Ivory's job was to do freehand illustrations of Miss Raines's designs. She also accessorized outfits for fashion shows—such as the spring

showings that had just finished—and made appointments for Miss Raines. Because Ivory was only twenty-
two, Miss Raines considered her too young to make
contact with buyers and kept that chore for herself. Nor
was she receptive to suggestions from Ivory on any
designs, despite the fact that nothing new or particularly
original ever came from Miss Raines's mind.

Ivory was walking briskly to work one morning carrying a portfolio of drawings. She had some ideas for
the summer line that would be shown in January—if
only she could get Miss Raines to take a look at them.
Ever the optimist, she was cheerful even if she knew
her cause was probably hopeless.

She came to a halt in front of the church half a block
from Kells-Meredith. A man sat on the wide stone steps,
wrapped up in what appeared to be a fairly expensive
gray overcoat. He stared straight ahead at nothing with
his one good eye. The other was covered by a black
eye patch held in place by a band that cut across his
lean, handsome face. He looked like a film star, she
thought idly, with his wavy black hair and smooth olive
complexion and even features. He had nice hands, too.
They were clasped on his lap, the nails very flat, very
clean. On the right little finger was a ruby set in a thick,
oddly Gothic gold ring. A thin gold watch peeked out
from the spotless white cuff over his left wrist. His
black shoes had a polish that reflected the sheen of his
gray slacks. He was leaning forward, as if in pain; and
although people who walked by glanced curiously at

him, no one stopped. It was dangerous to stop and help anyone these days. People got killed trying.

Ivory looked at him indecisively, her portfolio of drawings clutched to the front of her buttoned old overcoat. Her jaunty white beret was tilted just a little to the right over her short, wavy golden blond hair. Her gray eyes studied him quietly, intently. She didn't want to intrude, but he looked as if he needed help.

She approached him slowly, dodging the onrush of people on their way to work, and stopped just in front of him.

He glanced up. His one eye was black as coal, and it glittered with anger and coldness. "What do you want?" he demanded.

The abruptness of the question caught her unawares. She hesitated. "Well . . ."

He sighed roughly, sizing up her lack of financial wherewithal in a cold scrutiny that took in her shabby coat with the spots she couldn't erase on the lapel, and her scuffed, old shoes with their worn heels. He dug in his pocket and handed her a five-dollar bill.

"Get yourself some breakfast," he said shortly. "You look like a starved kitten."

He got to his feet. She hadn't realized how big he was until then. His size was intimidating, but not as much so as the look he gave her.

"I didn't want anything," she said, trying to give back the money. "You looked as if you were in pain. I wanted to help . . ."

"Sure you did," he scoffed. He rammed his hands into the pockets of his overcoat and strode off down the sidewalk, muttering every step of the way.

Ivory smiled ironically. "Well, I guess that puts me in my place," she murmured to herself. "I really will have to get myself a new coat!" She pocketed the five-dollar bill; she could give it to Tim when she went to the shelter on Saturday.

When she saw the stranger go into the building where she worked, she hung back a little before she entered. She didn't want him to think she was following him!

Ivory worked on the first floor of a converted warehouse where seamstresses on an assembly line sewed sample garments. Pattern-makers, markers, and junior designers had small offices there; Miss Raines's office and those of the two other senior designers were carpeted and more luxurious. The executive offices—art, promotion, and production—were on the second floor. That was where the vice president and manager of this division, Harry Lambert, worked.

Adjoining the elegant room occupied by Miss Raines was Ivory's small cubbyhole. The space was cramped and furnished with cast-off pieces that had apparently been designed to depress the most optimistic of workers. One of the two straight chairs had a loose leg, and the desk had a rough finish marred by careless hands with sharp implements. The curtains were windowless; not that it mattered, because the view was of a rough red brick wall less than twenty feet away. At least Miss Raines had a view of the street outside. She never looked, though, because she said it depressed her. No doubt she hadn't paid much attention to the furniture in Ivory's office, or she'd have discovered real causes for depression!

Ivory had sorted out the accessories that she'd been told to match with the simple outfits for the upcoming summer fashion shows. She was trying to decide which of two scarves to pair with a nice silk suit when her door opened.

"Miss Keene," Miss Raines said formally, her cold eyes unblinking behind her stylish glasses, "why were these designs placed on my desk?" She waved the portfolio at Ivory.

Ivory paused with the scarves held before her like a shield. She hesitated, and then rushed ahead before her courage gave out. "I'd hoped you might like one of them," she began.

Miss Raines put the portfolio on Ivory's desk with the air of someone disposing of nasty garbage. "Hardly," she said. "As I've told you already, the other two senior designers and I make up our new lines each season. Junior designers may contribute, but not someone on your level. Perhaps when you've been here a few years, we might consider something of yours. However, you will have to prove yourself first."

Ivory wondered how she was going to prove anything by matching scarves and suits. She studied the older woman from her short hair and simply cut but very expensive mauve dress to her polished calf pumps. Miss Raines had never married, and the business was her life. Perhaps it was all she had, Ivory thought, trying to be kind.

"Kindly keep your . . . drawings . . . out of the way," Miss Raines added as she left, and Ivory's impulse to be kind vanished at once. "And do clean this place up," she added as an afterthought. "Mr. Kells is in the building."

The door closed firmly behind her. Ivory stared at it with resignation. She'd been here six months, and it felt like six years. Mr. Kells might be in the building, but she was hardly likely to get to see him. She'd had no contact with anyone except Miss Raines, Dee Grier, who was the head seamstress, the seamstresses who made reality of the mental creations of the designers, and the various salesmen who frequented the office. Mr. Kells had no reason to come here. There was no suggestion box. Wages were paid, frugally, every other week. Insurance was bare-bone. Holidays were, apparently, few and far between. Hard work was the order of the day.

Ivory toyed with the label of the silk scarf in one hand. Gucci. She wondered how it would feel to be able to walk into an exclusive department store and buy several of these. Even one was far beyond her means, and the outfits that carried the Kells-Meredith label, even in the casual line, were so expensive that the price of one leisure dress would pay Ivory's rent for a month.

She put the scarf down and opened the portfolio. She'd designed a collection based on sixteenth-century Tudor costumes, having become intrigued with them when she'd first seen them in her local library back home. Her adaptations had a definition that was like a signature, and everyone she'd shown them to had exclaimed over them. Everyone, that is, except Miss Raines, who had the power to bring them to the attention of those in charge of the company's lines. She released a long sigh over her favorite, a heavily embroidered gown with mutton-leg sleeves and a square neckline. Ideally, it would be done in silk for summer and a heavier fabric, perhaps satin, for winter evening wear. The long sleeves might be too hot for summer. But, then, nearly every building was air-conditioned now and silk was so summery.

She closed the portfolio reluctantly and picked up the scarf again, only to be interrupted by Miss Raines, who asked her to take three sample gowns to the showroom where models were doing a special showing for some society matrons. Ivory did as she was told, and in her absence Mr. Kells walked through the sample room. He stayed only briefly and left before Ivory returned.

"I told you to clean this mess up," Miss Raines said impatiently when Ivory entered the room. "Let me tell you, Mr. Kells wasn't impressed. He said that even a sketcher-assistant should have more to do than pile accessories on desks. I agreed with him that you have too much free time, even with my work, so I'm going to let you do alterations as well. You sew of course?''

It was like a sudden demotion. Ivory felt sick to her stomach. ''Well, yes, but . . .''

''Then we'll get you started first thing tomorrow,'' she said. ''The regular girls have too much contract work to stop for repairs. This will work out nicely. Mr. Kells thought it would.''

''Miss Raines, I came here to do design work,'' Ivory began.

''Yes, yes, and you will, one day,'' she was promised indulgently. ''But we must crawl before we can walk, Miss Keene.''

Ivory sat down at her desk with an expression of pure anguish. If she had to do repairs as well as accessories and illustrations, she was never going to have time to work on her own designs. But what was the use, anyway? Miss Raines was doing everything in her power, apparently, to make sure that Ivory didn't have any successes. And so was the elusive Mr. Kells.

Miss Raines had admitted to Ivory early on that she had disagreed with Mr. Kells's decision to offer a job as a first prize in a nationwide design contest. It had all been a stunt, a promotion, to bring a fading design house back into the limelight. Ivory felt cheated. She'd expected more, somehow, from the description of the prize when it was given to her at graduation.

''You'll have a dream job in New York at Kells-

Meredith,'' Mr. Wallace, the president of the school, had assured her after the award was presented at the school's graduation exercises. ''And a nice apartment, rent-free for the first month until you start drawing your salary!''

''I'm very honored that I won,'' Ivory had told him.

''And so are we, young lady. It's a feather in our cap to have one of our graduating seniors do so well.'' He'd looked around curiously, because Ivory had come to the awards ceremony alone. ''Didn't your, uh, family care to come tonight, to see you get your design diploma?''

She hadn't blinked an eye. ''My mother is ill and couldn't make the trip,'' she had lied. ''My father died years ago.''

''You're an only child, then?''

She'd studied her feet. ''Yes.''

''Sad for you, especially at holidays, I guess.''

She'd composed her face and looked up. ''The job . . . how soon will I start?''

''As soon as you like,'' he'd said, beaming. ''Next week?''

''That would be fine,'' she had assured him.

The dream job was less than dreamy, and the promised apartment too expensive for her to keep on her salary. Her present flat, while clean and comfortable, was hardly a penthouse. It was in a nice part of Queens, though, and not too long a bus ride from work. There was a kitchenette, a living room, and a small bedroom with a double bed. It was a furnished apartment, but Ivory didn't really like the faded yellow-flowered sofa. With one of her first purchases, a sewing machine, she'd made slipcovers for the sofa and chair and a tablecloth for the small round table.

Ivory had scraped together enough moderately priced dinnerware and silverware to use, and she now had a small, refinished coffee table. It was the best accommodation she'd had in her twenty-two years. Someday, she'd promised herself as she looked around her living room, she would have new wall-to-wall carpeting.

Even if the apartment was less than elegant, the neighbors were something special. Mrs. Horst was an elderly German widow who had immigrated to the United States just before World War II. She made wonderful breads and cakes and liked making them for Ivory, whom she considered delightful company. Two doors down from Mrs. Horst lived Mr. Konieczny from Wisconsin, who worked as a bank clerk and had a small poodle for company. Mr. and Mrs. Johnson occupied a third apartment. He was a World War II veteran who had to get around in a wheelchair. He had lost his legs at Guadalcanal, but he was cheerful and liked to make wooden toys for the three small children who lived on the same floor down the hall with their parents.

It would have been nice to have a handsome young bachelor in the building, Ivory had mused wistfully, but she liked her neighbors very well.

A tap on the door interrupted her thoughts. Dee Grier stuck her blond head in and grinned. "Did you catch hell, too?" Ivory, disconcerted, just stared at the head seamstress.

"Mr. Kells," Dee explained. "He came. He saw. He grumbled for fifteen minutes. Everybody caught hell. Miss Raines was almost on her knees trying to placate him."

"Did you . . . ?"

"I hid out in the bathroom," Dee chuckled. "But I heard him. What a temper! Apparently, we're sluggish, uninspired, and hopelessly strait-laced. Our clothes are being passed over for fresh designs by new designers. Miss Raines actually sputtered trying to think up excuses."

"It isn't my fault," Ivory pointed out. "I have some designs, new and original, that Miss Raines won't even consider."

Dee recognized the hurt in the younger woman's voice and smiled reassuringly. "Cream always rises to the top," she said. "Don't give up."

"She says it will take years," Ivory groaned.

"If she has her way, it will. She knows talent when she sees it. She's afraid of you, so she'll hold you back if she can. Go over her head," Dee advised. "Take your sketches to Kells himself."

Ivory's eyes widened. "She'd fire me."

"Not if he likes your work."

"All or nothing, huh?" Ivory murmured.

Dee nodded. "No great risk, no great reward, and something about 'daring greatly.'" She frowned. "Who said that? I can't remember."

"Helen Keller and Teddy Roosevelt, I think, but not at the same time."

"Well?"

Ivory sat down. "I'm not brave enough yet," she said with a rueful smile. "I have a job and an apartment and Christmas is next month."

Dee laughed. "Okay. How about in the spring?"

"Good enough. The homeless shelter should be pretty warm by then."

"You idiot. A woman of your talents won't have to go on the streets."

"I can name you three people who felt that way, and they ended up there," Ivory said solemnly. "You ought to remember, too, because you introduced them to me at the shelter. Two of them had five-figure salaries and the third worked in real estate. They went from Lincolns to park benches in a few weeks."

Dee shuddered. "It's scary."

"Scary, indeed," came the reply. "What does Mr. Kells look like, do you know?" she asked Dee curiously.

"I caught only a glimpse of him. He's tall and visually challenged. I'll ask around, if you're really curious."

Visually challenged. Did Dee mean that he wore glasses? Probably. "I just wondered if he was old and set in his ways or young enough to entertain new ideas," she replied.

Dee fingered her collar. "He took over the company months ago, just before you came, and he hasn't fired Miss Raines yet," she said firmly. "What does that tell you?"

"That he admires loyalty to the company and that he doesn't like change, even though he would like to see some originality."

"Bingo."

"Then why did you suggest that I take him my designs?"

"Because you're talented. And I think any man brave enough to take on a failing design firm is brave enough to stick out his neck for something different." Dee added a remark about a two-man team of Italian designers who'd just burst onto the fashion scene with some romantic Spanish-inspired designs that were selling like hotcakes. "Who'd have backed them last year when women's suits looked like those communist Chinese uniforms?"

"They did not!" Ivory protested.

"Plain straight-skirted suits with scooped-neck blouses of various colors, and no trim. Yuck! I wouldn't be caught dead in one!"

"Beats miniskirts."

Dee reluctantly agreed. "Especially with my legs . . ."

"Miss Grier!" a strident voice called. "You are not paid to converse with other employees!"

"Yes ma'am, Miss Raines, I was just asking Miss Keene if she wanted to have lunch with me at the new

Japanese sushi place." She smiled sweetly. "You could come, too, if you like."

"I never eat fish, especially raw fish. God alone knows what pollutants are in the water where they're caught." She kept walking, her back like a poker.

Dee's face reddened as she tried not to laugh. She looked at Ivory, and it was fatal. Mirth burst the restraints, to be quickly disguised as coughing.

Ivory watched her retreat and turned back to her own work before Miss Raines had time to notice that she wasn't doing what she'd been told. Would it be worth a trip to Mr. Kells's office to show him those designs? Or would she lose her job? If only she weren't so afraid of being out of work.

But she was. A homeless shelter was a poor accommodation in November, when snow flurries had already come calling, along with sub-freezing temperatures. No, she decided. It might be better to wait just a little longer before she risked everything on such a gamble. Besides, Dee's description of Mr. Kells as visually challenged niggled at the back of her mind. What if she meant that he only had one eye? It would be just her luck to walk into his office and discover that he was the same ill-tempered, despondent man who'd mistaken her for a beggar and handed her a five-dollar bill for a meal!

CHAPTER
TWO

ON Saturday morning Ivory set out for the homeless shelter, where she was to meet Dee and work for a few hours. The volunteer work kept her mind off her own problems and gave her something to do with her free time.

There was a small corner grocery store near the shelter. She stopped there just as Mr. Galloway, the tall, elderly owner, opened up behind the strong iron bars that protected his shop from vandals.

"Good morning!" she greeted in her now accentless voice. "I thought I might take the children at the shelter some fruit."

"Got in some fresh oranges yesterday," he said, smiling at her over his narrow glasses as he indicated them. "Nice and sweet."

"Just the thing," she said, and picked out a handful. "When I become very rich, I'll come back and buy several cases for all my friends."

He chuckled at the mischief in her face. "I believe you." He handed her an orange with a flourish. "Compliments of the management."

"Thanks! I wish I had something to give you," she said wistfully. He really was an old dear, so kind to everyone who patronized his store. An idea lit her face. "I could design you an apron," she offered.

He looked down at his ample girth. "Better make it a tent."

Her eyes narrowed in thought. "Just you wait," she promised, measuring him with her gaze. She was good at estimating sizes. "Come Christmas, you'll be the smartest-looking grocer around."

"Nothing fancy," he cautioned. "I cut meat in the back."

"I know." She picked up her bag and put the change he handed her from a five-dollar bill into her purse.

"Be careful going down the street," he added. "We've got some roughnecks around here lately."

"I know. Tim told me."

He knew Tim. Most everyone in the neighborhood did. "Pity about him, isn't it?"

She nodded. "All children should have someplace to live . . ."

"No, I mean about what he's got."

Her hand stilled on her purse. "What has he got?" she queried. "He was cheerful and laughing the last time I saw him."

"He didn't find out until today. His mama came in

about an hour ago for some formula for the baby. She told me.'' He grimaced. ''Social services ran some tests last week on a few kids at the shelter, including Tim. Got the results this morning. He's HIV-positive. She said she'd have to tell him. Poor woman. She was scared.''

She caught her breath painfully. ''No wonder! But he's just eight years old.''

''Some babies are born with it,'' he reminded her. ''But his mama doesn't shoot up. In Tim's case, they think it was a contaminated needle . . .''

''Tim doesn't shoot up!'' she exclaimed.

''I know that. But he has a friend who does.''

Ivory recalled with disquiet the conversation she'd had with Tim and his question about contaminated needles, and her vague reply. Oh, the poor little boy! ''He told me about his friend. I wasn't listening,'' she said miserably.

''He told his mama that he picked up one of the syringes, you know, just out of curiosity, and accidentally stuck himself with it.''

''And that was all it took?!''

He nodded. ''Hell of a disease, ain't it? Kids getting it, that's the worst. Kids are the very last people who should get such a terrible thing.''

''If he's only HIV-positive, he hasn't necessarily got AIDS,'' she said stubbornly. ''Tim's very young and they're coming up with new treatments all the time. All the time!''

He smiled gently. "Sure."

She shifted the bag to her other hand. She felt empty inside. She started to go and hesitated. "You won't tell anyone else about Tim? Some people get funny when they know."

"I haven't told anyone else." He shrugged. "I knew you wouldn't treat him like a leper, or I wouldn't have told you, either."

She smiled. "Thanks, Mr. Galloway."

"For what? I like Tim. He's special."

She heard the metallic sound of the bars being slid into place behind her and spared a thought for Mr. Galloway, who'd been robbed twice and burned out once. Gangs seemed to target small businesses these days. It was a pity that anyone would want to hurt a kind man who went out of his way to help anyone in trouble.

She walked toward the shelter despondently and hesitated at the foot of the steps, looking around. Tim was nowhere in sight. He was usually waiting for her when she came, and she'd told him that there would be some of Mrs. Horst's gingerbread left over for him today. She'd tucked a slice, wrapped in plastic, in her purse for him. Had his mother made him stop coming? Unlikely. She was too busy trying to take care of a baby and the toddler to watch him all the time. If she had told him about his disease, maybe he thought Ivory might not want him around anymore. But Tim knew Ivory. Surely he wouldn't think it would make her avoid him.

She secured the bag of oranges under her arm at the entrance of the shelter and opened the door. It was a sad sight, all those rows of cots and hopeless people who had no place to go. Some of them were mentally handicapped, some were addicts. But most were just victims of circumstance with no education and no jobs.

Dee hadn't arrived yet, but it didn't take long to spot Tim and his family. She made her way through the clutter, past small colonies of Hispanics and other whites of all ethnic backgrounds, over to the side where groups of blacks huddled together. Some were Haitian, some Jamaican, some African.

Tim's mother was originally from Zaire. She had a nobility of carriage that Ivory had always envied. She was an elegant woman for someone in her circumstances, and she had a pair of hands that could handle the most delicately detailed work. She crocheted lace. She could even tat. Her handiwork fascinated Ivory, who could sew but not crochet.

Ivory smiled. "Hello. I wondered why Tim hadn't come to meet me."

"Ah," was the soft response.

Tim smiled and waved at her, but he didn't come close. His dark eyes were hesitant, uncertain.

Ivory stuck her hands in her pockets and made a face at him. "I know. Mr. Galloway told me. You silly boy, do you think it matters to me? Friends don't turn away from each other, do they?"

Tim shrugged and looked at his feet.

"Listen, wouldn't you still be my friend, if I had it instead of you?" she persisted.

He looked up at her. "Sure, Ivory!"

She smiled. "Enough said?"

He smiled back. "Okay."

Ivory looked at his mother, who seemed to relax. She shifted a sleeping baby girl in her arms.

"Here," she said, handing him the gingerbread and the bag of oranges. "Those are for you and your friends. You can't desert me," Ivory told Tim gently. "Okay?"

He nodded. "Okay, Ivory."

His mother, Miriam, lifted her face proudly. "There is a risk." In the older woman's eyes were the pain and resignation of years; there, too, was the pride that had made it all bearable.

Ivory nodded. "There is a risk in living at all," she said. And she allowed the other woman to catch just a glimpse of the pain and humiliation in her own past. "And I know all about judgmental people. Probably almost as much as you do."

Miriam managed a tired smile. The baby cried, and she rocked her, while the toddler, another girl, napped on the cot nearby. "Tim stuck himself with a bad needle." She took a deep breath and let it out. "God in heaven, he only stuck himself." She glanced around her with world-weary eyes. "If these people knew, they would not want us here. There was a man from Haiti who had the virus. He was beaten and his things were stolen. He had to leave to save his life." For an instant there was fear in her face. "The children are very small . . ."

Ivory never touched people. Only rarely did she put an arm even around Tim. But now she put her arm around Miriam. "You're a strong woman," she told her. "You can do what needs doing. And no one will know unless you tell them."

Miriam met her eyes. "It was there, for just an instant."

"What?"

"An accent," Miriam said. "A way of speaking. You are not from here."

"The accent comes out only when I forget." She forced a smile as she removed her arm.

"And now you go away, here." She touched Ivory's forehead. "There is no need. We understand each other, you and I." Her eyes sparkled with pride. "You know, I am the granddaughter of a chieftain in my country, not the beggar I have become in yours. Let me tell you, if I had not dreamed of living in a big city and having pretty clothes and if I had not followed my dreams to America, I would not be in this shameful condition."

"But you would not have Tim, either, or these two," Ivory reminded her with a smile.

"Ah, yes. That is so." And she smiled back.

Dee came later, and the two of them helped serve lunch and then clean up afterward. Ivory was waiting for Dee to join her late that afternoon on her way out, and she paused to wave at Tim and his family. A ragged old woman was putting a needle to a quilt she'd made of fragments of cloth that Ivory had brought her from the company—throwaways that the janitor had given her.

"What do you think, Ivory?" the old lady asked with twinkling eyes as she held up the latest circle she'd completed of the Dresden Plate design.

"Beautiful, Mrs. Payne," she said, running her fingers over it.

"This is my fourth. Perhaps nobody will steal it," she said with resignation, looking around. "That's the terrible thing about having no locks, dearie. Even honest people will take something when they're desperate."

"If you could sell one of these . . ." Ivory began.

Mrs. Payne smiled wistfully. "The extra money would mean a cut in my Social Security, you know. They cut your check if you make extra money."

Ivory, blissfully ignorant of the endless red tape of Social Security, patted her awkwardly on the shoulder and murmured a good-bye.

Dee got off at her stop and Ivory continued on to her neighborhood. When the bus stopped, she huddled deeper into her coat as she started back down the sidewalk toward home, noting the cracks in the pavement and the chalk marks where children had been playing hopscotch. A little farther down there were chalk marks of another sort. There was a dark red stain where the head would have lain, a reminder of the turbulence of the city and the brevity of life.

Voices called deep in an alley. She quickened her pace, almost running when she reached her apartment building. It might be wise not to show fear, but it was stupid to pretend walking alone at night wasn't danger- ous, even in a good neighborhood like this one.

She had her key out when she reached the top step. She inserted it deftly, dashed inside, and locked it back. Looking out the window, she saw three big, older boys on the sidewalk glance up toward her front door. The one who seemed to be the leader said something and then laughed. He shrugged, as if he didn't think it worth the effort to pursue her. They walked down the street, laughing raucously, talking loudly.

The leader had a pistol in his hand. He was showing it to the others. Ivory watched in resigned disgust. Tim had told her that any kid on the block could buy a gun if he had the money, and even his parents wouldn't know he had it. Used guns were the real problem in social violence. The great unregulated, steady stream of guns obtained in pawn shops and back alleys made up the arsenal of the street gangs. And the gangs could be found in cities a lot smaller than New York. So could the guns.

She went slowly upstairs to her apartment and fixed herself a meager supper of a ham sandwich and some yogurt, washed down with a cup of coffee.

Somewhere, a loud voice yelled and a shriller voice

answered. A baby was crying. Outside on the street, a car backfired—or was it a firecracker, or a pistol shot? Ivory turned on her radio and found some elevator music. Then she picked up her sketch pad and charcoal pencils and went to work on more designs that no one would ever see.

The designers were working feverishly to get ready for the showing of the spring and summer lines that would take place after the first of January. Ivory watched the seamstresses become more harried by the day as they tried to cope with changes and more changes. The pattern-makers threw up their hands and threatened to quit. Dee had said it was the same with each new collection. What looked right on paper became a nightmare when it was translated into patterns and cloth. A pocket might mean so much extra work that it would make the garment too expensive to produce profitably. A few pleats might interfere with a smooth line. A kick-pleat in back might not be deep enough, or might be too deep for comfort. A neckline that looked elegant in a drawing might be nearly impossible to sew so that it would lie flat around a neck.

All the adjustments had to be made in the designs long before a garment was put into production. Even couture houses had to keep costs down in a slow economy. Every penny counted even in the production of an expensive garment. Rich people were like the poor, not willing to pay more than they must for a piece of clothing. Mr. Kells, they said, was a fanatic about fads and frills that added to production costs. One of the older designers had cried with frustration when one of her innovative dropped-shoulder designs was scrapped because it took too long to sew properly.

"Ah, the joys of high fashion," Dee chuckled as they ate lunch at their favorite Japanese restaurant. "Don't you just love it?"

"It isn't what I expected," Ivory replied. "I had such dreams." She laughed softly into her hot tea as she sipped it. "Well, we live and learn." She reached for the delicate little teapot.

"No!" Dee exclaimed, taking it away from her. "That isn't polite. Never, never pour your own tea. Pour someone else's, but not your own." She filled Ivory's cup.

"I'll remember next time."

The waiter brought them more sushi and Dee grinned at him warmly. *"Domo arigato gozaimasu,"* she said, nodding politely.

"Do itashimashite," he replied with equal politeness, and withdrew.

"You sound so sophisticated when you speak Japanese," Ivory remarked.

Dee shrugged, pushing back her pale blond hair. "I love languages. Japanese is wonderful; so precise and logical and uncluttered with homonyms. I could teach you."

"Not on your life. I can scarcely speak fluent English."

"They say Mr. Kells speaks three other languages besides English, all fluently. His mother is from some Spanish-speaking country, we've heard." She studied Ivory's head. "You do very well at Spanish, don't you?"

"I picked up a little because we had some Mexican . . . neighbors for a while."

"Where?"

Ivory looked briefly hunted. "Back home."

"And where is back home?" Dee pursued with a smile.

"Out west," Ivory said, and changed the subject as quickly as she could. "I meant to ask you something. Miss Raines says that we have to go to some party the first week of December for the brass, did you hear?"

"Yes. We're going to mingle with the models and the designers like real people."

"Stop that. It's supposed to be an honor."

"And Mr. Kells will be there."

"I'll wear my best ragged gown."

Dee shook her head. "You never look ragged."

"I will at the party," she said miserably. "If only I could afford some fabric!" she blurted out.

"I have some pretty Christmasy green Qiana you can have. It looks like silk to the uninitiated."

"There won't be any uninitiated people at that party."

Dee rested her chin on her hand. "Well, it's pretty material. You'll look great in it. Got a design in mind?"

Ivory nodded. "One of my own," she said doggedly.

"Since you're kind enough to supply the material, I'll run up something for you, too, if you like. I've got a nice sewing machine at my apartment."

Dee had arranged to rent an expensive gown. She didn't want to hurt Ivory's feelings, so she hesitated.

"Actually, though," Ivory added quickly, sensing the reluctant refusal, "it will take a lot of time to do *two* gowns . . ."

"I'm renting one, and I've already put a down-payment on it," Dee confessed. "But next time, I'd love for you to design something for me."

"Super. Maybe by then I'll have managed to pay you back for what you're advancing me!" Ivory laughed.

Dee studied her face and thought how flawless that complexion was, creamy pink and beautiful, with those big pale gray eyes framed by thick curly lashes. If Ivory let her hair grow long, she'd be a knockout. Even with her hair cut short, she was very attractive. And she had a willowy figure that wasn't too thin or too voluptuous but seemed to mold itself to any sort of clothing. She was what old-timers would call a clothes horse. She would have looked good in a potato sack.

"You have nice eyes," Dee said unexpectedly.

Ivory laughed. "I wish I had green eyes," she confessed. "Lucky you."

"Thanks. I was just thinking how pretty your gray ones are, and how your hair would look if you let it grow. Then you could wear one of those white Grecian things and wear your hair in rows of tight curls . . ."

"You should have been a designer," came the dry reply.

"I'll drink to that." Dee lifted her tea and sipped.

Designing the dress became a prime project for Ivory in the two weeks that followed. She threw away many of her sketches before she finally settled on an updated copy of a gown she'd seen in Tudor portraits of the mid-sixteenth century. It had a square neckline with lavish embroidery, and puffed sleeves tapering down to tight cuffs. She left the length as it would have been in that period, but cut it down to a form-fitting silhouette that stopped at her ankles. It was a striking concept, but it wasn't suited to slinky Qiana. It needed to be made of white satin and embroidered with colored thread. But how could she afford that sort of fabric when she was hardly able to buy groceries? She'd just have to make do with what Dee was willing to give her, she thought, and resigned herself to the fact.

At work one day she showed the drawings to Dee, who stared at them open-mouthed.

"Will it do?" Ivory asked her, uncertain even now.

"*Do*?! My God!"

"I thought I'd start cutting it out tomorrow. It's Saturday. If you don't have any other plans, . . ." she began.

"You can't use a limp fabric on this," Dee said.

"Yes, I can," she argued. "The embroidery will . . ."

"It will pucker," Dee said.

Ivory hesitated. Dee was right. A light fabric embroidered so heavily probably would pucker. Maybe she could cut down on the embroidery . . .''

"It needs to be white satin," Dee suggested.

"Well, yes, but you've already got the Qiana. I can't afford . . .''

"I certainly can." Dee held up a hand when she started to protest. "It won't be that expensive," she said shortly. "You can make me another, in a different color, and I'll pay you for it. That will cover the cost of materials for yours."

"You want me to make you one?!"

"Is there a parrot in your throat?" Dee chuckled. "Listen, you dolt, that's the most beautiful thing I've ever seen in my life. Of course I want one, and in satin. Everybody will want one when they see you in it. I think it would make a sensational wedding dress as well! As an evening gown it will be a knockout. I'm just getting my order in first. You're going to start a riot when you walk in!"

"Well, I liked it, but I never know if something's quite good enough or not."

"*This* is good enough. Is it ever!" Dee shook her head as she studied the drawing. Her fingers traced its lines lovingly. "It's breathtaking. Just breathtaking!" She put it down. "We'll buy fabric on our lunch hour. I know just the place to go."

"Dee, are you sure?" Ivory asked worriedly.

"I'm sure!"

Miss Raines walked by as Ivory was putting the working sketch back into her portfolio. She gave it a haughty glance.

"Overdone!" she pronounced. "You'll have to do better than that if you expect to get a promotion here," she added as she swept out of the room.

Ivory bit her lip and didn't reply, but she was seething inside. One day, she promised herself, she was going to prove to Virginia Raines that she had what it took to become a top designer.

The pattern was complicated, but not so difficult to make. Ivory had learned a number of skills in design school, and pattern-making was one of them. She knew how to adjust one, as well, to ensure a customized fit. She worked with the pattern until she had it exactly the way she wanted it before she ever spread it on the pure white satin.

Then, it was just a matter of careful cutting. She basted it together and was delighted with the end result. It was a dress worthy of royalty, and she felt justifiably proud of her efforts, Miss Raines's biting comment notwithstanding.

The embroidery took the longest. She had to design that, too, and then choose colored threads to stitch it. She was particularly fond of a delicate ivy and wildflower pattern she had seen in an illuminated Book of Hours. It took up most of her spare time after work and she only hoped that she would be able to finish it in time.

Tim watched her nimble fingers work on the embroidery the Saturday before the party, while he played on the bare floor of the shelter with the wooden toy Mr. Johnson had made for him. Ivory had carried the dress with her to work on because she had so little time left to finish it that she couldn't waste a minute. Right now, she was babysitting with Miriam's children while Miriam looked for a job again.

"That sure is pretty, Ivory," he remarked. "Takes a lot of time, huh?"

"A lot. But it's the kind of work I like to do," she said, smiling.

"I think I'd like to be a doctor when I grow up, Ivory." Tim confided. "I could help cure people. But I don't think I'll get to do that." He was as cynical as a boy twice his age. As he slid the small wooden truck across the floor, his silence was heavy with despair.

Ivory watched him as she worked, wondering sadly if he'd live long enough—or if she'd live long enough— to see any of his dreams come true.

"Ivory, do you have a mama?" he asked unexpectedly.

She pricked her finger and had to move it quickly, before any blood got on the white satin. She sucked it and then wrapped it in a piece of thin paper she'd used to make the pattern.

"Most everyone has a mama, Tim," she said after she'd recovered.

"I'm sorry I made you stick yourself," he replied. He sighed because being stuck had led to his big problem.

His great, dark eyes searched her face. "You don't like your mama, do you?"

She let her eyelids fall over her eyes to conceal the expression in them. She put down the embroidery and went to get some toilet tissue to stick to the pinprick, because it was still bleeding.

She looked up and saw Miriam coming toward them with a resigned face. She didn't have to ask if Tim's mama had found work. "I have to go now. Help your mama with the girls, okay?" she said gently.

He got up, toy and all. "You ain't mad at me, are you?"

She hugged him. "No, I'm not mad. Come on. Let's find Dee and you can walk out with me. I think I'll stop by Mr. Galloway's to get some adhesive bandages. I don't want to get bloodstains on this dress."

At all costs, her dress had to be perfect. She would be on display at the party. With any luck, Mr. Kells would be there and he might see it and remark on it. If he did, she might get her foot in the door. All she needed was a chance, and she'd be on her way to a glorious career. She just knew it.

CHAPTER
THREE

B ELLE Harris was one of the models for the January fashion shows. She was being fitted with one of Miss Raines's new designs, a sheath dress, and while that was being done, she looked over the accessories that Ivory had chosen to go with it.

Accustomed to Miss Raines's constant criticism of her choices, Ivory waited for the gloriously beautiful redhead to make a stinging remark of her own. But she didn't.

"Why, you have a wonderful eye for color," Belle remarked, her green eyes glowing as she watched Ivory adjust the patterned green scarf and gold belt that she'd paired with the simple gray silk sheath. She looked around to make sure Miss Raines wasn't eavesdropping. "Honestly, when I saw the sketch for this dress, I groaned. Virginia Raines has no imagination. None whatsoever. Why Curry keeps her on is beyond me. Perhaps it's because she's the age of his mother."

"Curry?" Ivory ventured, curious.

"Curry Kells, silly," Belle explained. "He owns a lot of companies around town, and he's super rich. He takes me out a lot. He's a real gentleman. No kinky stuff, no fighting him off at the end of the evening—although, just between us, I'd love the chance! He's good-looking and cultured, and he smells like a male cologne commercial. He always wears one of those sexy scents that make you want to purr."

"One of the girls said he was . . . visually challenged."

"How politically correct!" Belle said with a laugh. "He's got one eye, Ivory. He lost it in a gang fight in his teens."

"Oh!"

"Don't look so dismayed. The other boy lost his freedom. He killed one of Curry's friends and was arrested for it. But not until after Curry caught up with him."

"Gangs never seem to go out of style," Ivory remarked. "I've seen them, and they scare me."

"It seems every neighborhood has one." Belle looked in the mirror, frowned, then swept her hair up and pinned it. "There, doesn't that suit the dress better?"

"Yes, it does."

"I'll have the hairdresser do it that way for the show. How about shoes?"

"I had these covered . . ." She produced a pair of pumps covered in gold satin.

"Elegant!"

"Trashy!" Miss Raines harrumphed when she saw them. "Black pumps, Ivory, not those vulgar things. Not with my dress!"

Belle and Ivory exchanged resigned glances and Ivory replaced the pumps. Miss Raines had no tolerance for people who disagreed with her ideas. In her world everything was structured, measured, with no allowance for spontaneity. The sad thing was that everyone around her was expected to comply with her design sense. Ivory despaired of ever using her creative abilities under that stifling control.

Later, when she had a little time to herself, she mulled over what Belle had said to her about Curry Kells. She began to suspect that the man she'd met on the cathedral steps was Kells. His presence at the company that day, only half a block from the cathedral, and the black eye patch clinched it.

If that was the case, how would she approach him about her designs now? He'd probably think she was pursuing him for another handout! On the other hand, the party would be the ideal time to catch his eye, and she wouldn't have to work too hard if her dress drew the attention she expected. He'd be bound to ask her who the designer was. And she'd tell him. She hoped Miss Raines would be standing right at her side when he asked.

* * *

In his Wall Street office, Curry Kells was just finishing a complicated financial report for his board of directors. He saved the file and turned off the computer, feeling as if he'd done two days' work in a quarter of the time.

He stretched and grimaced at the protest from his sore muscles. The leather chair was remarkably uncomfortable for something that was supposed to be both functional and luxurious. He remembered the ramshackle office he'd occupied years ago when he was only a clerk in a manufacturing company, and the tattered but very comfortable chair he'd used.

He looked around his carpeted office with its solid oak furnishings and black leather chairs and sofa. There were five awards in a cabinet against the wall, three of which were for humanitarian efforts in the inner city. The other two were from business associates: one was a Chamber of Commerce Man of the Year award, and the other was a youth club honor for organizing a sports club for underprivileged boys. He hadn't done the humanitarian work for the awards. To him, his community service was a payback. If it hadn't been for a successful businessman giving him a boost up the ladder, he'd still be an underpaid clerk. A man much like the man he'd become had made all his advancements possible by funding his education and supplementing his mother's meager income as a hotel housekeeper. He'd been able to see his sister through college and pay for a good nursing home for his severely retarded brother now that his mother was no longer physically able to look after him.

He stood up and looked out his office window at the city skyline that reached to the river. His mother's condition was far more serious than he'd realized. He'd thought she was indestructible, immortal. It had been her confidence in him, her quiet support, that had made it possible for him to rise above their hopeless poverty and make a success of his life. With little more than a good brain and some business sense, he'd made more than two million dollars already. He'd made sure that his mother shared his success, that she lived well. But now all the money in the world wasn't going to help her. He was helpless, and the fury he felt was spilling into his business life. It infuriated him that he could do nothing for the woman who'd worked herself almost to death providing for her family.

The buzzer sounded twice before it distracted him from his morose introspection. He turned impatiently and pushed the button on his telephone. "Yes?"

"You asked Miss Raines to come and see you, sir."

"Yes. So I did. Send her in." He'd had some comments from Harry Lambert, one of his vice presidents, on Miss Raines's treatment of the younger designers and her stranglehold on the company's seasonal designs. She was one of the senior designers he'd kept on from the old company. She was, in fact, the senior designer, and about his mother's age. She reminded him of Teresa Kells—salt-and-pepper hair and no frills, ever.

"Send her in," he said curtly.

A minute later, the door opened and his secretary admitted a visibly ruffled Virginia Raines. She was wearing a dark suit with a simple white blouse, probably one of her own designs. He wondered irritably why she didn't deviate from the same pattern she seemed to use for all her work. He didn't like dismissing senior staff or demoting them, but Miss Raines was costing him sales. The company was still operating in the red, which was really all that he expected from such a new acquisition; but he'd been hoping for some small rise in sales over the months since his takeover, and it hadn't been forthcoming.

"Come in and sit down, Miss Raines," he invited, motioning her into a chair.

"Yes, sir." She sat primly, her legs to one side, her hands folded neatly in her lap. "If it's about the new lines, they're coming along very well, Mr. Kells."

"They may be. Sales are not," he said bluntly. He leaned forward, his lean hands on the desk. "We need something exciting for our salesmen to push to the buyers for summer, Miss Raines. Our sales haven't risen one percentage point since I've been here. Our executives and our stockholders are getting worried. I can't say I blame them. Our competitors are gaining ground with some, shall we say, fairly outlandish designs."

She flushed a little. "Sir, elegance is still a matter of simplicity. I can't remind you often enough that frills and fads go out of style as often as they come in."

"And I can't remind you often enough that fads are a boon to the industry. As long as women purchase more clothes each season to keep in step, we make money. If we produce only time-honored designs that carry over for several seasons, we bankrupt ourselves."

She cleared her throat and lifted her chin. "I have been a fashion designer for twenty-five years . . ."

"And a very good one." In your day, he wanted to add. He forced a smile. "However, I feel that we need some new blood in our design staff. I want to see some outrageous fashions, Miss Raines, some eye-catching, controversial things that will make the top fashion writers look twice at us. On that note, I asked you here to check on the winner in that design competition we held in the spring. How is she measuring up? I can't say that I've had a single progress report from you since her arrival."

That had been deliberate, my dear sir. Miss Raines smiled with faint condescention. "Well, she's very young, of course; only twenty-two. And the contest was really more of a publicity thing, wasn't it? I mean, you hardly expect to find a creative genius come from a Texas design school."

He gave her a hard look, and she squirmed. He didn't relent. He'd found over the years that when it came to flat intimidation, a wordless glare got more results than volumes of words. He let her squirm some more before he answered the insulting remark.

"I should hardly think it matters where the design

school is, if the girl is talented. You sound as if she should never have been hired.''

''Oh, I didn't mean to imply that, sir! It's just that she's . . . causing dissention,'' she said firmly. ''I don't dislike her. She's a hard worker. But she interferes with my models and she's always trying to put herself forward as a designer. She's just a sketch designer, and she's only been with the firm for six months. It's impossible to let her have a hand in our new lines with so little experience. She's just twenty-two,'' she repeated, to emphasize the age. ''Perhaps you could find her another spot, another place in the organization. In another building,'' she emphasized.

Curry stared at her curiously. It was highly irregular for an employee to ask him personally to remove another employee. Miss Raines looked more than ruffled. She looked frightened.

''Doing what?''

''She might work well in sales,'' she said vaguely.

''You want her removed. Why?''

The question, so deftly fired at her, caught her unawares. She stammered. ''Well, she might be happier somewhere else.''

He recognized professional jealousy when he saw it. His gaze narrowed. ''The happiness of the staff is hardly a day-to-day concern of mine. Unless you have some tangible evidence of incompetence, you'll leave her where she is and work out whatever problems you have.'' He sat back in his chair, fixing her with that cold stare. ''In the meantime, Miss Raines, I want to see some new designs in our spring and summer line, something different and exciting.''

''Mr. Kells, perhaps when you learn a little more about design . . .'' she began with faint condescension.

''Perhaps you should learn a little bit more about spreadsheets and profit,'' he returned icily. ''If you can't or won't ditch your outdated designs and show me something new, then by God, I'll find someone who can. Do I make myself clear?''

Her face drew up like a prune. She cleared her throat. ''I'll do what I can,'' she said, almost choking. The former president of the company had been an elderly man with a kindly attitude toward her work. This barracuda was cut from different cloth.

She rose to her feet. He was dangerous, and she'd realized it just in time; but she couldn't resist one last gambit. ''One more thing, Mr. Kells. Surely you didn't mean to invite the *entire* design staff to this party you're giving?'' she asked hopefully.

''I did,'' he corrected. ''I don't play power games and I'm no snob. I want everyone connected with the company present. Everyone.''

She shifted restlessly. ''Very well, sir.''

He watched her leave, scowling. Odd question. He was still bristling at her tone. Something would have to be done about her. He admired loyalty, but there was such a thing as loyalty being detrimental to profit. Whole families depended on the jobs of his workers. He couldn't sacrifice them to Miss Raines's pride.

When the door closed he waited a few moments and then buzzed his secretary. "Rowena, get me the file on that girl who won the design competition we sponsored. Bring it right in."

"Yes, sir."

He put down the phone. The interruption had accomplished one thing, he told himself. It had diverted his mind from his own worries.

The penthouse where Curry Kells lived overlooked Central Park. It was big enough to allow for the entertainment of a small army; it took two maids and a valet to keep it in order, and the caterer had brought additional staff. Lavish tables were spread with platters of caviar and shrimp, dainty savory pastries, vegetable slices and dips, and little cakes and tarts. In addition to the amply supplied bar, there were soft drinks, fruit juices, and a huge urn of coffee for teetotalers. He seems to have thought of everything, Ivory mused as she arrived with Dee.

She recognized only a few faces in the colorful crowd. She was nervous, even in the exquisite white satin gown with its lavish, intricate embroidery, and the white satin-covered pumps that matched it. Clutching a small embroidered satin bag she'd made to go with the outfit, she looked exquisitely regal, even to Dee, who was wearing a couture silk sheath dress of taupe that went well with her flowing blond hair.

"You look like a visiting princess," Dee remarked under her breath. "Don't blow the image by letting your knees knock. Look confident. Smile!"

"I'm scared to death," Ivory whispered back. Even her voice was shaking, and for once, her carefully controlled accent was noticeable. "God almighty, Dee, the closest I've ever come to this in my life was a church party in high school! I don't even know what to say to people like these!"

"Don't panic," Dee said, squeezing her arm comfortingly. "Take deep breaths and don't look down!"

"Good advice for someone standing on a precipice," a silky deep voice mused behind them.

Ivory actually jumped, because the unexpected voice was right over her shoulder.

She whirled, and there he was—the man she'd seen at the cathedral.

He wasn't half as surprised as she was. His expression was one of amused mockery as he looked at her dress and then back into her flushed face. Her eyes were huge, gray as a sparrow's wing and full of apprehension. Her short golden blond hair circled her face like spun silk. She wasn't beautiful, but she was striking. Those gray eyes mesmerized him, but it was the faint fear on her features, the barely perceptible trembling of her slender body that touched him. He felt suddenly, shockingly, protective.

He caught Ivory's upper arm in a gentle but steely grip. "Come with me," he said. He looked over her shoulder. "Get her something non-alcoholic," he told Dee, taking charge. "Not coffee," he added dryly. "Something decaffeinated!" Dee chuckled as she went off to comply with the request.

"Don't faint," he said with soft mockery as he led her out onto the glass-enclosed balcony. It was icy outside, but this area was heated and filled with dozens of potted plants. It looked like a greenhouse.

"I wasn't about to faint," she replied, regaining some of her stamina. "I'm a little out of my depth, and strangers make me nervous, that's all."

He glanced back inside at the noisy crowd. "They're just people," he reminded her. "Some of them are probably as intimidated as you are."

"I very much doubt that." She looked up at him and allowed her eyes to linger. He fascinated her. She thought again, as she'd thought the first time she had seen him, that she'd never come across such a handsome man. He had a smile that made her insides feel warm, and there was interest and amusement in that black gaze.

He was looking, too. Her face was just a little rounded, just enough to make it vulnerable and soft without making it heavy. Her big gray eyes dominated it. She had high cheekbones and a straight nose and a firm little chin. Her mouth was a sweet curved bow that made his lips tingle just looking at it. Her figure was exquisitely displayed in that well-fitted gown, and he could not restrain his desire to linger just a moment too long on the line of her breasts. He was tall enough that he could see into the neckline, see the soft, firm swell of delicate pink flesh that the flat slash of the square neckline only enhanced.

"Please don't stare," she said in a quiet voice with a dignity beyond her years, clasping her hands over her bodice in quiet discomfort.

He lifted his gaze back to her eyes with a start. She was flushed with embarrassment. The white purity of the gown she was wearing seemed suddenly appropriate, and those annoying protective instincts began to stir in him all over again.

"Ivory Keene," he said.

Her eyes widened. "You know who I am?"

He nodded. He didn't add why. "I gave you a five-dollar bill in front of the church, didn't I?" She had a face that wasn't easy to forget. Neither was the kindness in those gray eyes.

She laughed at the memory. "I guess I did look tatty in that coat. I really must replace it." She didn't add that she couldn't quite afford something nice just yet, because she sent half her paycheck home to keep her mother at bay.

"Surely you can afford a coat," he chided. "Unless you're making payments on a yacht . . .?"

"I have . . . a financial obligation," she said evasively.

"We all have those." He turned as Dee came onto

the balcony with a glass of tonic water and a cup of coffee. She handed them to her companions with a grin. "The bartender mentioned that you never touch liquor," she said to Curry, "and that you liked your coffee black and strong."

"Thank you," he said, surprised.

"Yes, thanks," Ivory added belatedly with a smile.

Dee looked from one to the other quickly and excused herself. "There's a gorgeous male model over by the bar, and we share a hobby. I have to get back before someone appropriates him."

She was gone in a flash. Curry studied Ivory as she looked toward her departing friend.

"Dee and I came together," she said involuntarily.

"If her new acquaintance wants to take her home, I'll see that you get back to your apartment," he assured her.

She lifted her eyes back to his face with breathless excitement. There was something she should remember; something, someone . . . Belle! Belle was dating him. She couldn't infringe on the other girl's territory, no matter what the temptation.

"Wouldn't Belle mind?" she asked carefully.

He pursed his lips and smiled, balancing his coffee cup in one hand. "No."

"Oh. I thought, well, I heard . . ."

"That Belle and I are an item? We were. We're still friends," he said simply. "But she doesn't own me."

"I see."

"Probably not."

"Why did you look so sad?" she asked impulsively, and regretted it at once.

"At the church?"

She nodded. He sipped his coffee. "I'd stopped by to talk to the priest on my way to the office, but he was out on a visit. I was tired and I sat down on the steps because it felt comforting, somehow. My mother has cancer," he added stiffly.

"I'm sorry. Do you have other family?"

"A sister and a retarded brother. Severely retarded. He has Down's syndrome."

She frowned.

"That's what they mistakenly call a mongoloid child. It's caused by a defective chromosome. He was born late in my mother's life."

"You take care of all of them. All your family."

"Yes." He searched her uplifted face carefully. "I was rude to you."

"You were hurting," she said simply. "Wounded things always lash out."

"You sound as if you know a lot about wounded things."

She lowered her eyes to his spotless white shirt. "Oh, a little perhaps," she said with a smile.

His lean, immaculate hand started toward her shoulder, then hesitated. "I'm keenly aware that some people dislike being touched,'' he said when she looked up, surprised by this hesitation from a man who acted as if he never paused to ask permission.

"I don't mind," she said, surprising herself, because she was one of those people who didn't like it.

He smiled, and his hand smoothed over the shoulder of the garment. His fingers traced the embroidery. "Where did you get this?" he asked. "I haven't seen stitching like that since I was a child, watching my grandmother make blouses for my sister."

"I made it," she said simply.

He stared at her. "You made it?"

"I like the Tudor period," she said. "I don't have a college education, but I love history and I like to read about the Tudors. I saw a similar design in a painting of Elizabeth the First, and I adapted this from it."

His hand stilled on her shoulder. "You designed this? And embroidered it?"

She nodded.

His breath caught. "Good God!"

"It isn't too flashy or anything?" she asked uncertainly. "I mean, outlandishly so?"

His hand smoothed down the sleeve, savoring the soft warmth of her arm under the satin fabric. "It's virginal," he said. "Pure. I've never seen anything quite like it."

"Miss Raines thought it was overdone." She spoke without thinking, from pain.

His hand slid down to her fingers and tangled sensuously in them. "She's quite mistaken," he said, deciding to do something about Miss Raines before she destroyed this budding talent. "It's elegant," he added, his deep voice soft and reassuring. "Beautiful."

She smiled shyly. "Thank you."

His heart was acting up. He cleared his throat and withdrew his hand from hers. He'd never experienced such a feeling before, as if something inside him were melting sweetly.

She looked up at him with curious, trusting eyes.

His lips parted as he let out a breath he didn't realize he'd been holding. "You're twenty-two," he said involuntarily, remembering what Virginia Raines had told him.

"Yes. And you?"

"I'm thirty-seven," he said, smiling. "Ancient, in your young eyes, I imagine."

"Oh, no," she said at once. "You have the sort of face that age is kind to. You won't look old even when you are."

"Flattery, too," he mused, chuckling. "You're a charmer, Miss Keene." He was attracted and he didn't want to be. He moved away from her discreetly. "I want that design," he said.

She was reeling from the effect he had on her; that, and his withdrawal, his sudden coldness. "This . . . dress?" she faltered.

He turned. "Yes. I want it for the upcoming collection."

She was stunned, and it showed.

"I'll send word to Miss Raines. Furthermore, I want you involved in design projects from now on."

"She won't like it," she faltered.

"I don't give a damn if she likes it or not, I give the orders around here!"

His temper was quick and hot. She was reassured by it, rather than frightened, because she knew that a man who let off steam often was less likely to become homicidal all at once. Repressed anger was the dangerous kind, the psychologists said. She smiled.

"Well?" he asked. "You'll get a bonus if your design sells at the showings in January. I think it might; it has potential for a wedding gown as well as an evening dress. On the strength of its originality, I'm going to promote you to junior design status. That will mean a raise in salary, too."

She couldn't find the words to express her delight. Her open mouth spoke for her.

He chuckled at the rapt pleasure she couldn't hide. "You're welcome," he said with a grin. He glanced inside the apartment and found several pair of curious eyes directed toward them. "Uh-oh. I see a scandal developing."

"A scandal?"

"Us." He smiled down at her confusion. "I'm seducing you, my dear. Can't you tell, from the wolfish grins and the noses pressed against the windows?"

"Oh!"

"Not to worry. I'm not the rake I used to be. I'm too old and too tired for instant seduction. But watch those male models. Some of them are straight, and you're green for your age."

"A lamb among wolves?" she teased.

"Good analogy." He was moving toward the door.

"Thank you for giving me a chance, Mr. Kells," she said seriously. "I won't disappoint you."

He glanced at her. "Curry. Not Mr. Kells."

"Curry." She frowned. "It's unusual."

"It's my grandmother's maiden name," he explained. He opened the door for her. "Into the breach, as they say. Harry Lambert's drooling over you. He's the tall brown-haired man wearing the red tie with his dinner jacket—something of a roué, but nice people. You could do worse. He's one of my vice presidents."

"Yes, I know, he's in charge of our division. I've seen him in the elevator. I don't really want to get involved with anyone," she added honestly.

He closed the door. "Why?"

She shifted uncomfortably. "You ask a lot of questions."

"I'm a curious man."

"I don't really think I should offer you the story of my life."

"I'd hardly expect it from a casual acquaintance. But you and I are going to be considerably more than that."

Her eyes sought his and were captured by a glittery black gaze that seemed to penetrate right into her mind.

Her knees went wobbly at the intensity of emotion he kindled in her. She'd never known anything like it.

"You don't want involvement," he prompted in a terse, strained tone.

"I . . . didn't," she amended huskily, studying his lean, hard face with eyes that clung to it against her will.

He lifted his hand and touched her full bow mouth tenderly. His forefinger traced it and her lips parted on a soft murmur of pleasure.

"My God!" he bit off.

His finger trembled. She felt her body going taut, going rigid. She looked into his eye and imagined that she could see right through to his soul. Why, I've known you all my life, she thought inexplicably. I've known you since the beginning of time, and I don't understand how or why!

As if he could hear her jumbled thoughts, he moved away from her and turned his back. The night sky was misty. The streetlights had halos. Taxi cabs sounded their horns impudently on the streets below. He began to breathe normally again.

He heard the door open and close. He didn't turn around. It had been twenty years since a woman had had such an impact on his senses. But he had to remember that she was the wrong woman. He had his mother to care for. He couldn't afford the luxury of embroiling himself in a love affair right now, least of all with a naive woman not much more than half his age. And anything serious was out of the question. It was the night and the stress of the past few days, that was all. Besides, the girl had probably been playing up to him to get that job. She wouldn't be the first.

Having convinced himself that he'd taken it all too seriously, he went back to his guests and played the role of perfect host for the rest of the evening.

Still the promise he had made came back to mind when Dee left with her male model. Ivory was stranded, and Harry Lambert was buzzing around her like a persistent honeybee. Curry might have been able to ignore her, except that once she looked across the room at him with eyes that could have touched the cold heart of a statue. No silent plea for rescue had ever been more eloquent. He found that he couldn't ignore it.

CHAPTER
FOUR

"HELLO, Harry," Curry said with a polite smile as he clapped him on the back. "Having a good time?"

"Yes, sir," the younger man replied. He was watching Ivory with acquisitive eyes. "I was just about to ask Miss Keene if she'd let me take her home . . ."

"Sorry, but that's all been arranged," the older man replied suavely. "If you're ready to leave?" he added to Ivory.

"I'll say goodnight, then," Harry said stiffly, thwarted.

"I should have handled it better," Ivory murmured uncomfortably as she watched him walk away. "I'm sure he's very nice, but I didn't want to go with him and I couldn't find a polite way to say so."

"No harm done. He bounces back fairly well. Get your coat. I'll be right with you."

He excused himself and had another man stand in as

host until he returned; then he escorted Ivory out the door. Their departure was followed by several pairs of amused, interested eyes.

"That should provide them with enough juicy gossip for the rest of the month," he remarked as they reached his car, a silky white convertible Jaguar to which the parking attendant was just handing him the keys.

"This is your car?" she asked, touching it with wonder. "I've never seen a Jaguar close up. It's a sport model, too."

He chuckled as he unlocked the passenger door and helped her ease inside. "Do you think I'm too old for it?" he teased. "Or does the thought of riding with a sight-impaired driver unsettle you?"

She waited until he got behind the wheel to answer him. "I expect you see almost as well with that eye as I do with both of mine. And I'm not afraid to go anywhere with you, Mr. Kells."

"Curry." He cranked the car and put it into gear.

"Curry," she amended, smiling at him. It was still surprising that she felt so much at ease with him. Some men intimidated her. This one did, in an exciting way, but he didn't frighten her.

"Is Virginia Raines giving you a hard time?" he asked unexpectedly as he pulled out into the road.

"Why, no sir," she said hesitantly. "I don't think she likes me, but she's not hostile."

"Just catty," he ventured.

She grimaced. "Sometimes."

He let out a sigh. "She's one of the senior staff. She stayed with the company when she could have made twice the salary somewhere else. Loyalty these days is rare."

"Yes, it is."

"But I'm not stupid, either," he added quietly. "If she gives you any problems, come straight to me. I won't tolerate intimidation."

"I will, but only if I have to. Thank you."

"She won't like having your dress in the line," he continued. "If the pressure gets too hot, come and talk to me."

"I don't mind pressure, if I get a chance to design things," she told him. "From the time I was a little girl, it's all I've ever wanted to do."

"If that dress is any example of what you can do, I'm delighted to give you a start." He stopped at a traffic light. "Where are we going?"

"Oh, where do I live, you mean? Queens."

His expression was curious. "Queens?"

She didn't know what to say.

"I told the people in charge of the competition that you were to have an apartment near the office, damn it!"

"Please don't blame them," she said quickly. "They did arrange for one, but I couldn't afford it. I explained that I have to send some of my salary home. Queens is a fine place to live. I have a nice little apartment and good neighbors."

He made a rough sound.

"Well, of course, it's not a penthouse apartment," she persisted. "But, then, I haven't worked long enough or hard enough to deserve one yet."

He glanced sideways at her without speaking.

"I'll have a penthouse apartment, you wait and see," she continued. "And a Rolls, and furs, and diamonds on every finger."

He frowned. "Is that what you see at the end of the rainbow?"

"Of course!" She turned toward him in her seat. It was leather and even smelled expensive. She couldn't bear to tell him why, to explain the terrible poverty that she'd survived. "I've never . . . been poor, of course," she lied with a smile. "But I haven't been able to afford diamonds, either. I want it all," she added fervently. "I want fame and fortune and all the stars in the sky!" She hesitated, thinking why she really wanted to get rich. It was her only hope of being able to cope with her mother, ever. But she'd like to lavish some of those dreams on little Tim and his family, too, and on her friends in her apartment building. A new coat for Tim would be nice, too . . .

"A Rolls?" he mused.

"Figuratively speaking. I think I'd be very satisfied with a nice Jaguar," she added with a grin.

"The Ford people now own the rights to the Jaguar. They built the engine in this one."

"Really?!"

He chuckled. "Really."

She touched the dash gently. "I guess you aren't married."

"Why? Because I drive a sports car?"

"Maybe."

"I was married when I was twenty-four." His face hardened. "And I don't talk about it." He glanced at her. "I'm not married now. That's all you need to know. And you? No husband or lover or boyfriend?"

"I told you. I don't want to get involved."

He furrowed his brow. He could think of two reasons immediately that would explain such an attitude.

She saw his expression and looked down at her hands. "I'm not a lesbian and I haven't been raped," she said levelly. "But I just don't want anything to hold me back. I'm not ready for marriage and a family."

A lie. He recognized it without understanding how he knew, because there was nothing to go on except the faintest hesitation in her soft voice.

"There was a bad experience," he said quietly.

She glanced at him, surprised. "Well . . . maybe one," she confessed. Actually, there had been a few. Cheap remarks by her mother's boyfriends, leers and suggestive remarks, and once or twice even an attempted assault. Instead of finding the incidents disturbing, Marlene had just laughed about them.

"Is sex something brutal and ugly to you now?" he asked gently.

"Not sex so much as men," she corrected.

"Some men," he agreed surprisingly. He traced the finger-holds on the steering wheel while he waited for a light to change. "I had a father who beat me," he said unexpectedly. "I stayed around because of my sister and brother. I kept them out of the way. My mother wasn't so lucky. She took a lot of heat for us." His jaw tightened. "I won't forget the sacrifices she made. She held down two jobs, just to make sure we had enough to eat and decent clothes to wear to school. We were poor, but we were never ragged or hungry."

"She must be a good woman."

He shrugged. "Good. Kind. A little possessive. My sister had to run away to get married because Mama didn't approve of the man she wanted to marry. Mama didn't speak to her for six months." He smiled, remembering. "We're all she has, so she clings pretty hard. She always comes around, though."

Ivory felt a disturbing niggle in the back of her mind. A possessive mother could make things very difficult for a man if he became involved with a woman. She was glad that she wasn't involved with Curry Kells. She'd had enough of mothers to last a lifetime. And her battles with Marlene weren't over yet.

They both rode in silence for several minutes. She studied the beautifully lit storefronts along fifty-seventh street at night, the trees with their garlands of gem-like white lights.

"You turn right at the next light," she directed when they were across the bridge in Queens.

"What were you smiling about?"

"I was thinking that in New York, even the trees wear jewels," she said with a grin.

"Only at Christmas," he corrected.

"It isn't, just yet."

He glanced at her. "Will you go home for Christmas?"

She was still for a minute. "I . . . don't expect so. My mother goes to Europe with friends. I'll save the money," she said, amazed at how easily the lies poured from her mouth. "Besides, I have a lot of work to do, getting ready for the January showings!" she added with inspiration.

"Your dress is already in a showing state," he said, curious. "Your other duties aren't that hectic, surely."

"Well, since I'm also doing repairs . . ."

"Repairs!" He stared at her. "Who said?"

"Miss . . ."

". . . Raines." He ground his teeth together. "Never mind. When you're promoted I'll specify that you do design work and accessories only."

"I don't mind hard work."

"I mind when my employees are overworked. I'll handle it."

She started to argue, but thought better of it at the moment. It would be a relief not to have to struggle through the endless repair jobs, especially with a new job to learn.

He pulled up at her apartment building in the once-elegant area that was now middle-class, with a few trees lining the sidewalk. He turned off the engine, got out, ignoring her protests, and walked her to the front door.

"Got your key?" he asked.

She produced it and held it up. "Thank you for bringing me home," she said.

He was looking around. "It brings back memories. I grew up a few blocks from here. Of course, my apartment building wasn't this nice," he added with a grin.

He looked younger when he smiled. She looked up, a long way up, to catch his gaze. He had the look of a brigand in that eye patch, she thought; like a hero out of a storybook.

"The highwayman . . ." she murmured without thinking.

"And Bess with her long, night-black hair." He touched her short wavy hair wistfully. "Yours isn't black, it's like spun gold. And I don't suppose you'd let it grow to your waist if I asked you. Not on such short acquaintance, anyway."

She was surprised that he knew the poem, and its heroine.

"It isn't well known, you understand, but I have a romantic streak," he mocked softly. He tugged at her hair gently so that she moved closer to him to ease the pressure. He smelled of expensive cologne and soap; a clean, attractive—very attractive—man. Her eyes fell involuntarily to his firm mouth. It was thin, the lower lip almost square and very sensuous. There was a faint

shadow where he'd shaved, and his chin had a suggestion of a dimple. It was a firm, thrusting chin, arrogant
like its owner.

"I want to kiss you, Ivory Keene," he said quietly.
"I shouldn't try, and you shouldn't let me. I'm too old
for you and you don't want to get sidetracked from your
road to fame."

"If you say so," she replied. "But it will be a great
loss to my education if you don't. I haven't been kissed
very much. And I don't think I've ever been kissed by
anyone who knew how. You do, don't you?" she added
seriously, searching his face. "You know all there is
to know."

His chest rose and fell heavily. He traced her lower
lip and bent his head. Some things were inevitable, he
thought as his mouth parted and pushed down over hers.

She tasted of rose petals. Her mouth was faintly tremulous, hesitant, unsure of itself.

He checked his instinctive move to deepen the kiss
and brushed the side of her mouth as he lifted his head
just a fraction.

"Are you afraid I might force you?" he whispered.

Her hands pressed flat against his white shirtfront,
feeling warm, hard muscle and chest hair under the thin
fabric. "No. But you should be afraid that I might force
you," she whispered back outrageously.

He met her smile with one of his own. "I'm impressed. You're a better judge of character than I gave
you credit for." He bent again and nibbled softly at her

upper lip. "Open your mouth a little," he whispered, inhaling sharply when she complied. "That's it."

His lips came down again, caressing lightly. She could feel him smile as she did what he asked, rippling from the sensuality in the movement of his mouth, in the deep rumble of his voice.

A lean hand at her waist moved her lightly so that her body brushed against his while he teased her lips. She shivered and the deep, soft laughter became husky.

"You're . . . dangerous," she accused.

"Yes. I am." He pulled her close and cupped her head in his hand while his mouth stopped teasing and became intensely serious.

She shook inside with a heat she'd never known. Her legs trembled where they came into contact with his. She heard his breath sigh out against her cheek and felt the firm movements of his mouth with shocked wonder at its expertness.

Her hand crushed his lapel while she tried to control her own body and found that she was too weak. She let him part her lips and moaned when she felt the tip of his tongue tracing just inside her lower lip. The provocation was unbearable. Her mouth opened, hungry for something it had never known, never before wanted, intensely aware of the throbbing ache he'd aroused in her.

And at that moment, when she was ready to plead for more, he jerked his head up and looked into her half-closed, dazed eyes. He didn't say a word. He didn't have to. She was an open book, and all the sexual pages were blank.

He forced himself to let her go very gently. He held her arms until she seemed steady on her feet.

"I'll say goodnight," he said softly.

She looked at him helplessly. It took precious seconds to pull her dreaming mind back into place. "It was a lovely party," she said in an unfamiliar husky tone. "Thank you for inviting me, and for the ride home. And especially for the new job."

"My pleasure." He let her go, smiling with faint self-mockery at his own stupidity. He had no right to play games with her. His first impression, of stifled innocence, had been right on the money. She'd had a bad experience with men, but she didn't need any sexual healing from him. He'd stepped out of line.

"Goodnight," she said.

"Goodnight. I'll be in touch, about the show."

"Of course. Thank you."

He shrugged and went back down the steps to his car, taking them two at a time. He didn't look back as he drove off, but Ivory watched him all the way out of sight.

"He's probably a millionaire," she reminded herself on the way up. "He drives a Jaguar and owns several companies. He's almost forty and he has lots of girl-friends. So don't lose your head."

"You're talking to yourself again, Ivory," Mr. Johnson called from his open doorway as she went past.

She poked her head in, smiling as she watched his

hands work skillfully on a wooden bird. "Very nice,
Mr. Johnson. What's that one for?"

"My granddaughter. It's for Christmas."

"She'll love it."

He chuckled. "Yes, she will. Have a good time tonight?"

"It was very nice."

"I love your dress, Ivory," Mrs. Johnson called as
she joined her husband with her knitting in her hand.
"Did you make it?"

"Yes. Thank you."

"You'll be famous one day, my dear," the elderly
lady said with a smile. "I hope you'll still come and
see us then."

"You know I will." She called them a cheerful goodnight and went on to her apartment. She felt as if her
feet didn't even touch the floor, despite her own misgivings at letting a man who was practically a stranger
kiss her. It hadn't seemed that way, and she'd enjoyed
kissing him very much. But apparently, judging from
his reaction, he could take or leave her. It was probably
a routine thing for him, kissing women. She had to stop
thinking about that. She had a design to improve, and
the first real chance of her career. She wasn't going to
waste it, or be side-tracked, even by a very attractive
man like Curry Kells.

Miss Raines was venomous when she heard that Mr.
Kells had added Ivory's design to the collection. She

was even more venomous about Ivory being taken off repairs. They'd never make the schedule now. She shouldn't have mentioned the girl to Curry Kells. She'd inadvertently called attention to Ivory, which had been the very thing she'd tried to prevent.

Several people had remarked that Mr. Kells took Ivory home from the party and didn't come back for a couple of hours. No wonder the girl had been given a chance, she thought viciously. Ivory had seduced the boss and turned his head. Now she was reaping the benefits. But that design wasn't going to get her anywhere. Miss Raines knew good style when she saw it, and that dress would be the laughingstock of the company. Mr. Kells owned the company, but he was no fashion expert. His protégé was going to fall flat on her face, and Miss Raines could hardly wait to see it.

She wasn't openly hostile, however. She'd even smiled when she congratulated Ivory on her promotion to junior designer.

"She smiles like a barracuda," Dee remarked coldly. "You watch her. She isn't happy about this. I'll bet she's boiling inside. You don't know much about company politics, but I'll tell you, people can be underhanded in this business. Some of them will do anything to keep their jobs or prevent other people from promotion."

"Miss Raines isn't spiteful," Ivory protested.

"Her job isn't on the line—yet. If you're ever in the position of competing with her, look out. You've got

fresh and original ideas, and most of hers came out of
Chanel back in the sixties. Chanel moved easily into
the contemporary market, but Virginia Raines wouldn't
know modern fashion if it bit her on the nose. You
watch your back, so that she doesn't put a knife in it.''

"I'll watch," Ivory promised, smiling. "But I think
you're wrong."

"I hope I am," Dee said fervently. "But be careful,
just the same."

"How was your late date last night?" Ivory asked,
to change the subject.

Dee chuckled. "Well, it was a start. I like him, I
really do. He's a Midwestern farm boy who came to
the big city for a chance and found one doing commercials. With that face and body, I'm not one bit surprised
that he was discovered so quickly. I have contacts, too,
so maybe I can help his career along."

Just for an instant, Ivory wondered if Dee's escort
might have had that in mind. She decided that she was
much too suspicious of people and went back to work.

Teresa Kells had large black eyes, salt-and-pepper hair
that she wore in a bun, and hands that were twisted
with arthritis. In her simple black dress and her low-
heeled black lace-up shoes, she sat clutching her designer purse in her lap tightly as they waited impatiently
in the lab for the radiologist to come back and explain
the radiation treatment she was to have.

Diverted by the movement of her son beside her, she

turned her head and smiled at him uneasily. He was a good man. All his adult life he'd looked after her. She shouldn't be so possessive of him, she knew, but he was all she had left. Her daughter, married now to that overbearing computer executive she didn't like, and vice president of a major corporation, wouldn't listen to her anymore. Her retarded son had never recognized her. She had no husband, because the father of Curry and her other children had vanished twenty years ago. She had friends, but they were no substitute for this son of hers who cared so deeply for her welfare. She was keenly aware, as well, that her being Puerto Rican and Catholic had subjected her to discrimination far too often in the past.

Curry resembled her, with his black eye; but his wavy hair was more deep brown than black, and his olive complexion wasn't overly dark. Besides that, he had a well-modulated voice with no trace of an accent, although he spoke Spanish as fluently as she did, along with several other languages.

She put her hand over his. "Don't look so worried," she said, her speech softly accented. "Lots of people get these things and live for years. I want to see my grandchildren . . ." His whole body froze and she stopped in mid-sentence. "I'm sorry."

He turned away and looked pointedly around the room at all the machines. "Audrey will give you grandchildren one day."

"Audrey!" She smiled, remembering that she'd

named her little girl for her favorite actress, Audrey Hepburn, but the girl had grown up not to be sweet-natured and kind like her namesake. She made a motion with her hand. "She's too busy running companies and making money with that terrible man she married. What does she want with babies? It breaks my heart, that it will end with the three of you. I would be such a good grandmother to them, you know." She turned and stared at his rigid back. "Yes, I know, you won't discuss it. It was years ago and she didn't want to get pregnant, and you won't forgive yourself!"

His hands clasped even more firmly at his back while he tried not to hear her. "Mama, please," he said tightly.

"It wasn't your fault!"

He turned. His face was like stone. "It was my fault. Hell, yes, it was. And I won't discuss it."

He was implacable. She threw up her hands and lapsed into angry Spanish. "That's it, that's it, let the horse throw you and never get back on, walk instead of ride because it might throw you again!"

She was ill, and frightened. He had to remember that, and not take offense.

"You could get married again," she muttered, falling into English again as she calmed down. "Girls flock around you. Not that it can be just any girl," she added firmly. "Someone with a good background, it must be, a girl with a fine family name and money. I won't have you married for your fortune by some poor, flighty gold digger!''

"If I marry again, Mama, I'll marry whom I please," he informed her.

"Bosh! Look how you messed it up before," she said shortly. "I won't let you make a mistake like that twice.''

He raised an eyebrow, but she stared back unafraid. Then the radiologist returned, and her proud arrogance went into eclipse behind obvious fear and foreboding.

"Well, what are you going to do to me?" she demanded. "They've already cut me up and said they couldn't get it all, so are you going to make a miracle?"

The young man smiled sympathetically. "Not a miracle, exactly, but we're going to try a combination of chemotherapy and radiation to see if we can't prevent any more spread of the carcinoma. Today, we start the radiation treatment.''

"The cancer, you mean," she said, nodding.

He was reading over her file. "Dr. Hayes wants you to have a high dosage for two weeks, then we can reduce the intensity and length . . .''

"My hair will fall out?" she asked.

"Yes. I'm sorry. It's something we can't help.''

"Nausea? Headaches?" she persisted.

He grimaced. "Those, too. But we can prescribe medicine to help." He grinned. "In fact, we can prescribe marijuana. It controls the nausea very nicely, and you won't be arrested for using it.''

"I won't use drugs," she said haughtily. "None of my kids ever did, because I made sure they were raised right!"

"Uh, yes, ma'am," the technician agreed.

"Mama, get off the soapbox," Curry said.

She gave him a hard glare, but it bounced right off. She fixed the technician with cold eyes. "You're going to burn me up with that stuff, I guess, and I'll come out worse than I started."

"It's still better than dying," he pointed out.

"Who knows if it is?" she shot right back. "Have you died yet?"

Curry laughed involuntarily. "Mama, Mama, hush and let the man explain things to you."

She made a face at him. "Don't tell me what to do, if you please."

Curry stuck his hands in his pockets and exchanged a glance with the technician. "I wouldn't dare."

She turned her pocketbook over and smoothed it. "All right, young man, tell me what you're going to do, step by step."

He did, and while she listened to him, Curry watched his mother's tired, heavily lined face and remembered his childhood. She'd worked at two jobs, in all sorts of weather, but there was always something nice for the kids to eat and a lady to stay with them when their mother wasn't at home. They went to confession every

Saturday, and to mass every Sunday. There wasn't
much money, but there was so much love that it choked
him up when he thought about it. No problem was
belittled. No cry was ignored.

Before his father's desertion, they had lived with
some Hispanic relatives, two families sharing a big
room in a small apartment house. Privacy was impossible. The wallpaper was peeling; there were chips in the
linoleum floor. Water trickled from faucets, but it was
only cold water. The steam heat never worked. Everybody slept on the floor under quilts in the winter and
faded sheets from the Salvation Army in the summer.
Roaches and rats infested the building, despite the health
inspections, and the rent was exorbitant even so. Gangs
of young boys roamed the streets. Rape and murder and
theft were everyday occurrences. When his best friend
was murdered, Curry swore vengeance and went after
the boy who'd done it. He determined that one day he
was going to escape the impossible living conditions
and take his family out of there. So many other people
hadn't been able to escape the horrible cycle of poverty
that killed self-esteem and ambition, but he had.

Mama took good care of her kids, but no battles were
fought for them, at school or in the alleys. Only when
Curry's revenge on behalf of his dead friend landed him
in trouble for almost killing the gang member responsible did his mother have to intervene. She was more
eloquent than any lawyer as she pleaded for him before
the judge. Ironically, it helped his defense that his eye

was heavily bandaged and that a doctor testified that he'd never see with it again.

He was put on probation for aggravated assault, and turned loose. He kept his nose clean from then on because the money to pay the bail bondsman had cleaned out Mama's hard-earned savings account. Vengeance was expensive in many ways, he thought. He had a record for the felony assault, which he would carry with him all his life. It was the one and only time he had broken the law.

"You are not listening!" Teresa Kells muttered. "*¡Escucha!* Pay attention."

"Yes, Mama." He settled back into his chair and listened to the radiologist.

The cancer, which had started in the lower lobe of her left lung, had been surgically removed. But the surgeon wasn't sure that he'd excised every trace of it, so he'd recommended an intensive program of radiation treatment and chemotherapy, just to make sure.

She wasn't optimistic about her recovery, and it had taken Curry and his sister days to persuade her of the need for the auxiliary treatments. She'd rewritten her will and given all her prized possessions to the relatives she wanted to have them. She'd also signed a living will to make sure that she would not be kept alive by artificial means "to be a burden" on her children. It was like her, Curry thought, to be unselfish even at the end. It made her condition so much harder to accept. He'd always thought his mother would live forever. But she'd had cancer, and he had learned far too much about the statistics of survival among cancer patients from a friend who was a doctor. That was why he'd insisted on the treatments.

"I still don't think this is necessary," Teresa Kells was telling the radiologist.

"And I think it is," Curry replied with a smile. "Now be good and do what you're told. You can't leave us alone after all the years you've invested in us. You've a lot of spoiling still coming to you. How about that trip back to Puerto Rico to see our cousins, and the summer house in the Adirondacks that I promised to buy for you?"

"Oh, yes," she said, and for a moment her black eyes were young again. "Yes, I remember once your daddy and I rode up there on the bus for a weekend, before you were born. I did love it so."

He watched her smile with pleasure. She'd never said one harsh word against their father in all the years he'd been gone. She made excuses for him, apologized for him, but she was never censorious. He'd done the best he could, and it had been a hard life for him. He was uneducated, illiterate, a dock worker. They'd learned from one of his co-workers that he'd hopped a freighter one day after he knew that his youngest child was retarded. Mama had always said that he felt responsible and that was why he ran away. She felt just as responsible, but she wasn't the type to run from responsibility. Neither was her son.

"Your father was a good man," she added, pointing a finger at him as if he'd contradicted her. "He couldn't bear not being able to support us, and it was all so much worse when Andy was born so badly retarded. He felt guilty."

"Yes, I know, Mama," he agreed quietly.

"These treatments," she said, turning back to the patient radiologist, "how long must I have them?"

"Six weeks," he said.

She toyed with the handle on her purse. A long sigh passed her lips. "Very well, then." She looked at her son. "If you think I should."

"What a question!" he said with mild surprise. "You think I want to risk losing you?"

"My dear boy," she whispered, fighting tears as she reached out and took his hand in hers.

"*Mamacita, yo te quiero muy mucho,*" he said in his elegant, perfect Spanish, and he smiled.

CHAPTER
FIVE

THE sample room buzzed when Ivory presented her improved design for the evening dress she had created for the summer line. Only Virginia Raines was less than enthusiastic about it. She deliberately absented herself from the sample room while Ivory was finishing her nips and tucks to adapt the dress to the model who would be showing it.

"It's just dreamy," one of the girls sighed, staring at it. "I wish I could afford one, but with a Kells-Meredith label, it will be out of my price range."

"Mine, too," Ivory confided, and laughed.

"Yes, but you can sew yourself one any time you like."

She frowned. "I don't know that I can," she said. "Actually, since I've sold the design to the company, I think I've restricted my right to duplicate it."

"That's probably true," Dee said. "You could always ask Mr. Kells, of course."

Ivory felt herself going warm at the mention of his name. "Oh, he wouldn't bother with me," she replied. "I'm grateful to him for giving me a chance to design something. I wouldn't presume to ask for special favors."

Dee refrained from saying that she could probably get them anyway. Curry Kells had taken Ivory home from the party when Dee knew for a fact that he didn't ordinarily put himself out for minor employees. Ivory was young and pretty and she had a kind heart. She might very well appeal to someone with a palate as jaded and cynical as Curry's.

Dee worried about Ivory. She was unworldly and could be badly hurt by someone like Curry Kells. On the other hand, she was an independent sort who wouldn't take kindly to even the most well-meant interference in her private life. Dee turned her attention back to her own work. At times one had to trust that things would organize themselves for the best.

Ivory finished pinning the dress and gave it over to the seamstresses. She had one or two other ideas that she wanted to sketch, although she wasn't really expecting anything to come of them. Miss Raines might have no choice about giving the white satin gown of Ivory's a showing on Mr. Kells's say-so, but she could effectively halt any others if she liked. Ivory's career might hinge on this one design, and heaven help her if anything went wrong before the showing.

* * *

Thanksgiving Day dawned gray and rainy and cold. Ivory fixed herself a small baked turkey and some dressing, mashed potatoes, and cranberry sauce. She'd invited Tim and his family to come and share it with her, but they were getting a nice turkey dinner, courtesy of a group of people dedicated to helping the homeless. Because the weather was already cold and wet, Ivory had given Tim a new jacket early instead of waiting for Christmas, so that he could stay well when flu season began.

"For me, Ivory?" he'd asked, as if he couldn't believe that anyone would buy him such a nice coat.

"Yes," she said. "It's your Christmas present, but I thought you might like it early. It's very cold." She didn't add that with HIV, his immune system would start breaking down. A cold could go so quickly into pneumonia, and Miriam couldn't afford doctors or medicine unless she could go through a government agency to get them.

"Wow! Thanks!" He'd paraded around in it, his dark eyes beaming with delight.

Miriam had thanked Ivory for her kindness. "But someone will steal it, you know," she said sadly. "All that generosity will only go to waste."

Ivory hadn't considered that. In the small town where she came from, few people were mean enough to steal a jacket from a small boy with winter coming on. But this was a city where most people were strangers to one another. Hopeless poverty made thieves of some.

"Mrs. Payne can sew," Ivory said. "Let her stitch Tim's first name all over the jacket, with heavy thread, in some bright color. That will discourage some people, at least locally. Even if the thread is taken out, the holes will still spell out Tim's name!"

Miriam grinned. "Ivory, you have a devious mind."

"Well, sometimes you have to be devious," she replied. "As long as it's for a good cause." She smiled at Miriam, who smiled back.

The one hopeful fact was that Tim was still robust and healthy. Every day, medical science came up with new ways to combat AIDS. She could only pray that there would be time to find a cure before the disease kindled in Tim's small body.

Ivory ate her dinner and put part of the turkey in the freezer. If she ate it sparingly, it would last a long time.

She sat down on the sofa and balanced her checkbook, also totaling the amount she'd sent home. Her mother would certainly complain about the measly amount, even though it was half of Ivory's salary. When she'd started sending the money to Texas, she hadn't enclosed a note. It would only have been thrown away, unread. The money was all that mattered to Marlene.

As she fingered her ballpoint pen, she thought back to happier times, when her grandparents were still alive. She had always spent summers and holidays, including Thanksgiving and Christmas, with Grandmother and

Grandfather Howard. They were sharecroppers, in their mid-fifties when she was a little girl and finding life harder and harder as big corporations took over family farms all over the area. They hardly eked out a living.

Ivory hadn't realized until she was in school that they were very poor. The old, ramshackle house was so full of love that money never seemed to matter. There was plenty of food, because they grew their own; and if there was no running water and no indoor plumbing, that hardly concerned a little girl who adored them. It was so much better than being at home.

Her mind drifted to the rose garden that her grandmother had tended so lovingly. One renegade chicken liked to lay eggs under the thick branches, and Ivory had to crawl under to fetch them. In a mock orange tree in the backyard a family of mockingbirds nested every spring. The wild garden near the back steps bloomed with bachelor's buttons and sunflowers, zinnias, verbena, and black-eyed Susans in glorious profusion every spring and summer. And there was the kitchen garden, where she and her grandparents spent long, lazy hours weeding and tending, and then harvesting the fruits of their labors.

Grandma always had homemade fried apple pies in the cupboard to nibble on. Sometimes Ivory would sit on the back stoop and share one with her dog, while she watched the seasons pass over the fields and waited for life to come and get her. On lazy summer evenings, she would sit in the porch swing with her grandparents and listen to the crickets sing. Sometimes a thunderstorm would threaten, and from far away would come the deep bass sound of thunder amid flashes of magical-looking light in the dark clouds. Grandpa would smile as he smoked his pipe, grateful for the rain that would make his crops grow, ever hopeful of making a profit just one year. But he never had. He was eternally in debt to the landlord and always one season behind.

He was happy, though, working on the land and not being confined to an office and a timeclock. Being poor, he told Ivory once, was worth a lot, because at least a man had time to see the world around him in the way he was meant to see it. The glory of nature was much more vivid close up. Captive now in concrete streets and the steel skeletons of high-rise buildings, Ivory remembered the smell of rain coming across the parched fields and the scent of pink roses climbing the oak tree at her grandparents' house. She remembered the security of their love most of all.

Those memories had nourished her, fed her soul, in some of the worst times of her life. She could close her eyes even now and see the house, and them, safe and eternal in the cocoon of her thoughts. If her grandparents hadn't died tragically in a house fire when she was in the second grade, how much different her life might have been!

The clock struck eleven and she went to bed, but not to sleep. The nightmares had come back lately. They did, sometimes, when she was under a lot of stress.

She had to make a lot of money, to protect herself from any charges that might one day be leveled by her mercurial mother. Ambition had lifted Ivory from hopelessness. Now she had to trust that it would take her to the top and free her from the threat of her money-mad mother.

She hadn't much money, but she decided that she could at least afford a present for Dee, who'd been so kind to her. In one of the department stores that dotted the festively decorated streets she found what she was looking for—a beautiful silk scarf. It was more than she wanted to spend, but Dee deserved it.

She was getting ready to move to the checkout counter when something caught her eye. She paused in front of the display and stared and stared. A man like Mr. Kells wouldn't expect or want a present from her, she thought, and it wasn't even expensive; but it would suit him. He'd given her a chance to show her talent, and she wanted to do something for him. On an impulse, she reached out and took the small tie tack off the display. It was on sale at half-price and was 10-karat gold. The pearl, the sign said, was genuine.

She placed it with the scarf and held her wallet tightly in her hand while she waited for the harried clerk to ring it all up. The total was enough to take most of her spare cash, but she didn't mind. And they offered free gift-wrap, so that was an added bonus. She smiled and thanked the wrapper. It would seem like Christmas, now that she had presents to give, even if she knew she wouldn't get a present from anyone, except perhaps from Dee.

Now, if only she had a Christmas tree. She had studied them lovingly in the lot she passed on her way back to the office. It would have been so nice to have a tree. She could make paper chains to go on it and icicles, and she could afford a string of lights. It would make her spartan apartment so much prettier. But the trees carried price tags that would take half a week's salary or more, and that was just too much to pay for something that would last only days. She'd have to get herself a little artificial tree and settle for looking at the gaily decorated large trees in store windows.

She'd just started into the revolving door of Kells-Meredith when the door suddenly swung open and out stepped Curry Kells, right in her path.

With a shocked cry, she jumped backward, because he looked furious.

He frowned as he recognized her. "Ivory, isn't it?" he asked. His gaze landed on the small shopping bag with the two presents in it, glanced over her shabby coat and back up to her soft gray eyes and the golden hair peeking out from under the white beret.

"Been shopping?" he asked.

She nodded. "New York is so pretty during the holidays," she said with a wistful smile. "I love looking at the lights."

"Got your tree up yet?" he inquired indulgently.

"Oh, no, I can't afford . . . I mean, I don't really need one. They're so messy, you know, live ones . . ." her voice trailed off, and she smiled to let him see that she didn't mind.

"I've been down to see the progress on the summer line," he said, sticking his hands in his pockets as he shifted out of the path of passersby. "I can't say I'm overwhelmed with enthusiasm."

She bit her lower lip and looked worried.

"Your contribution is the only decent-looking garment I've seen," he muttered irritably. "The junior designers, except for you, all seem to copy Virginia's ideas."

She might lose her job if she told him that Miss Raines insisted on that.

He saw it in her eyes. His lips pursed as he studied her. "You're loyal. You won't say a word against her, even though I have a good idea what's going on."

Her face lifted. "My grandparents said that you should never say anything about another person if it can't be something good," she said with a smile that became a wicked grin. "So sometimes I didn't talk about people for years!"

He chuckled. She made him feel young and whole again. His gaze fell to her soft, bow-shaped lips and he remembered the delicious feel of them under his mouth.

She caught his eye and deep waves of sensation

pulsed along her veins as that blackness enveloped her in its unblinking intensity. She couldn't have looked away to save her life. She didn't now, and neither could he.

His face tightened. "You'll be late," he said.

She took a minute to absorb what he was saying. "Late? Oh. Yes. I should go."

He took a lean, beautiful hand out of his pocket and caught her arm. "Do some more designs for me. I'll stop by your apartment Friday night and you can show them to me."

Her breath caught. She beamed with delight, but that quickly changed to dismay. "But, Miss Raines . . ."

"Leave Miss Raines to me," he said tersely. "Will you do it?"

"Oh, I'd love to!"

He nodded. "Think of it as covert operations," he said. "Secret agent stuff. Industrial espionage. Except that we'll be doing it for the right reasons. I want something that will set the fashion world on its ear, something that will get us operating in the black. If you can put some life into those tired old designs, I'll give you senior design status."

"Miss Raines won't like it."

"She'll like having a job," he returned. "If our sales don't pick up, none of you is likely to have one."

"Oh, dear," she said.

"That's the situation. Get busy."

The sudden pressure of her job felt uncomfortable, even though the chance to do another series of designs was pure bliss.

He eyed the presents she'd bought again, and he lifted an eyebrow. "Only two?"

"Well, I don't know anyone well enough to give them presents," she explained. "Just Dee and . . ." She stopped, flushing as she looked at him and quickly looked away before her expression betrayed her.

But it was too late. He read the expression accurately. "And me?" he finished for her, stunned when she grimaced and verified his guess. "You bought me a present? And you won't even buy yourself a new coat?!"

She glared at him. "I'll buy a coat when I want one. And I can buy you a present if I like. Anyway, how do you know it's for you?"

He shrugged. "Wishful thinking?" He was smiling.

She grimaced again. "Well, it is for you, but it's not expensive. I can't afford anything really expensive. I just wanted some way to say thank you for what you've done for me." She looked up belligerently. "And I don't want a present back, either! That isn't why I did it."

His mind was full of women who expected diamonds or furs for a night on the town, rich women who didn't need any more glitter than they already had. Not one of them gave a thought to him. He couldn't remember ever expecting a present from one of his dates at Christmas, and here was this small-town sparrow pinching her belt tighter to afford a gift to give him. He was more touched than he wanted her to know.

"You should spend your money on yourself," he said stiffly.

"I've embarrassed you. I'm sorry."

"Embarrass me?" He chuckled amusedly. "Hardly."

"I can take it back," she began, knowing full well she couldn't return the present because it had been on sale.

"Don't you dare!" He led her to the door. "Get in there and go to work. And don't give away my present!"

"I'll bet you get carloads already," she muttered, stopping to look up at him. "What's one more?"

"My mother gives me a tie, my sister gives me a belt, and I'm lucky to get handkerchiefs or desk sets from the staff." He smiled. "I'll bet you didn't get me a tie."

"God forbid, the kind you wear cost sixty dollars apiece," she said without thinking, and put a hand to her mouth.

"They're silk," he told her. "I like silk. I like satin, too." His eye narrowed. "Do you have fabric preferences?"

"Yes. Those. Silk and satin, but I can't afford to make things out of them."

"The company will spring for the fabric, for God's sake," he said irritably. "You design. I'll pay."

"You're very grumpy," she said.

"I'm tired. You try going six rounds with the board of directors over the new budget."

She stuck her chin up and her gray eyes twinkled. "I'd love to! What do you want them to do, and when do I start?"

He chuckled. "I'll keep you in mind when I lose control."

She sighed. "I'll be dead of old age by then."

"I wouldn't be too sure." He checked his watch. "I'm late again. I've got to run. I'll see you Friday about eight, and don't tell anyone."

"What if I have a date?" she asked.

"Do you?"

"Well, not yet . . ."

"You do now. Me."

He turned and strode off without another word. Standing at the revolving door, she stared after him hungrily; she came to her senses just in time to avoid a collision with a couple coming out of the building. A hopeless longing for Curry Kells filled her. She couldn't fight it. She decided to take the days one at a time and hope for the best. At least, she was going to get a shot at more designs. She could hardly wait to get her sketch pad out!

She started that afternoon, her hand moving rapidly over the paper as she began to visualize the many styles and effects she could create drawing upon the Tudor paintings that were her inspiration.

It was bad luck that Virginia Raines should see what she was doing and pause to glare over her shoulder.

"Too flashy," she remarked haughtily. "Simple lines, Miss Keene, simple lines. No frills and flashes, they're faddish and they don't carry over from one season to another!"

Ivory looked up at her solemnly. "And if women buy dresses that they can wear for five years, don't we defeat the purpose of designing new ones? If people buy fads that go out of fashion quickly, we sell more clothes, don't we?"

Miss Raines gaped at her. She sounded just like Curry Kells. "You . . . you really have no idea about how to design properly, and you are impertinent!"

"That's fortunate for you, isn't it?" she asked gently. "Because if I'm that bad a designer, I'm certainly no threat."

Miss Raines's thin face went scarlet. She lifted her chin. "Certainly not." She folded her arms across her chest. "The very idea . . . why are you working on the spring and summer lines? We have all we need. You should be thinking about fall."

Ivory didn't dare tell her that it was Curry Kells's idea. She had enough trouble with the woman as it was.

"I'm just trying out some ideas for . . . for next year," she hedged.

"You should be working on the fall line," Miss Raines repeated bluntly. "And scrap those way-out styles. Simplicity is the key to good design."

She walked away, having had the last word. Ivory watched her, so stiff and set in her ways, and hoped that she wouldn't ever become so rigid. It was important to be flexible. Creativity was the true key to good design. She supposed that Virginia Raines had long ago decided to play it safe, with no deviation from the tried and true. But it was the pathfinders, the risk-takers, who made progress in any field.

As she finished two new drawings, keeping an eye out for Miss Raines's return, she felt vaguely guilty. It was uncomfortable to deceive Miss Raines. On the other hand, she recognized with a cynicism far beyond her years, that she had been deceiving people ever since she left home for design school.

Dee stopped by her office to take a look at the new designs and was enthusiastic enough to make Ivory smile.

"Has she seen them?" Dee asked, peering out the open door.

"Yes. She doesn't like them." Ivory hadn't told Dee about her talk with Curry Kells, and she wouldn't. The fewer people who knew, the better. She smiled at Dee. "Well, they're fun to do, and I'm being productive. I suppose I'd better do as she asked and sketch something for the fall line."

"Optimist," Dee muttered. "The lack of enthusiasm on the line for Miss Raines's new summer dresses is scary. If the seamstresses don't like them, how does she expect the buyers to? You'd better do some smashing accessories, Ivory, or we're all going to be standing in line at the local welfare office come February.''

Exactly what Curry had said, Ivory thought sadly. Probably it had been sticking to the old ideas all these years that had brought the company to the brink of bankruptcy. Styles changed with the times, and many of the buyers for the luxury stores who swore by the old designs had either lost their jobs as buyers or retired. The new buyers wanted trendy fashions, things that sold to a younger clientele. Kells-Meredith was still designing for wealthy women to wear to club meetings, not for female executives to wear to business meetings.

"Everything you've done is for evening," Dee pointed out. "Have you any ideas for executive office wear? Please, not straight jackets and skirts with round-necked silk blouses . . . !''

Ivory chuckled at Dee's prejudice. "In fact, I do have some ideas. I was doodling and one just popped out. It isn't like the Tudor inspirations, though," she added a little worriedly. "Those are strictly evening wear. This design is just a very simple off-white suit, made of a silk blend or linen, with wide lapels, and a jeweled butterfly design on the bodice beside the lapel. Something like this, worn with a soft-necked open silk blouse.''

She sketched it quickly and Dee loved it. "Why, that's elegant. It's appropriate, but feminine, and it

would go from a conference room to a banquet. It's
. . . incredible!''

Ivory grinned. "And you don't like suits."

"Well, I like this one."

"I thought that we could apply the butterfly in gold
tone or silver tone, and fill it with Austrian crystal."

"Yes," Dee said, catching her enthusiasm. "And
perhaps a nice black crepe or silk suit for evening—with
pants or a skirt. You could use a black onyx butterfly,
outlined in sapphires and diamonds and rubies . . ."

"Oh, what a great idea!" Ivory said, delighted. She
roughed out another sketch, incorporating Dee's butterfly onto the suit design. She showed it to the head
seamstress, who oohed and aahed.

One of the seamstresses, passing by, peered over
their shoulders. "Do I get to work on that?" she asked,
beaming. "How beautiful!"

Ivory flushed. "Thank you!"

"That would be a joy to sew," the woman sighed.
"For a change." She exchanged grimaces with Dee and
kept walking.

Dee reviewed the sketches thoughtfully and pursed
her lips. "Ivory, you have to show that to somebody
who has the authority to buy it. Mr. Kells, perhaps."

"You know," Ivory said carefully, glancing around
to make sure Virginia Raines wasn't listening, "I just
might do that!"

CHAPTER
SIX

THE rest of the week went by all too quickly. Ivory was kept busy working with accessories and helping fit models. Because the Christmas holidays were coming up and the plant would close down for at least a week, preparations for the shows the second week of the new year were being rushed.

When she got home on Thursday evening, she realized that she'd better get busy if she was going to get the apartment cleaned up and bake a cake. She wouldn't have time the next day before Curry arrived. She intended to serve the cake with the imported coffee she'd hoarded, and the real cream she'd bought for it. Afterward, she could give some of the cake to her neighbors, and save some for Tim.

She worked through the next day with her mind whirling as quitting time approached. She rushed home and dusted again, and then she sat and waited, all nerves, for her expected guest to show up.

Eight o'clock came, but Curry Kells didn't. She didn't know him well, but she was certain that he was usually on time. He seemed so efficient and conscientious. Perhaps something had happened. She didn't think he promised to do things and then just forgot about them, but perhaps people in his social echelon didn't value promises made to lowly junior designers. He didn't know her well, after all. She was just someone he'd met a couple of times.

Ten minutes went by. Fifteen. She straightened the skirt of the blue jersey dress she was wearing. It was calf-length, its neckline and long sleeves edged with white lace. The black pumps she was wearing with it had scuffinly, but not like Curry's sort of date. He probably would be ashamed to be seen with her in public, especially in that ratty tweed coat she still hadn't replaced. She wondered if that was why he'd wanted to come to the apartment, instead of offering to take her out somewhere. She intended to buy a new coat at the year-end clearance sales, when some of the smarter ones would be in her price range. Such a rich, influential man as Curry would hardly want to be seen with a woman who wore department store clothes anyway.

His disappointing her was a blow to her pride, but she couldn't afford pride if she wanted to rise in the company ranks. Here was the major executive, willing to look at her designs and possibly put them into his line. If he didn't regard an appointment with her as important, she had to swallow the insult until she was no longer in danger of being fired for speaking her mind. She'd come so far. She had to be willing to make the sacrifices necessary to take her the rest of the way to the top.

Waiting for Curry was beginning to feel like a career in itself. She looked at the small electric alarm clock on the table by the sofa. Eight-thirty. Perhaps he wasn't coming. She bit her lip as she looked toward the coffee pot, where the fresh coffee she'd made was beginning to darken. She'd have to make more.

A sharp knock at the door started her heart racing. She jumped up, almost falling in her haste to reach it.

"Who is it?" she asked cautiously.

"Good girl, you can't be too careful," said a familiar deep voice. "It's me. Open up."

She smiled as she threw the locks and opened the squeaky old wooden door. And there he was, resplendent in a dark blue pin-striped suit with a spotless white shirt and an elegant silk tie. He smiled reluctantly at her rapt expression, while he secretly deplored the clothes she was wearing. She would be pretty, if she had the money to dress properly. She looked nothing like the young woman in the elegant satin outfit she'd worn to his party.

"Your neighbor buzzed me in so that I could surprise you with this. Are we going to stand here all night, or may I come in?" he asked.

"I'm sorry!" She was flustered, fumbling with the

door chain. She stood back and Curry walked in, followed by a second man who carried a fir tree wrapped in wire.

Her mouth fell open as the man, in a neat suit, nodded politely, walked across the room, and stood the tree against the far wall.

"I'll go and gas up the car, sir, and then I'll be downstairs when you're ready," he told Curry politely.

"I'll page you," Curry replied.

"It's a Christmas tree," Ivory said in wonder, touching it lightly.

"Looks like one, doesn't it?" he said with an indulgent smile. "Do you always react like that to gifts?"

She whirled, her face bright and open and happy. "How?"

"As if you don't expect anything, ever, from anyone."

"Well, I don't," she said honestly. "Oh, you shouldn't have done this!" She touched the tree again. "It's so lovely!"

He chuckled, then went back out the door and returned with two large shopping bags. "I didn't know what you'd like, so I brought an assortment. There's a tree stand in this one."

She peered into the sacks, astonished at the variety of ornaments. Some appeared to be the kind that moved. She'd drooled over similar ones in department stores.

Curry sat down on the sofa and watched her with more pleasure then he'd experienced in years. She "oohed" over one ornament, then another like a kid turned loose in a toy shop with an unlimited budget. Her sounds of pleasure were music to him after the bored acceptance of other, more sophisticated women.

On the floor among the wrappings, heedless of the crumpling of her dress or the faint dust that was clinging to it, she examined every single item individually, handling each reverently.

Dumbfounded, she lifted her face to his. "I don't know what to say. There are no words." She fought tears and lost. They ran down her cheeks unashamedly. "No one ever . . . *ever* did anything like this for me." She was remembering Christmases past, when Marlene refused to have a tree in the house, much less any decorations for it.

He scowled. He hadn't expected such an overwhelming show of feeling, and he didn't know quite how to respond to it. She made him feel more masculine, somehow, with her unexpected vulnerability.

"It's only a tree and a few trinkets," he said carelessly, hiding his faint embarrassment. "Nothing to get so excited about."

Suddenly, she felt childish, dimming the joy of the surprise. She wiped the tears from her cheeks and carefully put the ornaments back into the bag. "I'll enjoy them very much. It was kind of you."

"You bought me a present," he reminded her. "I don't like owing things. Ever. So I reciprocate favors, or gifts."

That sounded stiff and almost unfriendly. She'd have to remember not to obligate him again. No wonder he'd bought her the tree and the ornaments. She'd put him in a difficult position and offended his pride.

She rose to her feet, ignoring the helping hand he extended. "I made a cake and some coffee," she said, without looking directly at him.

"Coffee, black," he said. "Thanks for the offer, but no cake."

She wouldn't think about her wasted effort, to say nothing of the expense. There were plenty of friends to enjoy the cake. As for the cream . . .

While she poured coffee he looked around the apartment. It was sparsely furnished. As he surveyed the small area she used for a kitchen, he realized suddenly that she'd probably had to borrow from her sleep time to make that cake since they'd been so busy lately. Unless he missed his bet, she had real cream in the refrigerator, too, and she'd probably bought that specifically for him. He had been thoughtless.

He got to his feet, hands in his pockets, and sauntered into the kitchen. "On second thought, I think I will have a slice of cake. And if you have cream and sugar for the coffee . . ."

She looked up at him, beaming. Yes, he thought,

he'd been right on the money with that guess; she'd shopped for him. He'd have to make a point of doing something equally nice for her. He smiled back and watched her take the cake out of its wrapping.

"Devil's food," he mused, emphasizing the first word, "with white icing. Well, well, am I being got at?"

"You don't look like a man who'd eat coconut cake," she said, and laughed at his expression.

She poured him a cup of coffee and put out the ceramic sugar dish and the matching creamer, filled with cream.

"Real cream," he said appreciatively. "I usually take my coffee black, but occasionally I like it sweetened and creamed."

"I didn't know how you took it," she replied.

"You'll know next time, won't you?" he asked gently.

That sounded promising, as if he meant to come back. She handed him a slice of cake on a nondescript saucer, with a fork, and they went back into the living room to eat it, using their laps for the cake and the coffee table for the coffee mugs.

"I know that you're used to a lot better than this," she said apologetically, "but my budget really doesn't run to silver and crystal and china just yet."

He studied her and then smiled curiously. "When I was ten, we lived in a tenement, two families of us in

one room not much bigger than this,'' he began, and
the smile grew as her expression changed. ''We had rats
the size of small dogs, roaches that carried hardware. I
had one decent pair of jeans that I wore all the time,
except when Mama washed them at the coin laundry,
a pair of boots with cardboard in the soles to keep the
cold out, and two faded shirts that belonged to my
uncle.'' He looked around her apartment. ''Lucky you,
to have all this space and nobody but yourself to live
in it.''

She burst out laughing. ''I'm sorry!'' she said, when
he gave her a questioning look. ''It's just that I've
seen where you live, and you drive an expensive car.
I thought you'd be horrified even to be seen here.''

''Surprise,'' he returned. He sipped his coffee and
his expression was flattering. ''Just right! So many people think coffee should taste like hot brown water.''

''I didn't mean for it to be so strong, but I made it
a half-hour ago.''

''I had a dinner meeting,'' he explained. ''A business
deal had almost fallen through, and I was busy persuad-
ing the other party that it would be mutually beneficial.
I won. But I couldn't get away as quickly as I wanted
to and then I had to stop at a tree lot and the store.
That's why I was late.''

''Oh, I didn't mind,'' she said quickly.

He gave her a level look. ''Of course you did. I have
good manners. I don't forget appointments.''

''I didn't think you did.'' She looked at the tree

lovingly. "It's been so long since I've had a tree," she mused.

"You surprise me," he murmured. "I thought most people had them."

She caught herself, remembering almost too late the pose of sophistication she'd adopted, with her invented wealth and social standing. "Well, we traveled so much, you see, when I was younger. It wasn't practical to put up a tree when we weren't home to enjoy it."

"I see." He'd wondered at her emotional reaction to his gift. It seemed rather odd that a monied young woman would be so overcome by such a small token. He would have expected her unusual delight if she'd been poor as a child and never had expensive trees or decorations. But perhaps if her family had traveled often at Christmas, it was the newness of being home to celebrate that had brought tears to her eyes.

"Where are your people from?" he asked casually. "You don't seem to have an accent.

"They're from . . . Louisiana. From Baton Rouge." She smiled, and the lie even sounded real. "My mother's people were French. My father's were British. At one time, our family owned one of the largest plantations in the state. After the Civil War," she added hastily.

"Then you had a wealthy upbringing?"

"Oh, yes. I could still have anything I want, you understand," she said, "but it's very important to me to prove to my moth . . . to my people that I can make my own fortune. I don't want to count on inherited wealth you see. I want to develop my talent and make a name for myself."

"And enough money to buy a Rolls and a few diamonds," he teased.

"Yes!"

"Do you still have relatives there, besides your mother?"

She sipped her coffee without answering, and her face paled. "My mother?"

He frowned. "You said that she was only traveling in Europe, didn't you? She doesn't live there?"

"Oh! Oh, of course not, no, she lives in Baton Rouge."

"You're very reticent about yourself."

"I'm not used to talking about myself, that's all," she prevaricated. "I'd really rather know about you."

His eye narrowed on her flushed face. "I don't have to know every single thing about you and I don't pry. You're safe with me. Safer than you might realize, and that's not a statement I make lightly. I've thought of pretty young women as fair game for years. When I was younger, I fancied myself the Latin lover; I was here today and gone tomorrow, never any ties. I'm older now, and I don't have to seduce every woman I meet. Does that reassure you?"

"You don't want to seduce me?" she asked. "Why, how insulting!"

He chuckled. His dark eye ran over her slowly, appreciating the slender curves of her body and the fine bones of her face. "Well, that isn't quite true," he confessed, "I would like to seduce you. But you're off-limits."

"Because I work for you?"

He looked solemn. "Because of that, and because despite your wealthy background, you don't seem particularly sophisticated, or worldly," he corrected, faintly curious about the way she paled when he said that. "You really are green for your age, and I don't like taking advantage of it. Besides that, I've just had a fairly traumatic event in my life and I'm not emotionally stable enough right now for a love affair. My mother comes first. She has to."

She searched his face quietly, curiously. It was odd how at ease she felt with him, how secure.

"What are you thinking so intently?" he queried gently.

"That you're beautiful," she said, grimacing when he burst out laughing. "I shouldn't have said that. I meant that you're remarkably handsome."

The smile faded and cynicism replaced it. He'd heard that line too many times from women who wanted something from him. He'd become distrustful over the years. "Do you think so?"

"The eye patch only makes you *look* dangerous," she added.

He didn't smile. If anything, he looked angry. "If I took it off, you'd faint."

She hated the pain in his face. Presumably, the

women he knew were squeamish. In her young life, Ivory had seen worse than a cut eye. "Do you think so?" she replied gently, turning his own question back at him. She folded her hands serenely in her lap. "Go ahead, then. Call my bluff."

The serenity pricked at his hot temper. "All right. Feast your eyes!" he snapped, and, impulsively, he ripped off the patch.

Her expression didn't change. She studied the damaged eye with quiet curiosity, but no revulsion. She moved closer, to his surprise, and her fingers came up lightly, hesitating at his cheek. He didn't move, or try to catch her wrist, so she touched the scar that ran through the eye. The lid was closed, and she imagined that it concealed a glass eye now, considering the obvious depth of the wound. He shivered faintly, to her surprise.

"How did it happen? Or don't you like to talk about it?" she asked softly.

His jaw tightened even more. She was the first person, outside his family, who hadn't flinched at the sight of him like this. Powerful emotions ran shuddering through him at the feel of her soft fingers on that ugliness.

"A knife fight," he said tautly. "In my late teens."

"I'll bet the other fellow looked worse."

"Considerably."

Her forefinger traced the thick black lash over the eye. It moved slightly under the contact. "Can you open it?" she asked.

"It's not glass," he said shortly. "There's no artificial eye because its uncomfortable for me to wear a glass one."

"Of course." She smiled at him softly.

He took a slow breath and levered the eyelid up.

She studied it quietly. It wasn't as horrible as he seemed to think. She thought of his pain, though, not of the scar and puckered flesh. The smile was still there. "It isn't so bad, you know. You could leave the patch off."

He glared at her. "People would stare at me!"

"Of course they would stare," she said impatiently, "you look like some Latin movie star."

Both eyebrows jerked down this time, and stayed there.

"You aren't that unsightly, at all. Heavens, one of my favorite actors has a glass eye and you'd never know it to look at him. You could probably even get used to one if you tried."

"The scars are too bad," he said irritably.

"And you won't have plastic surgery on them, of course," she agreed impishly, "because then you wouldn't have an excuse to go without that rakish eye patch."

"Damn you!"

She never saw it coming. He had her across his lap in a heartbeat, and his hard mouth ground into her lips before she could get out a protest. It wouldn't have done any good, anyway, because the hunger and passion of the kiss worked very quickly on a body that had never known either. The shocking thing was that she wasn't offended, or repulsed. In fact, she did something totally unexpected. She went pliant in his arms and her hands went up to tangle in the cool, clean strands of his thick, wavy black hair. He tasted of coffee and faintly of some after-dinner liqueur, licorice-flavored. His mouth was warm and hard and exciting. She felt a lean hand in her own hair, angling her face just where he wanted it. The other hand smoothed with shocking possession right over her breasts.

She struggled a little and his head lifted.

That one good eye was shattering as it stared down at her red face and swollen mouth. "I didn't tell you the other night that you taste like a virgin, did I? But you do."

His hand smoothed up past her ribcage and her frantic fingers caught at his.

He just looked at her, without lust, without amusement. "Grass-green, aren't you?" he murmured gently.

"Please . . . !"

He smiled. "You're very old-fashioned," he said. "Most women can't wait to open the buttons for me."

She pushed at his hand and he let her move it. "I'm not most women!" she said, angry at the innuendo.

"So I noticed." He traced her cheek instead, but he didn't offer to let her up again. He leaned back, still holding her against his chest, and pulled her protesting hand to his mouth. He kissed it. "You had a bad experience," he recalled. "Was it bad enough that you don't want to be a woman?"

The easy tenor of his voice was comforting. She felt less threatened and relaxed a little. "I don't think it was that bad," she said honestly. "It frightened me, although I was very young when it happened. But intimacy is dangerous, isn't it, even if I weren't old-fashioned about that sort of thing . . ." She flushed at the expression on his face. "Don't laugh."

"I'm not." He pushed back her disheveled hair. "I'm thirty-seven. I haven't lived so long without learning a lot. I always, always, use protection when I'm with a woman," he said firmly. "I have no diseases of any kind that I could give to you. Maybe a cold in winter," he added, teasing. The smile faded. "If we made love together, I'd use something or I'd insist that you use something; maybe both. I never want to make a woman pregnant." He didn't add the word "again." There was no need to bare his soul to her. Not yet.

The vehemence in the words was puzzling. "You mean, out of wedlock," she fished.

"I mean ever," he said shortly. "I don't want children."

She wondered if it was because of his retarded brother, if it was a genetic thing that worried him. She didn't know him well enough to pry. She could understand his feelings, though. Childhood could be so terrible. She wasn't sure that she wanted a child, either. But, then, she didn't want marriage. The thought of her childhood made her wary of any sort of family life. Her mother and father had hardly been any sort of advertisement for "happily ever after."

He touched her soft mouth. "What?" he prompted.

"I was thinking that I don't want to get married."

"Why?"

She shifted. "I can't tell you."

"We both have secrets," he replied with a soft sigh. He traced her eyebrows and then her straight nose. His lips tugged into a smile. "Will you want a lover one day?"

Her body tingled with the thought of it. "Yes, I think so. But . . ."

"But?"

"I haven't felt that way with anyone, except you."

His chest swelled. He traced her soft mouth and then bent to brush his lips over it in a way that made her spine tingle. "When you're ready to take that step, you can tell me."

"And be one in a line," she said on a sigh.

"Never." His gaze was steady and unblinking. "If you take me as a lover, I won't have women on the side. It will be you and only you."

"For as long as it lasts."

He looked thoughtful, searched her face and scowled. "I don't even know that I could live with myself if I had an affair with a virgin your age," he said, thinking out loud. "It might be a very lengthy love affair. It might last a long time."

"You wouldn't want to get that mixed up with some-one like me," she said sadly.

"Explain that."

She didn't dare. She faltered for the right words. "I'm a nobody in the fashion world," she amended, wanting to tell him about her background of poverty and deprivation, but afraid.

"Then we'll make sure you become a somebody first," he replied. He chuckled at her expression. "Isn't that what you want? To be a very rich and famous designer?"

"More than anything," she confessed.

"All right, then." He put her off his lap and sat back. "Let's see those new designs," he said, with a lightning change from prospective lover to employer that left her staggering.

CHAPTER
SEVEN

IVORY handed him her portfolio. "They aren't terribly good designs," she began worriedly.

"Let me be the judge of that." He felt uncomfortable without the eye patch. He reached for it, but she touched his hand lightly.

"Don't," she said gently. "You don't have to do that here."

He caught her hand roughly and pulled her down beside him. "You make me hungry when you say things like that. Watch out."

She smiled with scarcely contained excitement. He searched her eyes for a moment, then made a sound under his breath and released her hand, devoting his attention to the new drawings.

He whistled softly when he saw the suit. "Nice," he said. "Very nice. The inspiration for this wasn't Tudor."

"Actually, it was a pin I saw in a jeweler's window," she confessed. "It was a tiny bee made of gold and diamonds. They presented it on a field of oyster satin. I thought how gorgeous something similar would look on a suit jacket of that shade. So I changed the design to a butterfly, used silver beadwork instead of gold, and added a few flourishes. I didn't copy the artist in any way. This could all be beadwork instead of crystal if you'd rather.''

''You'll do Austrian crystal,'' he said, touching the drawing with a thoughtful expression on his handsome face. ''What a unique device. It reminds me of diamond pins created for the Duchess of Windsor, but she favored leopards, as I recall.''

''I like crystal,'' she said.

He lifted his head and studied her thoughtfully. ''That's what we'll call your designs: the Crystal Butterfly Collection. We'll do the butterflies in silver and gold and crystal . . .''

''How about in onyx? That was an idea Dee had for an evening suit . . .''

''Wonderful! You could even design a line of evening wear with the same motif as the suits.''

She caught her breath. She hadn't considered so monumental a scope.

''Not that I don't like the embroidered satin gown you did. I do. It's unique and very elegant. We'll keep it, but only as an haute couture piece; it's too expensive to produce the embroidery by hand and I don't like machine stitching. It's cheap.''

She laughed with unbearable delight. "Oh, I must be dreaming."

"Hardly," he mused. "You're quite talented. I begin to understand how you won our competition. We'll get out of the red and you'll be a top name in the industry. I have dreams of my own."

"You've made mine come true." She grimaced. "Miss Raines," she said through her teeth, "is not going to like this."

"Miss Raines won't be a problem," he said simply.

"She's a senior designer and she has all kinds of authority. She'll stick my designs in the back and use the ugliest models she can find. They'll trip going down the runway and everyone will laugh."

He burst out laughing himself at her remarks. "Do you think so? Leave Virginia to me. I'll handle this. I'll move her from designing to managerial duties. It *is* my company," he added.

"And you run it so well, Mr. Kells!" she murmured dryly.

"Don't I, though?" He looked very wise as he studied her, and a little arrogant. "I didn't get where I am without learning how to read and manipulate people," he said bluntly. "I'm good at it. You know why? It's because I know what motivates, what produces quality work."

She glanced in the corner. "Christmas trees?"

"And kisses," he chided gently, smiling.

She looked wounded. He reached out and took her hand in his.

"I'm teasing. You'll have to get used to it." He pressed his mouth to the palm of her hand and got to his feet, bending to retrieve the eye patch. This time he put it in place. It seemed to remove him, somehow, to make him less accessible. He was like a man hiding behind a mask now, his expression unreadable, his dark eye inscrutable as she rose from the sofa to stand beside him.

He looked down at her warmly. "Trim your tree. I've got a hundred things to do." His expression tautened. "Mama has a nurse, but I like to be at home with her at night. She's not having an easy time with the chemotherapy and radiation treatments. They make her very sick."

"I'm sorry. It must be difficult for you and your sister," she added, "having to stand by and not being able to help her."

"Very." He took her face in his hands and tilted it up to his quiet gaze. "We can't make a habit of this," he said as he bent down to her. "But I think an occasional taste of each other won't hurt so much."

He kissed her softly, and felt her body melt into his, felt her mouth part, inviting, submissive. She wasn't a woman who demanded. It went to his head. He lifted her a little roughly against him, and his mouth bit into hers with revealing hunger. When he heard her gasp, he put her back down, reluctantly letting her move away from the corded strength of his aroused body.

He had to fight to breathe normally. Her own emotions were easily seen. She was trembling.

"Do you like it, feeling this way with me?" he asked huskily. "It's narcotic. You begin to need it after a while, in larger and larger doses. If we kiss each other like that too often, we'll have each other, eventually."

"You make it sound like a threat," she said, trying to laugh off the shattering pleasure.

"Oh, it's more than that," he assured her solemnly. "And neither of us is quite ready for it. So let's keep things cool for a while. Okay?"

She managed a smile. "Okay."

"You see, the trouble is that you don't know how it feels to go all the way. I do." His smile was rueful, amused, tender.

She glared at him, suddenly jealous, possessive.

"You're jealous. I like that," he murmured quietly. "You'd fight for me, wouldn't you?"

The expression on her face puzzled him. She didn't answer. He couldn't know how much fighting she'd had to do over the years. She toyed with the skirt of her dress and turned. "I guess you're anxious to get home and see about your mother," she said. "I hope she's not feeling too bad."

"Yes. So do I." He opened the door and hesitated, his gaze narrowing. "I'll have to have some cost studies done. One of my assistants will get in touch with you on Monday to go over materials and labor with you.''

"What about Miss Raines?"

"I told you; leave her to me."

"Thank you, for the chance," she said sincerely. "I'll work very hard."

"I know you will." He touched her cheek. "I'm suspicious of people, did you know? When I first started out, people tried to use me for various reasons. I'm sensitive about being a stepping stone."

Her eyes didn't blink. She nodded. "I would be, too."

He relaxed, and smiled a little. "Thanks for the coffee and cake."

"My pleasure."

He was remembering the way she'd trembled in his arms, the furious beat of her heart, the way her breath caught when his mouth bit into hers. No, he decided. She couldn't have faked it, not for all the career chances in the world. She was basically honest, a rare trait. He recognized it, because it was one of his own.

"Goodnight," he said.

"Goodnight."

He closed the door behind him and walked, preoccupied, to the elevator. As he passed an open door, a man in a wheelchair waved at him. He waved back. It was like the old days. He'd done his share of apartment living. He knew the family feeling it gave to know all the people down the hall. This man looked kind. He smiled as he thought that Ivory was, too. She wasn't beautiful, but she was talented and she had a kind heart. If he were still a marrying man, she'd be at the top of his list of possibilities. But that was something he'd never be. And now, with his mother in such a desperate condition, he couldn't even think about having a private life. What he was beginning to feel for Ivory would have to wait.

The office was strangely quiet when Ivory walked in on Monday morning. She looked around her warily, fully expecting Miss Raines to jump out of hiding. The older woman might not react as Curry expected to the news that she had been given managerial duties. Miss Raines had been a designer, apparently, most of her adult life. She wouldn't like giving it up.

A faint noise in her dark office caught her attention. She checked her watch. She was an hour late, because her bus had been delayed in traffic. Surely someone else was in the building. She felt nervous as her hand reached for the doorknob and slowly opened the door.

The lights came on, and everyone who worked in the sample room was waiting for her.

"Congratulations!" Dee called out, hugging her. The girls behind her echoed their best wishes.

"But how did you know?" Ivory asked, aghast.

"We have our ways," Dee murmured dryly. She

laughed. "Oh, all right, I have a friend in the executive offices. She called first thing and told me, just about the time Mr. Kells sent for Miss Raines."

"She hasn't come back yet?"

"She won't be back," Dee replied. "My friend said that they had a nasty argument. He won. She told one of the assistants to pack up all her things and send them to her apartment. She's had another offer, apparently, and was going to take it right away. Bad luck, but she never should have shot off her mouth to Mr. Kells about you. They said he was furious!" Dee shuddered with mock horror. "God forbid I should ever get on the wrong side of him!"

"Me, too," Ivory said wholeheartedly.

"Anyway, you'll be tossed in at the deep end right away. You're to get her old office down here and as much staff as you need to rush that suit into production, along with at least six more pieces to start the collection. We're all just overwhelmed!"

"Well, so am I," Ivory said, thinking to herself that Curry Kells had put his weekend to amazingly good use. "I have to sit down," she added in a subdued tone. "My goodness, maybe I've gone mad."

"Not yet. You will, trying to get these designs into production. Harry Lambert is on his way down to discuss figures with you," she added. "And you watch yourself, because he liked yours at Curry's party, if you remember."

* * *

Indeed Harry had liked her figure, and still did, but he was very businesslike as he shook hands and sat down with her in her old office. She had yet to move into the new one; and despite Dee's assertions, she wasn't taking a single step until someone with authority told her to.

"Curry sent me to look at some cost figures," Harry said with a grin, and didn't mention that the older man had done so reluctantly. The man he'd intended to dispatch wasn't free, and Harry was. Curry's reluctance to have him talk to Ivory had irritated Harry. He couldn't forget how Curry had appropriated her at the party. "You're a wonder, aren't you?" he added, with more than a hint of spite. "Nobody knew your name before you came to Curry's party, and now you're a senior designer." He was insinuating things that Ivory didn't like.

"I haven't done anything that I'd mind reading about in the gutter press," she informed him with a straight face. She couldn't afford to let him see that she had, actually, but it had nothing to do with the present or Curry.

"You have to admit that it's a great leap," he continued.

"Yes, it is." She smiled politely. "Let me show you why it happened."

She brought out her portfolio and opened it, spreading the new designs out before his stunned eyes. He couldn't stop staring. He knew genius when he saw it. He looked at her and scowled. Amazing that with that sort of talent she'd been overlooked for even six months.

"These are like nothing I've seen in years," he said seriously.

"I should hope not," she replied. "I don't copy other designers."

"Indeed you don't need to." He picked up the suit design with the Austrian crystal butterfly emblem on the bodice and shook his head in wonder. "This will be a runaway success. You won't be able to meet the demand."

"A prediction or wishful thinking?"

He laughed. "Well, call it a prediction for now. I do know salable goods. The cost is going to be the problem. It's going to be expensive to produce, as I think you are already aware."

"I could show it to a few buyers . . ."

"And risk having the design stolen? Bite your tongue."

"I didn't think about that." She chewed on her index nail thoughtfully. "I showed it to Dee, though," she confessed.

"Oh, Dee." He laughed. "She's a clam, like the rest of us. No, you can't show it to buyers until it's in production. And that's what we have to work out right now—getting it there." He opened a notebook. "Curry wants no skimping, either. He wants satin-lined oyster linen for the jacket and skirt, and Austrian crystal for the butterfly. What sort of buttons?''

"Silver, to match the outline of the butterfly," she said at once. "And no pockets. It's to be a simple, straight design with only the necessary darts for fit. The jacket is collarless and I've designed an oyster silk blouse to go with it, an open-necked one with a soft collar. See?" She indicated it on the design.

"Hmmmm." He was studying it with an eye to price. "You've shown it mid-calf. Is that where you want it?"

"I can compromise on length. It might be well to shorten it, but not above the knee," she added firmly.

"No, I like it as it's drawn and so did Curry. It won't mean that much difference in price if the length remains as it is here. The buttons . . . how do you feel about having them crystal, too, instead of silver?"

She pursed her lips. "I like it."

"Or fabric-covered, to enhance the butterfly?"

She looked at him approvingly. "You know, I like that idea best of all."

He didn't mention that it was Curry's idea. The man wasn't a designer, but he did know what looked good on women. And no wonder, he'd had so damned many of them. Harry shifted, trying not to think about his own lackluster love-life.

"Let's do fabric-covered, then." He made some notes. "Thread?"

She told him, gauge and color, and added information about the zipper and skirt button.

"You want silk for the blouse?"

"Silk charmeuse," she emphasized. "Yes."

He sighed. "That will be expensive."

"All of it will be expensive. But if it impresses anyone, it will be worth it. If I could afford an expensive suit, I certainly wouldn't want one that was cheaply executed to cut costs."

He chuckled. She was forthright. And she had a point. "All right. I can see your position." He studied her quietly. "You'd be a knockout in something like this," he said abruptly.

She laughed. "Not me. I like blue jeans and sweatshirts when I'm not working."

"If you make a name for yourself, you won't. You'll need to wear the clothes you design and be seen by a lot of people."

The thought thrilled her, because who better to show her off than Curry? She dropped her eyes before she betrayed her renegade hopes to Harry.

"I suppose so. But getting known—that's a long way off."

"Only a month off. We'll know very soon after the January showings if you're a success or a failure."

"If I'm a failure, I won't be around very long," she observed quietly. "I will have been a flash in the pan, and I'll be looking for a job."

"Oh, Curry will find you something," he said.

"Only if he's short on bundle-girls," she returned dryly.

He burst out laughing. "You've got a sense of humor. That will help." He turned back to the costing and conversation took a serious turn.

After Harry finished, word came from the executive offices on Wall Street that Ivory was to go and see Curry right away.

"But I don't know how to get there," she said to Dee, her expression one of consternation.

"Any cab driver will." She jotted down the address on a piece of scrap paper and handed it to Ivory. "There'll be a security guard. You'll have to go to the desk and sign in, and they'll give you a visitor's badge to wear. It's that way everywhere these days, especially since the World Trade Center bombing. You can't blame people for being super-cautious."

"No, I guess not." She looked around and smiled at Dee. "You don't suppose he'll scrap the whole idea when Harry's figured the cost?"

"I don't really think so," Dee mused. "Go on. He'll tell you why he sent for you."

He could have come himself, Ivory thought, and then was ashamed of herself for thinking it. A man in Curry Kells's position was hardly expected to go and see employees. Still, he'd gone to see Ivory at home and given her that wonderful tree. She'd spent the evening decorating it, and she hated the thought of Christmas coming and going because she'd have to take it down. Then she remembered something: she'd forgotten to give Curry his gift on Friday.

The thought disturbed her all the way over to his office. She signed in, got her badge, and went up on the shiny elevator all the way to the thirtieth floor where his office was. A secretary in the spacious waiting room showed her into the big room where Curry sat at a polished oak desk.

He rose as she walked in and motioned her to a black leather chair. She knew the black-and-white-striped dress she was wearing was not very elegant, but she had altered it to fit perfectly and felt self-assured when she wore it. That assurance vanished when she saw Curry's face. It bore an expression that was cold and businesslike.

"You're firing me," she said with resignation.

He leaned back in his chair with a smile. "Hardly," he replied. "I wanted to know how things went with Harry."

She blinked. That was a surprise. Harry should have arrived at Wall Street at least a half hour before she got there. "Haven't you talked with him?"

He nodded. "He was here a few minutes ago, and he looked guilty. I want to know if there were any innuendos made about how you got to be a senior designer so quickly. I won't have women harrassed here— especially you."

His concern made her feel warm inside. "I showed him my designs," she offered.

"That wasn't what I asked, Ivory."

She crossed and uncrossed her legs. "He wasn't insulting."

"I was," he replied. "I was damned insulting. I didn't want to have him talk to you and he knew it, but everyone here in the executive offices was busy."

"Yes, well, isn't Mr. Lambert head of our division?" she asked warily.

"He is. But I usually have one of the financial people do cost estimates."

"Oh."

"I want to know if he upset you."

She lifted both eyebrows. "What did you intend to do if he had?"

"I enjoyed firing Virginia Raines," he said arrogantly. "Maybe I haven't fired enough people yet."

She couldn't believe she'd heard that.

He didn't blink. "I know. It isn't quite rational, is it? But that's how I feel. I don't want you hurt by anyone."

She smiled gently. "Thank you. But I can take up for myself when I have to. I'm not helpless."

"Let me feel protective," he said quietly. "It isn't something I indulge often, and it's usually limited to family."

She shrugged. "Suit yourself, but I don't listen to gossip and as long as I know how I get where I'm going, nobody else's opinion matters."

"An interesting attitude," he mused. "It makes me

wonder how it was developed. You've been exposed to public gossip before, perhaps?''

She stared at him with cold eyes. ''There was no scandal in my family,'' she said with practiced hauteur. ''I come from a socially impeccable background . . . !''

He sat up, his hands folded on the desk. ''I'm sorry,'' he said at once. ''That was unforgivable. The reason I asked you over here was to explain what we're going to do with you,'' he said, smoothing over the awkward moment. ''I'm going to have your new office redecorated. You can pick and choose your own furnishings, paintings and such. I'm sure that you don't share Virginia's taste. An office is an extension of the person. It should suit you.''

The statement prompted her to look around his. The black leather furniture was complemented by white curtains with red and black ties. On one wall was a painting of a stone fort surrounded by palm trees, and crossed swords, antique-looking, hung on another. The whole office had a Latin flavor, right down to the few pieces of small statuary that graced its tables.

''My mother is Puerto Rican,'' he told her, and waited for any hint of prejudice to show on her face. It didn't.

''And your father?'' she probed gently.

''His great-grandparents were Irish immigrants. He was illiterate.''

''A lot of people are,'' she said. She averted her eyes. He had a background very similar to her real one.

She longed to tell him the truth, but it was already too late. She was trapped by the past she had invented.

His gaze narrowed as he studied her. "You have a vague Southern accent. It's hardly noticeable unless you're upset or excited. You hide it well. Are you ashamed of it?"

"Not particularly, but I went to a very good private school. Before I started at the fashion design school," she added quickly.

His firm lips pursed as he studied her. "You're a lady of many mysteries," he said absently. "Before I'm through, I'm going to know you right down to your bones, and you're going to know me the same way."

Her eyes lifted in faint surprise. He sounded very serious. He looked serious as well.

"Don't start looking for places to hide," he said with a gentle smile. "We've got all the time in the world. And right now, I have more on my plate than I can handle, anyway. You'd be a terrible complication."

She let her eyes fall to his dark wine-colored tie. "So would you, for me."

"But it won't always be this way. And that's all the more reason to be honest with each other," he said.

She picked at a short fingernail. "I know." She smoothed over the picked place. Her conscience was already killing her. "Goodness, is that the time?" she said suddenly, checking her watch. "I promised Dee I'd help her with the new pattern."

He saw the subterfuge for what it was. "All right, *querida*. We'll leave it there for now."

She searched his face with faint pleasure. "Why did you call me darling?"

He pounced on that understanding of his mother's native tongue with a suddenness that she couldn't foresee.

"*¿Cuando aprendiste español?*"

"*Cuando era una niñita,*" she replied without thinking, and then caught her breath at being caught out so easily.

"Well, well," he murmured. "I would have thought French would be more natural to you than Spanish, being from Louisiana. *Parles-tu français?*"

When she stared at him questioningly, he looked back at her the same way. "No, you don't speak French, do you?"

"I've . . . forgotten most of what I learned as a child," she said ingeniously. "I didn't know that you spoke both Spanish and French," she said hastily, trying to divert him.

"I have something of a knack for languages. But I can't claim Spanish as a real accomplishment, since I've been speaking it all my life. Unless I miss my guess, so have you."

She ground her teeth together. She hadn't wanted to give herself away.

"You said your mother had French ancestry, and your father had British. Where did you learn Spanish?"

She scarcely heard him. She was choking in a stranglehold of memories of her mother. She jumped to her feet, gasping for breath. Her eyes were hunted.

He stood up, too. "Ivory," he said sharply. "Ivory!"

She looked at him, and finally registered who he was.

"It's all right," he said gently. "Sit down, now. Sit down. Calm down. I promise you, I won't ask another question."

She fumbled her way back into the chair, pitifully aware that her face was ashen. She clung to the leather arms, seeking security.

He buzzed for his secretary. "Send Bill for coffee, will you? Cream and sugar," he added.

"Yes, sir."

Curry picked up a pen on his desk, toying with it while Ivory composed herself.

"That was not fair," she told him.

He sighed roughly. "I know. I'm sorry. It's just that you're so damned full of contradictions. It was only a simple question, Ivory."

"A man taught me Spanish, all right?!" she asked angrily.

"A man. But not a lover."

"Not a lover," she muttered.

"But he wanted to be?"

She folded her hands in her lap, fighting for control. She looked at him after a minute, her face composed. "About the designs," she said, grasping for conversational gambits, "is the cost going to be acceptable?"

He hesitated, but in the end he let her get away with it. She was too upset already. He wanted to know more about her, that was all; but she was like a clam about her past. Perhaps there had been a bad experience, and he was causing her pain. He decided to let it go.

"Hell, no, the cost isn't going to be acceptable." He grinned. "But I'm going to pay it anyway. I've always been a gambler, when I had a sure thing. This is no gamble. I can feel it."

"What if you're wrong?" she worried. "What if nobody likes the designs?"

"Everybody will." He leaned forward intently. "I'd better not find out that Harry insulted you," he added, unexpectedly returning to their earlier discussion.

"He didn't. Not after he saw the designs," she said with a faint smile.

"I'm not surprised. Don't let him bother you. He's a junior executive, and expendable if he harrasses you. He came on strong at my party, but that was a social affair. In the workplace, a man has an obligation to be no more than a co-worker."

"Thank you. But you won't have to fire him."

He sat back in his chair. "Now. I've been going over the design for the suit. I've got people out scouring the country for Austrian crystal, and the pattern-makers are busy on sizing. I'm having the sample room run up two or three suits in various sizes for the showing. If we lose a model, I don't want any last-minute snags about fitting."

"Neither do I."

"We can do the suit in wool or cashmere for winter," he continued. "But for summer, it has to be a silk blend or linen."

"I'd love to do it in wool," she said dreamily.

"And we will, if it impresses the buyers." He chuckled. "It will. Stop backsliding. You have to have faith in yourself."

"I always have had, to a point," she said. "It's a gift, you know, not something I struggled to learn how to do," she added. "And Harry had some very good ideas about altering the design just enough to cut costs. Like having self-buttons."

He tossed the pen onto the desk. "My idea," he said. "I'm glad you liked it." He lifted an eyebrow. "Harry didn't mention that?"

She sighed. "I should have known."

"Of course you should. I'm not a designer, but I made damned sure I knew something about designing when I took over this company."

"You have a lot of companies."

"Ten," he said carelessly. "This is the only design firm."

"How do you keep up with them all?"

"I put in good managers and scare hell out of them with surprise inspections," he confessed. He sat forward a little. "How does the tree look?"

"It's beautiful. I forgot to give you your present," she added.

"Suppose I come over Christmas Eve for it?"

Her eyes lit up. "That would be so nice. But . . . but you'll want to be with your family, your mother."

"Yes, but I can spare an hour," he said gently. "I'll look forward to it."

"So will I."

The door opened and Bill, the office boy, came in with two cups of coffee and sugar and cream on a tray. He put them on the desk, staying only long enough to deposit them.

"Drink your coffee," Curry invited. "And while we're doing that, I'll explain the cost estimates to you. I think this is going to be one of my more profitable ventures." And, he added silently, as he watched her put cream in her cup, in more ways than one.

CHAPTER
EIGHT

IVORY'S life took on the semblance of a dream. She went to work each day with a light step and a smile, overjoyed to be doing what she loved most and getting paid for it. With Virginia Raines gone, the office was more relaxed and even more productive. The girls on the line were sewing clothes that they really liked, and they tried harder to do a good job.

The suit she had designed turned out even better than Ivory had expected. She added pleated puff shoulders to it, to emphasize the smooth line from shoulder to waist. Although the change was an extra expense, Curry didn't say a word about the cost; he was so pleased with the improvement.

Ivory had no intimate contact with Curry on the job, although he spent a lot of time in the building, overseeing production. They had coffee in her office from time to time, and his quiet gaze lingered longer and longer on Ivory, who noticed and became painfully shy. He had a way of looking at her that made her toes curl up in her shoes, and the attraction between them became more intense every day. She couldn't forget the warm hunger in his kisses, and she dreamed of him at night.

There were long conversations when he came to her office, or when she went to his, about work and politics and the world at large. She found him easy to talk to, and despite the excitement he engendered in her, she felt more comfortable with him than she'd ever felt with anyone else. He shared that contentment, it seemed, because often he sought her out for no more important reason than to share a cup of coffee with him.

He didn't see her away from work, however, and he didn't invite her to go out with him. He'd said that he didn't want complications. Obviously he meant it. But he spent enough time with Ivory that she didn't mind so much. They grew closer every day, in ways far removed from any physical attraction.

Belle was chosen to model the new suit. Ivory fitted it on her the morning of Christmas Eve, before the noontime closing. It was disturbing to Ivory to see the woman here now and to remember her connection to Curry, who had become so very important in her own life. She was jealous and insecure, especially when the gloriously beautiful redhead mentioned that she'd been to an art gallery showing with Curry just the night before.

Although Ivory had already made so much progress, she hadn't made her mark yet and was still a long way from affording designer clothing and the kind of accessories she'd need for a high-society night on the town. She realized that quite suddenly. Curry couldn't take her to an art gallery show because she dressed like a street person and he'd be embarrassed. Why hadn't she thought of that until now?

The model frowned as she studied the other woman's bent head. "You look worried. Doesn't the suit fit me the way you think it should?"

"You know very well that it does," Ivory replied calmly. "You're lovely. The suit really was designed for a brunette, you know, but you have the flair and height that add elegance. And I think it would look almost as good on a blond."

"I love it," Belle said with a smile. "It's the most dramatic outfit I've ever modeled for Kells-Meredith!"

"Thank you."

She finished her minor adjustments and left Dee to run it up on her machine. The other seamstresses were very good, but Dee had a special touch.

Belle's fitting left Ivory depressed and sad. She hadn't seen Curry for two days except at a distance as he was passing through the building. She supposed that she'd read too much into the Christmas tree, a few light kisses and sweet words and the extra time he spent with her on the job. He wouldn't have taken Belle on a date if he'd had any real feelings for Ivory. She had to remember her place. She was just a member of the staff, after all, not his lover. He liked being with her, but that didn't mean he wanted a permanent relationship. He was an attractive, worldly man. She couldn't expect him to be a monk.

Besides, she'd been so busy designing and dreaming of fame and fortune that she'd forgotten her real status here. She wasn't what people thought she was. Her carefully modulated voice and good manners had been acquired at design school. The Ivory who'd presented herself at the front door of the Paris Design Academy in Houston had been an oddity and even something of an embarrassment her first few days there. She was literate, but her clothes came from yard sales and she did not know how to use makeup, how to dress, even how to behave in civilized company. She spoke with the kind of drawl that was the mark of the uneducated, and the pronunciation of some of the basic fashion words was almost beyond her. If it hadn't been for the kindness of one of the female instructors, who taught Ivory speech and social graces, she might never have made the grade. No one knew that the scholarship she'd won had been the only opportunity in her deprived, and abusive, childhood.

She'd always had the gift of being able to draw what she saw; but her drawing and studying weren't encouraged by her mother. Marlene was too busy with her own life to consider what Ivory could achieve in hers.

After her husband's death, she'd used the insurance money to buy expensive clothes and cosmetics. Her investment in her looks had led to several dead-end love affairs, the last of which was with a rich landowner named Larry, who'd paid the bills for her and given Ivory a job working in the fields—at Marlene's insistence. She needed the extra money to pay liquor bills she didn't want Larry to know about.

When that money wasn't enough, Marlene became proficient at shoplifting around town. It was easy to blame Ivory for it and then put on her martyred face, so that people felt sorrier for her and agreed not to have Ivory arrested. Those charges had hurt, because Ivory was honest. Marlene had never been.

Ivory had to fight her mother to get to finish high school. Then, two years of hard labor went by before the design scholarship contest was announced in one of the state newspapers. Ivory had entered, secretly. When she won—to her astonishment—she spent every penny she had on a bus ticket to Houston and promised to reimburse her mother for her room and board when she found work.

What a laugh—to be asked to reimburse her mother for raising her own child. But it was no joke. Marlene Costello was vicious and unpredictable. She seemed to have no scruples, and she'd spent her life creating trouble and scandal for the people around her. Before Ivory's father died, Marlene had been a little more stable, sometimes even kind.

After her husband died, Marlene's kind periods grew farther apart until they all but vanished. Marlene had allowed Ivory to go to design school only on the understanding that she would begin repaying her debt to Marlene from the minute she got her first paycheck. Ivory would have agreed to anything to get away. And once in Houston, she'd changed her name legally to Keene in a halfhearted attempt to escape her mother. But she'd been too intimidated to run away completely. She sent small checks home, cashier's checks from the bank, and tried to put the past behind her.

One incident, however, was impossible to forget— or forgive. Not too long after Larry had died, Marlene found a new boyfriend. She and her new man got roaring drunk the same week Ivory was accepted to design school. Marlene decided then on a ménage à trois. She helped her boyfriend hold her daughter down, laughing all the while. Fortunately, he was too drunk to do much. Also fortunately, an off-duty policewoman who had been passing by, heard Ivory's screams and rushed to her assistance. After Marlene's cursing, drunken boyfriend was taken away in a squad car, Marlene became hysterical and claimed to be the victim. She blamed the whole episode on her daughter's attempts to seduce the man. Because Marlene had built such a tissue of lies to belittle her daughter, she was believed again. That was the last straw for Ivory. She accepted the scholarship by letter and when she received the paperwork, she announced her plans to leave despite all of Marlene's threats. Perhaps Marlene realized that she'd crossed the line during her last drunken spree, because she didn't really try very hard to deter her daughter.

Ivory had escaped and nothing on earth would make her go back. Still the thought of her mother kept her sleepless some nights. Ivory had built a good life for herself here in New York. People accepted her as someone with a decent background, as a person in her own right. Marlene could ruin it with her lies. To keep her away, Ivory had no choice but to split her check with Marlene. The threats came by mail, regularly. Pay up or else. She knew that her mother wasn't bluffing.

Marlene blamed everyone, especially Ivory, for her lack of wealth. She could have had a career if it hadn't been for her ugly daughter keeping her in prison, she raged. It was Ivory's fault. She wished the girl had never been born. Once, she pulled her father's old shotgun out of the closet in one of her drunken bouts and threatened to kill Ivory. Fortunately, there were no shells for it. The pale blue eyes staring at her down that long barrel had screamed murder.

There were no social services offices in Harmon and no close family to report the mistreatment of her child. The school officials knew nothing of Ivory's home life, and Marlene made frequent trips to PTA meetings and activities to show everyone what a good mother she was. Early on, she'd learned how to convince people that Ivory was a pathological liar. The small Texas community was full of people who only shrugged when Ivory ran out in the road from time to time crying that her mother was hurting her. Marlene had told them that Ivory did it frequently, for no apparent reason. She

made sure that the bruises didn't show. By the time
Ivory was in her teens, Marlene had destroyed her credi-
bility.

Even today, if she were to go back to Harmony,
Texas, people wouldn't think any better of her. She'd
heard from the one friend she had that Marlene told
everyone how ungrateful her only child was, and it
hadn't gone unnoticed that Ivory never even came to
see her.

After her husband's death, Marlene had been allowed
to stay in the small house, which was owned by Larry,
who had been her husband's boss. The job Marlene had
induced him to give Ivory was picking and packing fruit
in the orchards with a family of Mexicans who worked
on his farm. It had been hard work, but Ivory had had
no choice. She wasn't badly treated, she was away from
Marlene all day, and she was paid. Of course, Marlene
took the money; but some of Ivory's few happy memories were associated with that loving Hispanic family.
That was where she'd learned her Spanish. It was part
of the past she felt obliged to hide from Curry, although
he made the lowliest profession seem noble if it involved
sacrifice. His mother had been a housekeeper, and he
thought her a paragon. He didn't seem to care very
much about social position, but he cared about people.
Ivory smiled at that thought and then grew sad remembering that he and Belle had been out on the town.

She went home that afternoon, Christmas Eve, with
her heart around her ankles, imagining Belle out at some

glitzy party with Curry. He might spend some of the evening with his mother, though, considering her condition. She mustn't be jealous of him, Ivory told herself firmly. She had no right.

Curry had mentioned that he planned to drop by on Christmas Eve for his present, but Ivory didn't believe he really meant it. She was sure that he'd forgotten all about her, so she didn't bother to dress up.

After she made herself a meager supper, she sat in front of her gorgeous Christmas tree with a cup of instant cappuccino and listened to Christmas music on television. She had developed a love for opera, and Luciano Pavarotti was singing arias, along with Plácido Domingo, on the educational channel.

The buzz at the intercom came just at the end of "Nessun Dorma," from her favorite opera, *Turandot*, by Puccini. She grimaced at the interruption in the middle of the exquisite crescendo, and she lingered just a moment before she got up, reluctantly, to answer the signal. It must be a neighbor, she thought, offering good wishes.

"May I come up?" a familiar deep voice asked.

Her heart skipped a beat. "Y . . . yes! Of course!" She pressed the buzzer next to the intercom to unlock the outer door.

A minute later, there was a knock on the door and she ran to answer it. Curry was leaning there against the wall, in the sort of evening clothes she had seen only in store windows. Her heart ran away at just the sight of him. He was unbearably elegant, from his white tie to his tuxedo, an overcoat with a white silk opera scarf thrown carelessly over one arm. Even his black dress shoes were polished so brightly that they reflected the hall light overhead.

He lifted a dark eyebrow, letting his curious gaze wander down her body in the jeans and bright red T-shirt she was wearing.

"There didn't seem any need to dress up," she faltered. "I didn't expect anyone . . ."

He smiled lazily. "Not even me? I told you a while back that I was going to stop by for my Christmas present, didn't I?"

Of course he had, but she hadn't really believed he would after she'd talked to Belle. "Oh!" She opened the door and let him inside, closing it gently behind him. "The tree, it's lovely," she rambled as she watched him drape the coat and scarf over the back of her one straight chair. He was studying the tree intently.

"Yes, it is," he agreed. "You did a good job." He turned, watching her closely. "Belle said that you looked worried when she went for her fitting."

She lowered her eyes before he could read her feelings in them. "I couldn't get the darts in the jacket straight," she lied.

He didn't believe that for a minute. "She told you that I took her to a gallery showing."

She drew in an impatient breath. "Look, you have

no ties to me," she said. "It's none of my business. I only work for you."

He moved toward her slowly and stopped a foot away. He tilted her face up to his searching gaze, watching her color. "Don't. I know how I'd feel if someone told me you'd been out on the town with another man."

Her expression was fluid. Surprise finally won it over.

"I told you at the beginning that Belle and I were friends, but I think I'd better qualify the relationship. The gallery showing was all business. Belle was wearing one of the pieces from another of our collections. I wanted to show off some of our designs. I had two other models there as well, not just Belle."

"O . . . oh."

"I don't usually bother explaining myself. It's different with you. You're very vulnerable. I don't want to hurt you unnecessarily." He traced the soft flush down her cheek to the corner of her mouth and let his finger explore the shape of her soft lips.

"We aren't . . . involved," she whispered, made breathless by his intoxicating nearness and that maddening finger tracing her mouth.

"We could be, if I were more of a roué," he replied with a faint smile. "I'm very protective of you. Even against my own base inclinations."

"Are they so base?"

He chuckled. "You might think so." He bent and

brushed his mouth lightly over her lips, drawing back much too soon. "Where's my present, Ivory?"

"Mercenary man," she accused.

"Well, I don't get presents often," he explained. "I told you."

She reached under the tree and drew out the small package. The other one, for Dee, had already been given away. She placed it in his hands with trepidation.

"It's not much," she said worriedly. "Don't expect . . ."

He kissed her softly. "Hush," he said, his deep voice tender.

He opened the package and opened the small box. He smiled, and with genuine appreciation.

"It's a real pearl," she pointed out.

Odd that she seemed to think it was, when he knew from the setting that it was cultured. Perhaps she didn't buy pearls often. Well, she'd know the difference after tonight. And not for all the world would he have admitted that his jewelry case had a dozen or so tie tacks made of South Sea pearls set in 18-karat gold. He examined it with the same satisfaction he'd have felt if she'd given him a new yacht.

"Do you like it?" she persisted, nervous.

"Oh, I like it, all right." He bent and kissed her again, a little longer this time, with breathless patience. "I have something for you, too."

"But you gave me the tree! And all those decorations!"

He waved the expense away. "Hardly a proper Christmas present. Here."

He handed her a box. It had a jeweler's label on it, and inside was a black velvet-covered box. Her hands trembled and almost dropped it as she forced the lid open and saw what was inside. She kept looking, unbelieving.

"Great minds run in the same direction, don't they? Try them on."

Her fingers touched the pearls. They had the palest pink sheen, like the inside of a seashell. They felt hard, and strangely warm. "They're . . . real?" she faltered.

"Yes, they are. And I mean real, not cultured."

She had a vague idea of the expense. "But you can't!"

So she did know the difference in price. That reassured him. A woman from her wealthy background would have to, of course, and she would hardly have spent hundreds of dollars for a tie tack on such short acquaintance.

"Of course I can do it," he replied. "You'll be going to shows, meeting buyers, representing the company. You can't dress properly without a good string of pearls. Presumably you don't like jewelry, because you seldom wear any."

She had to agree because she couldn't admit that she couldn't afford nice jewelry; she was supposed to be from wealthy Louisiana society. She took the pearls reverently out of the box and put them on, uneasy at handling something so beautiful and costly. She'd never had a good piece of jewelry in her life.

"The catch is tricky, isn't it?" she asked with an apologetic laugh as she fumbled with it.

"Here." He fastened it for her, breathing in the faint floral scent that clung to her hair, which was almost as wavy as his own. His hands on her shoulders were heavy and warm, lightly caressing. "Do you have a mirror?"

"A hand-held one, on the dresser." Her voice sounded husky.

He let her go, reluctantly, to fetch it, and held it so that she could see the way they looked against her throat. She had a slender neck. He'd been right about the color, too. It suited her skin tone much better than a silver-gray tint would have.

"These, too," he added suddenly, producing a second box. "I noticed that your ears were pierced."

"Oh, no, Curry, you can't," she pleaded, embarrassed by how expensive the gifts were.

"Yes, I can. Don't argue."

She opened that box, too, and discovered a pair of pearl studs that matched the necklace. There was such a difference between these small pearls and the one in his tie tack that she felt mortified. Hers was so obviously a cultured pearl, but she hadn't known until she'd seen the real thing. She hoped he didn't wonder why she didn't know the difference. She still had so much to learn about wealth.

She fitted the earrings into her lobes and then stood looking up at him with anticipation.

He nodded. "Yes. They suit you, all right. I'll have to take you out one night, so that I can wear my tie tack. We'll be perfectly matched, like the pearls," he teased.

Her face fell with her eyes. "I couldn't go out with you."

"Why?"

"Well, look at me," she said on a groan, indicating her clothes. "Curry, I can't afford the clothes I'd need to go out with you! I'd be an embarrassment to you at an exclusive restaurant, without the clothes I left back home. You see," she lied convincingly, "I wanted to start from scratch. I wanted to earn my place in the world, all the way, so I brought nothing with me." She laughed nervously. "Why, you wouldn't want to be seen with me at the local fast food joint in the sort of clothes I wear . . ."

"*Querida*," he said gently, pulling her back when she would have walked away. "You're lovely as you are. The clothes are not important."

She smiled. "Thank you for the compliment but you know how important clothes are; you make them."

"And you design them. You can wear the beautiful satin dress you wore to my party," he reminded her.

"I sold you the design . . ."

"And I'm telling you to wear it," he returned.

She brightened. "You'll have to wait for warmer weather, though."

He framed her face in his lean hands. "What sort of coat do you want? I'll buy one for you."

She colored furiously and tried to move away. She remembered Marlene teasing her married lover, begging for pretty dresses and coats and new shoes.

He held her securely. "I embarrass you. Why?"

"I'd feel like a kept woman," she said. "Without honor, or pride."

"Ah. I see." He drew in a slow breath as he studied her. "No woman such as you has come into my life since I became wealthy," he mused. "I don't know how to deal with someone who wants nothing material from me."

"The pearls are too much, already," she said. "I'll be able to afford a coat in a month or so."

"The financial obligations you mentioned—are they serious?"

"Heavens, no!" she laughed, flushing a little. "I send money to a poor relation back home, that's all."

He watched her closely. "You do this because you choose to?"

"Of course!"

Her reply was a little too quick. He was a shrewd man, with a keen intellect, who knew when an answer was less than the truth. But he was a good poker player as well. He smiled. "Of course." He pursed his lips.

"Since you will not permit me to buy you a coat, will you permit me to lend you one?"

She blinked. "Well . . ."

"Only for an evening out," he promised.

"I suppose I could do that," she said, yielding to his persuasion, while inside she was churning with excitement. "I haven't been out at night since I've been in New York. Just to a movie occasionally."

"New York at night is not a thing to miss," he said. "After the new year, we'll make a point of some evening entertainment."

"I guess you're busy with family this time of year, especially now," she added gently, remembering his mother.

His face darkened for an instant. "Yes." He touched her soft hair. "It's a sad time for us, but we mustn't show it. Mama gets upset if we pamper her too much. I want you to meet her."

"In the new year," she agreed.

He looked gently on her uplifted face. "We're like family already, aren't we?" he asked in a whisper. "Two lonely people who find such joy in being together that it's difficult to keep the distance between us, even at work." He chuckled. "My secretary remarked the other day that I spend more time drinking coffee with you lately than I do on the telephone."

Her eyes brightened as she searched his lean, solemn face. "I've felt that way too, about being close to you,

I mean. I didn't know you did. You have so many friends . . ."

"Not like you," he explained gently. "I feel comfortable with you, safe." He laughed. "What a thing for a man to admit."

"But you are a man," she replied quietly. "Very much a man. You don't have to prove it, do you?"

His powerful shoulders rose and fell. "Once in a while," he confessed. "Big business has its challengers and some are devious and bad-tempered."

"I suppose I'll learn about that soon enough."

He nodded. "If you climb in the company, which I fully expect, you'll have to learn to deal with the board of directors. I have no doubt you'll do that quite well."

"I'm not very assertive."

"It comes with age." His expression changed as he looked at her. "You're so young," he said softly. "And I'm thirty-seven."

She reached up and touched his firm, warm mouth. "I've never known anyone like you," she said in a voice as quiet as his. "It wouldn't matter if you were fifty . . ." She hesitated. "I don't know how to say it. It hasn't anything to do with age. It has to do with what people are, inside."

He held her palm to his mouth and kissed it hungrily. "Perhaps it does, but you're very unsophisticated and I know too much about women."

"Such as?" she asked, deliberately provocative for the first time in memory.

His gaze held hers intently while he drew her arm toward him and pressed his mouth against it, moving slowly from her palm down her wrist to the elbow and back up again. She felt shivers down her spine at the lazy intimacy. He bit softly at the mound of her thumb and then teased the thumb with his tongue and finally took all of it slowly into his warm mouth.

She gasped. She'd read about such caresses, but had never experienced them.

He drew her arm up again and draped it around his neck while his free hand slid in at her waist and brought her body in between his legs. He turned her, ever so slowly, as if they were dancing, and all the while holding her eyes with his. She felt his legs brushing intimately against hers. Even through her jeans the pressure was feverishly arousing. When his hand slid over her spine and down to move her rhythmically against his hips, she felt her knees give way.

He caught her up in his arms and held her like that, off the floor, unprotesting, shocked by her own sensuality, by his mastery of her senses. The look he gave her made her heart beat loudly but she couldn't utter a word.

"Well?" he asked quietly.

She forced her lips to move as she stared up at him. "I didn't realize," she whispered huskily.

"It doesn't make you afraid?"

She shook her head. "Not in the way you mean." She bit her lower lip. "I'm a pushover, I guess."

"Only with me. That's how it should be." He drew

her close and walked to the sofa, easing down to sit with her across his lap.

She clung, devastated by her intense need of him. It went so far beyond a simple physical attraction that she couldn't comprehend it fully.

His arms were warm and comforting now, not arousing. He smoothed her golden hair and after a minute he lifted her chin. "Kiss me," he said quietly.

She reached up to put her mouth softly to his. He gave the kiss back just as gently, savoring her warm lips as if they were the key to paradise. He paused long enough to remove his tuxedo jacket and put it aside. Then he pulled her back against him and kissed her for a long time in just that way, as if they were both adolescents, exploring the right pressure, the right contact, to give each the maximum pleasure.

He lifted his head finally, and laughed softly. "Even this is different," he murmured. "Kissing like children."

"It's so sweet," she managed, her eyes lingering upon his mouth.

"Sweet," he echoed, and bent to kiss her again.

But he was a man, and inevitably, his arm contracted and the kiss became slow and deep and hungry. She felt his breathing change, heard the soft groan against her mouth, almost at the moment his long, elegant fingers slid under the T-shirt and up to trace the curve of her breast in its lacy covering.

She shifted to give him access, yielded completely

to his lazy ardor. It wasn't until the cool air became uncomfortable against her skin that she realized he'd bared her breasts while he kissed her.

Embarrassed, she tugged at the fabric, but he shook his head. "Only this," he promised softly. "And it will cause me some pain. But I want you to know."

He left her pondering the curious statement and bent to open his mouth and press it down hard over her taut nipple.

She cried out like someone being tortured. Her body arched up in his arms and shivered, and her hands caught frantically in his hair as he drew the nipple into his mouth with gentle suction.

Time dissolved in heat. She arched her body again and gave him liberty to do anything he liked to it. She was weeping and trembling all over when he finally paused to look down at her.

His hand rested on her belly, just above the fastening of her jeans. He stared into her flushed, tear-stained face for a long moment, unspeaking, and she returned his gaze. He looked like a lover, his white shirt unbuttoned to the waist, his mouth swollen, his dark face drawn with lines of desire.

"You said . . . it would hurt you?" she managed to ask.

"And it does. Like hell," he answered. "But it's the sweetest hell I've ever tasted." His eyes fell to her breasts. "I want you."

"I want you, too," she said, so emotionally out of

control that her voice broke on the words and ended in a sob.

"So much." He drew her close and held her, rocking her, as he savored her warm weight. "So much, so much . . . !"

Her short nails bit into his broad shoulders. Against her bare breasts she could feel the wiry thickness of the hair on his chest, and she nestled there, awash in another in a series of new and frightening pleasures.

"What . . .?" He lifted his head and looked, and realized. "Ah." He chuckled softly, a wicked sound that, added to the gleam in his eye when he looked down where they touched, made her flush.

He held her upper arms and deliberately moved her against him with the sensuality of a dancer. "Who could put into words the glory of skin against skin?" he murmured huskily.

She couldn't reply to that. Her mind was spinning. Her body was greedy, demanding more of these sensations she'd never before known. She closed her eyes, already lost in a sensual paradise, his willing conspirator, ready to yield whatever he wanted.

"Talk to me," he whispered at her ear.

"I . . . can't. It's like . . . dying," she faltered breathlessly. "I want it never to end!"

His arms slid completely around her, and he held her close without moving, his head bent over hers, his body corded with urgency. But he conquered the fierce, sharp desire after a minute and began to relax.

"No," she groaned when he started to move away.

He caught her protesting hands and put them to his mouth. "*Querida*, we can't," he whispered huskily.

She looked at him from a daze of swirling emotion. "Why not?"

He held her palm to his hard cheek. "For half a dozen reasons. But the most important one is that I don't have anything to use with me." He kissed her palm. "I'm a stickler for prevention. Almost a fanatic. I told you that once."

She searched his face. There was something he was hiding. "It isn't only because you're worried about diseases. It has something to do with babies, hasn't it?" she asked hesitantly, without understanding how she knew.

Shocked by her perception, he looked straight into her eyes. Pregnancy. Ivory, pregnant with his baby. Images flashed into his mind. He thought of her body racked with pain, her voice accusing him, blaming him . . .

With a rough groan, he put her aside and stood up.

CHAPTER
NINE

HE fastened the buttons of his shirt absent-mindedly. "It doesn't matter what all my reasons are," he said quietly. "I have my hands full with my mother. I can't afford complications in my private life. And you're career-minded, aren't you? The last thing you need right now is something to distract you from those designs."

She rearranged her own disheveled clothing, a little shyly. "Well . . . yes. I want to see what I can do, even if I fall flat on my face. It's important to me, to make my name known, to be somebody. Away from my family background, of course." She sighed. "I appreciate the chance you've given me. I guess a lot of people think the same thing Harry did, that I've come too far too fast not to be involved with you."

He glowered. "So that's what he said. Damn him!"

"It's all right, you know. I told you that he changed his mind when he saw my designs." She stared down at

171

her lap and saw in her mind the image of her greedy mother, scarcely kept at bay. With enough money, she could get her mother out of her life for good. She could buy her off. "I want to be rich," she said with determination. "I want it more than anything in the world."

She felt his intent gaze on her. "But I want to make my own fortune," she emphasized quickly, so that he didn't think she was asking him for anything.

He picked up his tuxedo jacket and slid it on with a rueful smile. "Being rich isn't all it's cracked up to be, Ivory," he said. "The thrill wears off pretty quickly when you realize how much hard work it takes to keep what you make. And being famous has its drawbacks, too."

"I won't mind finding out the hard way," she replied.

He chuckled. "I see. You want the furs and diamonds you mentioned before?"

"Oh, yes," she said lightly. "I'll get there."

He saw that light in her eyes and recognized it. He'd had the same look once, when he was lean and hungry. "Yes. You'll make it. Just be sure that what you find at the end of that rainbow is what you really want."

She frowned. "Why, of course it will be what I want. Money is the most important thing. If you have that, you're safe; everything else just falls into place."

"And will it be enough to make you happy?" he asked softly.

"Certainly!"

He didn't argue with her. But he knew that the glitter wasn't real. She'd have to learn it the hard way.

He ran a comb through his dark hair, picked up his overcoat and scarf, and looked at her intently. "I lose all my common sense and reason when I touch you," he mused. "I never meant that to happen."

"It's Christmas," she said gently. She fingered her pearls. "Thanks for my present."

"Same here."

"Are you going to a party?" she asked curiously.

"I was at one before I came here," he replied. "I left the family at the Rainbow Room. I have to go back for them. Mama probably hasn't missed me yet, but she will."

"But that's in the middle of Manhattan! You came all this way . . . !"

He pulled her up from the sofa and kissed her softly. "I wanted to see you," he murmured, searching her eyes. "It wouldn't have been Christmas if I hadn't."

She touched his face lovingly, hating the thought of letting him leave. "We can be friends, can't we?" she asked seriously.

He smiled. "The very best of friends," he said with faint wistfulness. He searched her soft eyes, drinking in their gentle adoration. He bent and kissed her again, but on the forehead this time, with tenderness. "Happy Christmas."

"Happy Christmas to you, too."

He let her go with deliberation. She really was too green for a man his age, and too vulnerable. Probably everything she felt right now was hero worship. After all, he'd given her a shot at fame and her first taste of desire. It was natural that she'd be infatuated with him.

But it was different for him. He found her irresistible. He wanted to be with her all the time. He'd never felt like that with other women. He couldn't afford to become obsessed with Ivory, though. Not with his own hangups about children and marriage. So friendship was really all he had to offer. But he could live for a long time on the memory of her body in his arms. And if she ever grew hungry for a physical relationship with no permanent ties—well, he'd be around.

He put on his coat and his white silk scarf. He really did look elegant, she thought.

"I'll be in touch soon," he assured her. He walked to the door, hesitated for just an instant, then went out without looking back.

Ivory spent Christmas day visiting other people in the apartment house. In the late afternoon she went down to the homeless shelter to see Tim and his family.

Miriam had a new scarf that Mrs. Payne had made for her, and she'd given Mrs. Payne an embroidered silk handkerchief. Tim still had his beautifully embroidered jacket that Ivory had given him, although it had a tear from a fight at school. His mother had sewn it up neatly. Ivory thought as she sat talking quietly to them that Tim looked very tired for a child his age. It worried her, all the way back home.

On Monday, everyone was on the job again. Christmas was over and New Year's Eve was coming up. Ivory had no plans to celebrate, and she didn't expect to see Curry, either. The grapevine had provided the information that Christmas had proved exhausting to his mother, and she was confined to bed following her latest round of treatment.

While Ivory often thought of Curry's mother and hoped that things would go better for her, she concentrated on her designs. Refreshingly, none of the other senior designers seemed jealous of her. They were remarkably creative themselves, and optimistic about the new lines bringing the firm out of debt and into the black. For all their sakes, Ivory prayed that it would. Her career would be well on its way if they were right.

New Year's Eve came, and Ivory planned to greet it alone in her apartment with a glass of eggnog laced with a finger of whiskey that Mr. and Mrs. Johnson had given her for the occasion. But her plans didn't work out as she'd expected. Just after eight o'clock, there was a sharp knock on the door.

When she opened it, there stood Curry, resplendent in his tuxedo and overcoat, his gleaming white silk scarf around his neck. He carried two dress bags bearing the distinctive red and black script "KM," Kells-Meredith's logo, and a gaily decorated Christmas shopping bag.

"Am I allowed to come in?" he asked with a smile.

Her heart went wild at the sight of him. She hadn't expected him, and she deplored the picture she must make in faded jeans, T-shirt, and thick socks. She hadn't even combed her hair.

"Oh . . . of course." She stood aside to let him in, feeling small and shy.

He chuckled at the telltale flush of her cheeks. "You didn't expect me, I gather."

"No. I . . . thought you'd be with your family, or maybe that you had a date."

"I do. You."

She gnawed her lower lip. "I can't go out. I haven't anything to wear, and that's the truth."

"Not any more it isn't." He handed her the bags. "A late Christmas bonus. And before you refuse out of hand, let me tell you I've already made reservations at the Rainbow Room. Just think of yourself as Cinderella and me as the fairy godfather."

She'd been expecting a dull evening at home and all at once, there was magic in the night. She caught her breath when she opened the bag and found one of her own gowns in it—a beautiful white silk with her signature crystal butterfly. There were matching pumps, in her size, and the coat he had brought was deep-piled black velvet.

"That coat must have cost a fortune," she faltered when she saw the label. "I can't . . ."

"On loan," he said easily. "It's my sister Audrey's

and she's delighted that I have someone to spend the evening with. She's generous and sweet. You'll like her.''

She sighed as she stared up at him. "I'm dreaming."

"No." He flicked back his cuff and looked at his Rolex. "Hurry."

She picked up the dress and rushed to the bathroom with it, pausing along the way to dig in a drawer for lingerie.

It only took her five minutes to dress. She made up her face, just lightly, and then came out in her stocking feet to slip on the shoes.

"Wear your pearls," he said softly, admiring the look of her in the exquisite dress.

"Of course." She dug them out, too, and put them on, fumbling with the catch just as she had when he'd first given the necklace to her.

He chuckled with delighted amusement as he fastened it for her, and his warm hands on her throat played havoc with her pulse.

His mouth drew lightly along the side of her throat, making her gasp. Without conscious thought, she leaned back against him and tilted her head to make room for his warm face.

His hands tightened on her shoulders and he made a rough sound deep in his throat as his mouth lingered on the pulse where her shoulder joined her neck.

"You smell like heaven," he whispered gruffly.

"So do you."

He turned her slowly and looked down into her eyes, drowning in their gray softness. If she didn't love him already, she was well on her way to it, he thought delightedly and without conceit. And he didn't think it had one thing to do with the help he'd given her career. This was physical as well as emotional and he'd have bet his life on its sincerity.

His unblinking, intent stare made her breathless, and his grip on her shoulders was beginning to hurt.

"Is something wrong?" she whispered.

He didn't move for an instant. Then his face relaxed into a smile. "Something," he murmured. "Nothing that concerns you." He forced himself to let her go. "We'd better be on our way."

She let him drape her in the velvet coat, drinking in the warmth of it, the luxury. She was going to own one of these one day, she promised herself.

He ushered her down to the street, and she stopped dead at the sight of the long black stretch Lincoln sitting there, with a liveried driver getting out to open doors for them.

"You should be used to these," Curry said with a chuckle. "Surely they have them back in Louisiana."

"Oh, yes. But it's been a long time," she said, glad that he couldn't see her face. "That is, it seems like a long time since I've ridden in one!"

"It will all come back to you. In you go."

The interior was black leather with room enough for six people facing one another. It had footrests and a bar, a television set, a record player, and a telephone. The glass partition between driver and passengers could be raised and lowered.

Curry sat back and watched her explore her surroundings with amusement.

"It really has been a long time, hasn't it? I'll have to send you around town in a limo and get you used to it again," he said. "Having fun?"

She laughed delightedly. "Oh, yes."

"They're only exciting the first time or two, aren't they? After that, it becomes routine," he returned.

"Yes. Of course." She glanced at him. "Is this one yours?"

He nodded. "The driver's name is Tommy. He's worked for me for several years. Ever since I bailed him out of jail."

She gasped.

"His mother is our cook," he explained with a smile. "She's a fine lady. Tommy's a good boy. He got in with the wrong crowd and had to be salvaged. He's turned out very nicely. He's going to night school, and I think he's going to be a lawyer one day."

"You *are* a nice man," she said with genuine feeling.

"Well, I think of it as reciprocation. If a nice man hadn't bailed me out when I was a teenager, I might have ended up in jail for life. If we pass a kindness along, it multiplies."

"What a good thought."

"You operate on the same principle, don't you?" He

pursed his lips and studied her in the beautiful gown. "Dee tells me that you spend Saturdays helping her as a vounteer at a homeless shelter."

"Yes," she confessed. "I get a lot of satisfaction from helping people less fortunate than myself. It's much the same for you, I guess, planning a way to make me happy tonight."

"My intentions are not so unselfish, I'm afraid. I just want to be with you," he murmured.

That was just what Ivory wanted to hear; and for tonight, it was enough.

The night lights were beautiful. She stared out the window like the small-town girl she'd once been, wrapped up in expensive clothing and dreams. She smiled as she contemplated the hard climb she'd already made, from a small farm to a chauffeur-driven limousine in New York City, with one of its most handsome and eligible bachelors sitting beside her. The fact that she was able to cope so well in an unfamiliar setting made her feel even better. Dinner lay ahead with its unfamiliar utensils set out in bewildering array, but she could watch him and follow his lead in selecting the right ones for each dish. For a woman who'd come from such poverty, she was doing amazingly well, she thought.

She felt his gaze and turned her head in the shadowy confines to look toward him. He wasn't smiling now, and the way he looked at her made the pulse throb in her throat.

With frank desire, he let his gaze linger where the deep neckline cut across her creamy breasts, giving a tantalizing glimpse of their soft pink curves. Then he looked back up, catching her eyes, and watched her lips part on a breath she couldn't quite contain.

He held out his hand and she laid hers within it. He took her hand to his mouth, kissing the palm with sensual tenderness.

Ivory thought that she'd never known such happiness. Her eyes adored him, tempted him, pleaded with him; but he came not a step closer. Even though he must have known that she was ready for anything he asked of her, he kept his distance.

"Patience," he said quietly, still retaining possession of her hand. "We have all the time in the world."

She laughed self-consciously. "Am I that obvious?"

"Yes." He smiled at her expression. "I'll let you choose the time and place. Whatever you want, Ivory. Whenever you want it."

She understood instinctively what he was telling her. He was prepared if she wanted the night to end with more than kisses. She averted her face. It wasn't fair to put the responsibility all on her. On the other hand, he was telling her subtly that it wasn't going to be seduction. He wasn't the sort of man to take what he wanted and walk away without looking back. He was offering much more than a night in his arms, but she didn't know if she was ready. She was wary of starting something that might jeopardize her career, regardless of the fact that she would have done anything for the man beside her.

"Don't worry so," he chided. "We're going to have a delicious dinner and dance for a while."

"And then?" she asked softly.

He searched her face. "Ask me later."

She nodded and changed the subject by commenting on the holiday lights reflected in the fountains of the tall buildings they passed. He answered in kind and kept the conversation light all the way to the fabled restaurant high above the city.

Ivory wondered a time or two during the evening if she weren't still dreaming. The city spread out below them, glittering with a million jewels. They ate prawn cocktails, followed by beef Wellington with new potatoes and julienne carrots, and then an exquisite salad. For dessert, he had a chocolate mousse and she ordered English trifle. They finished with a delicious aged port. After living on a budget that permitted no luxuries in food other than an occasional visit to the Japanese restaurant near the office, Ivory savored every bite.

"It seems almost sinful to eat this well," she confessed to him.

"Don't look so guilty," he said gently. "I'm a rich man, haven't you noticed? I can afford treats like this."

"It's more than a treat to me. Thank you."

"My pleasure." He glanced toward the dance floor,

where several couples were moving slowly to music provided by a celebrity band. "Do you dance?"

"A little."

"Come on, then."

The lazy rhythm of the dance, added to the delicious fullness from the meal and the effects of the heady port, made her reckless. She slid both arms around his neck and moved closer, pleased by the sudden stiffening of his body that told her he was affected by her closeness.

"Is this an invitation?" he asked at her ear.

Her fingers tightened where they were linked behind his head. "I . . . don't know," she said, hesitating. She drew back and looked up at him. Sparks of pleasure darted through her at the way he was watching her. "If it is an invitation, it's to something I've never done before."

"Yes. I know."

She lowered her eyes to his mouth. "I don't even know if I can."

His lean hands drew her close and he listened to her sharp gasp. Her breathing grew quick and stifled.

"Do you want to find out?" he asked quietly. "There won't be any risk. I promise you."

She laid her forehead against his jacket and drank in the sexy fragrance he wore. "Yes," she whispered. Under her fingertips his chest heaved. "Yes, I think . . . that I'd like to find out." Her eyes lifted. "But you don't need to worry that I'll cling, or make demands . . ."

His finger came up to press against her lips and stop the words. "I know you better than that."

She smiled gently, shyly, and pressed closer. Probably he did. She refused to think about tomorrow. The gossips all thought he was sleeping with her anyway, so what difference did it make? She was lonely and very much in love with him, and he obviously felt something special for her. He'd even said once that it would be more than a physical thing. Just for once, she was going to do what she really wanted to do, and not worry about the consequences.

He took her back to his apartment and dismissed the driver. He didn't try to sneak her up the back stairs. He held her hand and appeared totally unconcerned about gossip.

"You look lovely," he said huskily as they rode up in the elevator. "I was proud to be seen with you tonight."

She beamed.

Inside his apartment, it was cozy and warm, and dimly lit. He lifted the velvet coat from her shoulders and tossed it over the back of the sofa.

"Care for a drink?" he asked.

She shook her head. She shouldn't be nervous, she told herself. He wouldn't hurt her. All the same, it was a monumental step in her life. She hadn't thought that she'd ever want this with any man. Giving up control of her body was like giving up control of her life. But

Curry was different. Very different. She had dreamed about him night after night. She loved him so much. What they shared tonight would be something to remember in the lonely years ahead, because she knew he wasn't the kind of man who wanted or needed marriage. After him, there would be, could be, no one else for her.

Her eyes came to rest on a length of oyster-colored satin cloth draped over a chair. "What's that?" she asked.

"A sample of some fabric we're going to use in a promotional ad for your new collection," he said. He picked it up and ran it through his fingers with slow, intense sensuality. His gaze fell on Ivory and lingered until her heart ran wild in her chest.

"Come here, Ivory," he said quietly.

She went to him. In his expression was a deliberation that both excited and frightened her. He moved to unbutton her gown and gently slid it from her shoulders to let it fall around her ankles. Then he removed everything under it until she was completely nude.

Before she had time to be embarrassed, he took the length of satin and draped it around her, drawing it softly over her skin in sensuous brushes that quickly aroused her. He drew it over her breasts, so that her nipples contracted and went dusky. He slid it around her thigh and drew it lingeringly through and around the other leg and upward, between her legs in a whispery caress that made her tremble.

"Are you ready, Ivory?" he asked in a tone that made her whole body throb.

She looked into his face and knew that she had no will to deny him, not under the circumstances.

He needed no words. He found his answer in her half-closed, dreamy eyes.

He laid her gently, draped in the satin, on the bed. Then he stood over her, his gaze never leaving hers, and undressed for her.

She'd never seen a man without his clothing. Curry's body was lean and muscular, tanned all over, with thick hair beginning on his chest and running in a wedge down over his flat stomach, feathering his powerful thighs. She moved restlessly against the satin, feeling like a siren as she watched him become aroused. It was shocking and somehow beautiful and natural, all at once.

"I won't put out the light," he said quietly. "This isn't going to be sordid or casual. You won't be ashamed, afterward?"

"No," she whispered. "I love you."

"As I love you," he replied, his voice as solemn as his face.

Whether or not he meant it, her heart soared. He eased down alongside her, his hands sliding over the length of satin again. He smiled faintly as he began to draw it along her skin again, watching her reactions with tender pride.

"All these years of working with fabric, haven't you

even wondered how erotic it could be against your bare body?'' he asked.

"I couldn't have let anyone . . ." she began, and suddenly cried out when he touched her unexpectedly.

"Will you be afraid if I confess that I've never made love to a virgin?" he asked, doing it again. "But I'll try my best to make it good for you, even this first time."

"I love you," she choked. "It will be good . . . even if it hurts."

He smiled as he lowered his mouth to her stomach. "Oh, it won't hurt," he murmured. He felt her surging, sobbing response to his tongue as he began to trace soft, slow patterns there while his hand slid under her and drew the satin lazily against her taut breasts.

The minutes that followed were the most shocking and the most beautiful of Ivory's life. His mouth was all over her, against her breasts, her back, her thighs, her arms, there wasn't one space that he didn't caress. He whispered to her in Spanish, soft, sensuous love words that made her tingle. She breathed in the clean scent of him, savored the delicious touch of his hard-muscled flesh against her bare skin. She let him guide her hands, let him teach her how and when and where to touch him in return.

She didn't know what she'd expected of her first sexual experience, but it was nothing like the movies she'd seen or the books she'd read. He was beside her, inside her, around her, over her, behind her. She was so aroused that she couldn't even define the first instant of penetration, because the pleasure ebbed and flowed from his hands to his mouth to the slow, lazy thrust of his hips.

And all the while, that silky satin rubbed against her skin, making the pleasure so dark and sweet that she wept and wept against his chest, his throat and his mouth.

Only once did he lift his head to look into her eyes, at the very moment when she shot off into the sun, her eyes fixed on his face, her body convulsing uncontrollably under the measured thrust of his hips. As the urgency subsided, embarrassed, she started to turn her head, but his hands held it still.

"Watch," he ground out.

His face contorted. She felt him clench suddenly and shiver. A deep cry muffled in his throat and he sucked in a breath. All the while he held her fast so that she could see him.

When he relaxed, his weight was deep and warm and heavy upon her. His hands on her face fell away and he shuddered as he tried to breathe.

She was red-faced and weak. He brushed back her hair, but he didn't move.

"I've never let anyone watch," he said.

"But . . . people don't . . ." she choked huskily.

"We do." He kissed her eyes closed, savoring her wet eyelashes with his tongue. "Nothing we do will ever be more intimate than that. *Te quiero*. I love you."

She clung to him, her eyes closed, her body languid,

floating. He moved a little again and she groaned in response, her nails biting into him as her breathing grew rapid and her hips lifted involuntarily.

He raised his head and saw the helpless hunger that had returned to her eyes.

"All right," he said softly. "But we have to prepare for it first."

"Again?" She was surprised.

He reached beside the bed and let her watch him do what was necessary. "Every time," he said quietly. "I won't risk you. Not that way."

She stared at him, torn between curiosity and urgent need to experience again the racking pleasure he could give her. In the end, he took the burden of that decision from her by simply leaning over and placing his mouth softly over her own.

Later, after a leisurely bath in the sunken tub, she dressed again. He'd already showered and was dressed and pacing the living room. He greeted her a little remotely, now that the urgency of passion was removed. She was puzzled and faintly wounded by his manner. The phone had rung while she was in the tub. She wondered if the call had anything to do with the somber, disturbed look on his face.

He didn't say a word until he'd eased her into the velvet coat. "I have to take you home," he said. "Mama called. She wants me to come over. She's not feeling well."

It was New Year's Eve. She felt guilty that she'd taken him away from his mother on such an occasion when there might never be another New Year's Eve for him to spend with his mother.

"I'm sorry," she began.

He put his forefinger over her tender lips. "Don't ever be sorry for such an exquisite loving," he replied solemnly, searching her eyes.

She blushed a little and he smiled.

"What did you think?" he teased gently. "Did you read that men tell all sorts of lies to get a woman into bed and then become immediately disinterested when they've had what they wanted?"

She shifted restlessly. "Of course not."

He chuckled. "Liar." He pulled her close with a contented sigh and kissed her with breathless tenderness. "I told you that I love you," he said softly, holding her gaze while he said it. "Would you like to hear it again, when I'm not aroused?"

Her eyes twinkled. "Yes."

He kissed her eyes shut. "I love you," he whispered. "I love the way you talk to yourself and the way you worry about me. I love it that you gave me a present when every other woman I've ever known only asked what I was going to give her. I love everything about you."

She hugged him close and laid her cheek against his chest. "I don't want to go home."

He stiffened a little, because he didn't want to let her go either, but his mother's call had sounded urgent, and he was worried. He drew back, brushing her hair away from her eyes with a gentle hand. "I don't want to let you go," he agreed. "But Mama is dying, inch by inch. She sacrificed for me all my life. Now, when she needs me, I have to go to her."

She nodded. "It must be wonderful to have a mother you care about that much, one who cares about you, too."

"Doesn't your mother care about you?" he asked with surprise.

She smiled. "We'd better go."

"Okay. Keep your secrets, for now." He traced her eyebrows, a little darker gold than her hair. "One day, though, I want to know everything. All of it. People who love each other shouldn't have to keep secrets."

Her heart leaped in her chest. He was right. But how could she ever tell him about her past? The thought of it made her sick all over. He wouldn't want her anymore if he knew what she was, what her mother was. Right now, just the thought of Marlene was enough to make her panic.

"Stop worrying," he chided.

"Just a stray thought," she confessed with a smile. "Thank you for the New Year's celebration."

"My pleasure." He lifted her hand to his lips. "You can't imagine the pleasure it was, either," he added

with a smoldering, unblinking gaze that made her knees
weak. "I thought I knew it all until tonight. You were
a revelation."

"So were you," she murmured shyly.

He laughed with pure delight. "Did it shock you?"

She nodded. "It isn't like what they show in the
movies," she said.

"They'd all go to jail for showing it that way in the
movies," he said. He caught her hand in his. "I phoned
the driver while you were in the tub. He'll meet us
downstairs."

She let him lead her to the door. She looked back
into the open bedroom, where the satin cloth on the
disheveled bed gleamed in the overhead light. It had
been smooth and spotless at first, and now it was wrinkled and stained. She pushed the faint guilt she felt to
the back of her mind and followed Curry into the hall.
He closed the door behind them, and the echo of that
sound stayed in her mind all the long way home.

CHAPTER
TEN

CURRY'S mother was sitting up in bed when he arrived at her apartment. His sister Audrey was there, too, looking harassed and worried. She drew him to one side while the round-the-clock nurse took Teresa Kells's vital signs.

"You shouldn't have told her you were taking that girl out," his sister said worriedly. "She's harped on it all night long. That's why she called the apartment and told you she wanted you here."

"Hoping to break up anything that was going on?" he suggested with a smile.

"It isn't funny," she said. "She's convinced herself that your new girlfriend is a gold digger who's using you to get to the top of the design list."

"She belongs there," he said, faintly defensive. "If you don't believe me, you could look at some of the things she's created for us."

"You don't have to convince me," she said with a smile. "I'm not Mama. And you're no fool."

He chuckled. "Thank you." He glanced toward the bedroom. "The doctors warned us that the painkillers might cause some problems," he reminded her. "Her mind plays tricks on her."

"At least the medicine is holding the pain at bay," she replied, following his gaze. "I'm glad you came."

"What else could I do?" He ran a hand restlessly through his thick, dark hair. "We owe her so much. Why can't we do more for her?"

"It's the way life is," she said heavily. "I love her, too, Curry, you know I do. But she's so possessive lately, and so full of orders! I'm to give up my job and get pregnant, mama tells me. Ben would love that, just when we're finally getting into the black with his own business! My job keeps us solvent while he builds his up. She doesn't want us to wait until we can comfortably afford a family, she wants one right now."

"You have to overlook her eagerness," he said, pushing the reference to pregnancy right out of his mind. "Children can wait."

She studied his lean, hard face curiously. "At my age, yes," she began.

He held up a hand and his expression made him unapproachable. "I know my own age," he replied in a deceptively soft voice. "I no longer have a terror of it. But I have no wish for children right now."

"Considering the type of women you run around with, I'm not surprised," she retorted. "Models don't like to risk their figures."

He ignored her failed attempt at humor and watched until the nurse motioned for them to come in.

Teresa Kells glared at him. "So you finally got here," she said irritably. "Where were you, and with whom?"

"You know where I was, Mama, I told you," he said as he kissed her gently on the forehead and sat down in the chair at her side. "I took Ivory out to dinner to celebrate the New Year."

"Ivory," she scoffed. "What a name. Does she look like an elephant's tusk?"

He averted his gaze to his sister and tried not to let his temper get the upper hand. His mother was very ill. He had to humor her.

"How are you feeling?" he asked, trying to divert her.

"I feel terrible, and I'm going to die," she said flatly. "And I won't hold one grandchild in my arms before I go!"

He took a sharp breath. "That is in God's hands," he said.

"There are some good girls in our neighborhood," she persisted. "You could marry a good girl and try again to have children." She held up a hand when he started to protest. "I did have both of you, Curry, and I am still alive. Pregnancy is not always fatal," she added gently, when she saw his jaw start to clench. "Besides, you are getting no younger. This Ivory whom you have been out with tonight, what does she do?"

"She's a designer."

"Is she a model, too?"

He shook his head.

"I talked to Belle. Belle says the girl is not from New York."

He was surprised that she'd gone so far as to call Belle to find out about Ivory. It irritated him, but he didn't let it show. He had to remember his mother's condition, that her pain and the medications used to combat it reduced her inhibitions. "That's right."

"Where is she from?"

"Her family is from Louisiana. Her father is dead, and her mother spends a lot of time in Europe. They're very wealthy, but Ivory wants to make it on her own. She took nothing with her when she came to work for me," he added.

"Ahhh." Teresa relaxed back against the pillows with a wan smile. "Now I can relax. You have eased my mind. I had such thoughts, of a poor girl playing up to you to get you to give her things. A mother does worry. But is she Catholic?" she persisted.

He smiled. "I'll ask her."

"All right, but if you're going to get involved with a woman, you need to know a lot more about her than how she is in bed."

He glared at her and got up. "My private life is my

own," he said, striving to hold his temper. "You have never concerned yourself with it before."

"I was never on the edge of death before," she said, shifting painfully in the bed. She coughed, rested a minute, and coughed again. Her eyes lifted to his. "Some women will do anything to get money, to get position. It worried me when Belle said that only months ago this woman was in a very minor position, and now she is a senior designer."

"She earned her position," he said flatly. "When I come back, I'll bring some of her designs to show you." He smiled. "Even the fashion writers will love her, when they see the creations she makes. The company will get back on its feet. She is brilliant."

"You gave her Audrey's coat."

He glared at his sister, who grimaced. She hadn't told their mother voluntarily, but that wouldn't matter to Curry. "I borrowed it for her to wear tonight. I brought it back," he added. "She has nothing to wear . . ."

"Yet she has a wealthy background?"

"Mama, for the love of God!" He stopped. "I told you, she wanted to make it on her own. She refused to let me buy her anything, so I had to lend her a coat!"

"She refused to let you buy her anything?" She pursed her lips. "Well, well. Now this is a good sign. Is she a proud woman, then?"

"Yes," he replied. "Proud and fierce. And she loves me."

"And you?"

"I love her as well," he confessed.

"I want to meet her . . . !" She began to cough and couldn't stop. The nurse came quickly back into the room to settle her patient, asking Curry and Audrey to leave while she did so.

Out in the living room, Curry paced while his sister sat rigidly on the sofa, her consternation plain on her face.

"Did you mean it? Do you love her?" she asked him out of the blue.

"Yes."

She didn't say another word, but she smiled to herself. She'd never expected her taciturn brother to lose his heart, after his tragic first marriage. It delighted her that he had.

When they were allowed back into Teresa's room, the older woman was pale and very quiet. She looked at Curry with love and delight.

"If you have found a woman to love after all this time, I will say not one word more against her," she promised, and managed a smile. "It is enough that you are happy." She began to cough again, her face contorted with pain.

Curry held her hands while she coughed, wincing as if he felt every pain that showed in her lined face. It hurt him that he could do nothing for her.

The January showings of Kells-Meredith summer fashions took place in wintry weather. Ivory looked out at the dirty gray snow and chewed on a fingernail until she had gnawed it to the quick as she and Belle waited backstage for the model's turn to go down the runway in the suit Ivory had designed. Gathered at the Plaza Hotel were the top buyers from exclusive stores around the country. There had been two near-disasters already, and everyone's nerves were in pieces.

"It will be all right," Belle said comfortingly. "Don't be so nervous!"

"I'm trying, really I am," Ivory said in a small voice. "There! You're on!"

"I'll knock 'em dead," Belle promised, striking a pose that showed the suit off perfectly.

She walked down the runway, and for the first few seconds there was an ominous hush. The moderator's voice continued, unruffled, providing descriptions of the fabric and design. Ivory held her breath. Then, all at once, there was an excited clamor of voices and applause.

"Feel better now?" Dee murmured as she rushed past with needle and thread to alter a hemline for one of the upcoming models. "I told you so."

Curry came up beside her, quietly satisfied with the showing. He looked at Ivory and his body rippled with pleasure when she smiled up at him.

They had lunch together every day now, and they spent achingly sweet hours together on the weekends, but there were no more interludes in bed. This had puzzled her at first, until Curry explained that he thought it was important for them to really get to know each other, so that they didn't base their relationship on nothing more than the physical. Touched, she'd gone right along with him, because it sounded as if he had a long relationship in mind.

However, she realized that her fabrications about her past were not holding up under Curry's very close scrutiny. She spent some time writing down a believable life history one Sunday so that she could memorize it and answer any question he threw at her. He wasn't openly suspicious about her past, but he did sometimes ask pointed questions that disturbed her, and often she hesitated before she could answer them.

He gestured toward the enthusiastic crowd. "See them comparing notes?" he teased. "I told you so, too," he added. "You're a hit."

"We're a hit," she countered, thrilling to his nearness, even amid the excitement of her acceptance by the assembled buyers and press.

He nodded. "Yes. We're a hit. The other designs are making nice impressions, too. It's even more than I hoped for. How do you feel? Still standing on a precipice?"

She laughed, but she had a new worry. "Now more than ever. I'll have to live up to that applause."

"This is your hour. I'm going to take Belle out with me and let you glory in it."

"But . . . !" she protested.

"Listen," he said solemnly, "if we leave together

there's going to be talk. I don't want it said that you rose to the top in my bed instead of behind a drafting table.''

''Everybody at the office knows we go out together,'' she protested.

''Indeed they do. But these people can make or break you,'' he added quietly. ''Don't give them a stick to beat you with. Stand by yourself right now. Let them see that you don't need the crutch of my influence.''

So that was it. She smiled up at him with her heart in her eyes. ''You take very good care of me.''

''Of course I do, my own,'' he said softly. ''You gave yourself to me, didn't you?''

''Only once,'' she pointed out.

His dark eye glittered down at her. ''I want you, too,'' he whispered. ''But we're going to take it slowly. I like what I'm learning about you.''

What would he think if he knew how false it was, she wondered frantically. If they'd had a more intimate relationship perhaps he wouldn't look at her so closely or be so curious about her past.

''What's this little frown for?'' he teased.

''I have to meet some of the fashion writers after we're through. I'm nervous.''

''You'll do fine. Remember that you love what you do. That should make it easy to talk about your work.''

''I hope so.'' What she really feared was pointed questions from people who were used to asking them. But she'd memorized her story by heart, and she thought she could field any embarrassing or potentially damaging inqueries.

"Yes. It should make it easy," she agreed.

The end of the show came rapidly and Curry went out with his designers to take a bow. The applause was gratifying. Ivory saw flashbulbs going off all around her, and she smiled through a veil of happy tears. She was, after all, on her way.

But when Curry left, with Belle on his arm, everyone noticed. It was almost a public declaration of disinterest in his new designer, just as he'd expected that it would be. Curry Kells might adore his designer on the job, but he was making it apparent to everyone around him that his interest didn't extend to their private lives.

His judgment was right. No rumors spread concerning Ivory's meteoric rise in the company; but her success felt strangely flat without him to share it. She was on her way to the fame and fortune she'd coveted. It should have made her the happiest woman on earth. She was, she told herself. It was only that she felt so empty inside.

One of the barracudas of the fashion writing corps cornered her after the show and sat down with her near the runway. The brunette was chic, elegant, expensively dressed, and her dark glasses kept Ivory from seeing her eyes or any giveaway expressions.

"I understand that you're from the South," the woman said. "What part?"

"Louisiana," Ivory replied. "Baton Rouge."

"And your family? What do they do?"

"My father died when I was much younger, but our family came from France and England after the Civil War, and they owned a huge plantation on the river. Sadly, it was lost after the turn of the century. Then they invested in Texas oil and cattle and made another fortune."

"So many people did, before income taxes," the interviewer said blandly. "Did your mother influence your work?"

Ivory's heart leaped. She had to be very careful. This woman would see any tiny sign of discomfort and pounce on it. She smiled. "Yes, indeed," she returned. "She's quite a clothes horse herself. She's in Europe this season," she added.

"Where?"

Fortunately she'd just read the latest issue of *Town and Country* and she knew about the newest meeting places for the wealthy. She drew one out of her head and presented it.

The fashion interviewer was jotting down notes. "Where did the Tudor designs come from?" she asked, looking up. "Are you a history major?"

"I'm afraid I was too pleasure-oriented for college. After I graduated from high school, I went to Swiss finishing school and then I traveled extensively in Europe for a while. I settled back into local society afterward, and then I won a competition for a design scholarship."

The interviewer's pen paused on the page. "Why would you enter one?"

Because I was poor and couldn't afford the tuition, she thought, but she forced a grin. "For the hell of it," she bluffed.

The pen moved on, and there was a sound like a laugh from the other woman. "How did you end up at Kells-Meredith?"

"They had a competition, too. All the students entered. I won. I was really very shocked. And then," she added, carrying on the pretense, "I seized the chance to make my own fame and fortune, without having to rely on my mother's. I left it all behind me and came up here with nothing except a little talent." She sighed dramatically. "And the results are just more than I ever dreamed!"

"You don't have an accent, do you?" the woman queried. "I suppose finishing school took care of that."

"Yes, indeed."

The pen lifted. "Well, your designs are quite unique. I like them. So do a number of other writers, and buyers. But you're not what you're telling me, Miss Keene."

Ivory felt her face stiffen and her heartbeat race. "I beg your pardon?"

The dark glasses came off. Eyes as black as almonds stared right into Ivory's and nothing escaped them. "I've been in this business for twenty years. I have a sixth sense about people. You're no more high society than I was when I came up here from Alabama twenty-five years ago to make a name for myself.'' She laughed without mirth. ''Don't worry. I won't sell you out. But if you're using this pose with Curry Kells, you'll regret it. I'm famous now. But I wasn't always. I pretended to be an established business writer when I met Curry. He was already climbing to the top of the New York establishment, and he was good copy. I lied to get into his office, I lied to interview him.'' She swallowed. ''He found out.''

Ivory let out the breath she didn't know she'd been holding. ''What did he do?''

''I didn't work for a year,'' she replied. ''He had contacts everywhere and he used them. I didn't realize he'd be so vindictive, but apparently lies have that effect on him because of something in his past. I finally got work again, and I managed to get where I am despite his animosity. Just take it from me. Don't ever lie to him. Tell him the truth, while you have time.''

''He's my boss, not my . . .''

The other woman smiled. ''My dear, the two of you together would light up a city block.'' She settled her sunglasses back over her eyes. ''You have great promise, and an extraordinary career ahead of you. I'll be in to buy one of those Tudor creations myself, as soon as they're available. Best of luck. You're going to need it.''

Ivory watched her go with a sick feeling in the pit of her stomach. If she was that transparent, how would she cope with a really vicious reporter? She'd have to go over her story again and again until she plugged up all the holes, every single one. She'd been spared this time. Next time, she might lose everything.

But as for telling Curry, it was far too late now. She'd just have to bluff her way through and hope that he never learned the truth. In the meanwhile, perhaps it would be wise to spend a little less time with him. Once she made it to the top, then she could tell him what she'd come from. And maybe he wouldn't hold it against her, especially if the company was making a lot of money from her designs. It gave her a little hope for the future.

The weeks that followed reinforced her popularity as a designer. Orders started coming in from some of the buyers of the best stores in the country, just as the fashion writer who'd interviewed her had predicted they would. She wasn't Chanel, but the tentative orders were more than enough to reinforce her status with the company.

"I want more evening wear with that crystal signature design," Curry told her as he met with her in his office in late March. "And while we're on the subject, I think it might be an interesting idea to include a pants suit in the line."

"Dee suggested that," Ivory agreed. "I'd love to work up a design."

"Go for it. Do several."

She hesitated to ask him anything personal. She'd

been immersed in her work, developing new ideas. He'd spent nearly all his free hours at his mother's side as her condition deteriorated. They'd had little time for each other.

He looked more fine-drawn than usual, as if he had more than his normal load on his mind, as they sat in his office.

"How is your mother?" she asked gently.

His face closed. "Fine."

The polite snub made her self-conscious. "Good. Uh, I'll get back to work now . . ." She started to rise.

"Sit down."

She did.

He leaned back in his chair with a faint sigh. "She's not fine. She's had the radiation treatments—so many that they've all but burned her up. She went through one course of chemotherapy, but they checked her and said she needed more. They come to the house and draw blood for testing and come back the next day and give the chemotherapy. She's sick all the time. She still has headaches from the radiation and nausea." He clasped his hands on the desk and stared at them. "The only good thing is how kind people are to her."

Ivory was remembering Tim, who was HIV-positive, and how unkind some people had been to him since his condition had been acknowledged. He'd told his best friend at school, who had, like most young boys, spoken without thinking to other people. Now Tim was alternately taunted and avoided by his classmates, and every time Ivory saw him he was more morose and despondent.

"She's going to die, you know," he said abruptly. "They found cancer in her other lung. And it isn't responding to treatment. It's a matter of months, they said. Probably weeks."

"I'm sorry. I really am."

He pushed at a paperclip on some papers. "I know that. It's hard for me to talk about it." He searched her eyes. "I need you more than ever right now. But look at the complications. Your work takes up all your free time, and Mama and financial complications at work take up all of mine. I don't even have the energy to make love to you." He smiled at her expression. "Yes, I want to. I think you want to as much as I do. One day this will all go away, and I'll take you down to Nassau for a week. We'll make love all day and party all night."

"A lovely thought," she said with a sigh. "I've never been to the Caribbean," she added without thinking.

"Never?"

The question brought her up short. She had to stop letting herself be caught off guard. "It was always Europe," she corrected.

His eye narrowed but he didn't say anything.

"I'm sorry about your mother," she added gently. "I guess we all reach a point when we're beyond any human help," she said. Her eyes had a faraway look.

"I remember when my father died. They found him . . ." She didn't mention where; she couldn't tell him that her father had died in a field. "He looked like he was asleep. I had thought he was going to live forever. For a while, I hated him, because he left me behind." That had been because she was totally at Marlene's mercy after his death. She couldn't mention that, either.

"You loved him a lot, I guess?"

She nodded.

"It's hard to give up a parent. But a mother hits closer to the heart."

She couldn't agree with him, so she didn't say anything.

"I remember," he said abruptly, and smiled just faintly. "If you can't say something nice, don't say anything, right?"

Surprised that he'd remembered her saying that, she laughed with delighted surprise. "Well, yes."

He wasn't going to ask about her mother. It was too obvious that she didn't want to tell him. She kept so many secrets from him. He'd learned that he couldn't pry even one out of her. That quality of mystery intrigued him, but it also made him wary. What was she hiding? If she loved him, why didn't she trust him? The statement his mother had made on New Year's Eve, about Ivory using him as a ladder to get to the top, still niggled. He didn't think he believed it. After all, Ivory came from old money, and she didn't need his help. If she'd been poor, well, there might have been something to his mother's accusations. He was only being fanciful, he told himself.

"I have some news for you, by the way," he added. "Your suit design has brought us more new business than the company had for the past five years before I took it over. And it looks as though sales of that couture evening gown are going to go just as high."

"Really?!" Her expression was one of almost tortured delight.

"No need to ask if you're pleased. I hope the crystal collection is going to continue to be such a best-seller. In the meantime, whatever you need, you can have."

"I'm just overwhelmed!"

"You deserve to be. All a talent like yours needed was a showcase. I've given it to you. Now let's see what you can do with it."

"I'll try not to disappoint you," she said sincerely.

"I'm not worried."

She got up to go, pausing by the door.

"Was there something else?" he asked.

Her hand closed around the cool door knob. Yes, she thought, lots of things, such as: why don't we talk anymore except about business, why have you stopped coming to see me, why don't you want to take me out? Was I just a one-night stand after all? Didn't you mean it when you said you loved me? All those questions rolled around in her busy brain, but she hadn't the courage to voice them. He had enough on his mind with his mother so sick, and she knew there had been problems at his Wall Street office, because she'd heard about them through the grapevine. It wasn't really surprising that their time together had dwindled to lunch once a week, but it was disturbing that he didn't seem to mind.

She glanced over her shoulder at him as she left the room and smiled brightly. "No. No, there was nothing else, thanks."

As the spring and summer went by, the name of Ivory Keene became known in the fashion industry. Her Crystal Collection pieces were worn by everyone from film stars to socialites, both in America and abroad. She gave interviews, but with conditions, and then prayed that her mother wouldn't read about the lies her daughter had concocted. Since her mother's choice of reading material was limited to the local gossip columns and Harmony, Texas, was too small to have a bookstore, Ivory didn't expect that her mother would even see a copy of *Vogue* or *Elle* or *Harper's Bazaar*. Nevertheless, she worried. She'd spread her lies, however, and she couldn't take them back now. She'd just have to pray that her mother was satisfied with the increasing size of the checks she sent home and leave her alone.

She was photographed at showings; her name started cropping up in conversations on television when people wearing her clothes were interviewed. Inevitably, she was asked to appear on a program that dealt specifically with design. She refused, but Curry accepted on her behalf and made her go. Such publicity for the company was too good to turn down, he explained. She had to do it.

"We're just edging into the black," he told her as he explained the interview to her in his office. "We haven't any choice. I'm sure you realize that opportunities for publicity like this don't happen every day."

"I do," she agreed. "But I've never been on television before. I'm not sure how I'll perform when I'm on camera."

"You'll perform just as you should," he assured her, and a faint smile touched his mouth. "Relax and enjoy it. You're a celebrity. You're famous. Isn't that what you wanted?"

She stared at him with her heart in fragments in her chest. She'd thought it was. Money, fame, and glory, surely they were the end of the rainbow. But she couldn't forget that night in his arms, the tenderness, the passion, the love they'd felt for each other. She couldn't even imagine that with another man. And if the lack of tidbits from the grapevine was any indication, he wasn't on the town with other women except to show Kells-Meredith clothes, either. The curious thing was that although he'd slowly backed away from her after their intimacy, she was certain that he still felt something for her.

"You're staring," he said quietly.

She shrugged. "You're good to look at." She managed a smile. "Sorry, boss. I'm trying to manage the status quo. I get flashbacks sometimes."

"So do I," he replied gently. "But there's nothing I can do about it now."

"I haven't asked for anything," she reminded him.

He looked at the paperwork scattered across his desk; cost figures for the new line, production quotas, sales figures.

"I won't ask for anything, either," she added.

His face came up. He stared at her for a long moment, thinking how she'd changed in the months she'd been with the company. The clothes she wore weren't haute couture, but they were at least new; and she had a poise and sophistication that hadn't been there before, either. "You're different, somehow," he said after a minute.

She smiled. "Of course. I'm in a responsible position. Having to make decisions that could cost money and jobs does change people. I expect it changed you, too, when you started out."

"A lot of things changed me." He stood up and went to look out the window, his hands in his pockets. "Money and power make subtle differences in the way we think, Ivory. I like to hope that you won't become hard and inflexible as you climb higher in the organization."

"I won't," she said with assurance. Her eyes slid hungrily over his back. She wished that she had the right to go up to him and slide her arms under his and press close against his back. He was the only man she'd ever loved, or ever would, she was certain of it. But he'd backed away without any explanation and she didn't feel free to offer him comfort or love.

He seemed to feel her gaze. He turned his head abruptly and looked straight into her eyes. The muscles in his jaw moved convulsively.

"I'm going to send one of our promotional staff over to talk to you this afternoon about that TV interview."

"About what?" she asked curiously.

"You don't just go on television," he explained. "You have to know how to avoid questions you don't want to answer, how to manipulate the interview."

"Oh." She frowned. "Can't I just tell the truth?" she asked, to erase that odd expression from his face.

Sure enough, the question erased it. "Of course." He turned around and perched himself on the edge of the desk. "What do you say when he asks if you're sleeping with me to advance your career?"

Her lips fell apart. "He wouldn't ask me that."

"Don't you believe it," he fired back. "These days, the shows that get the best ratings are the controversial ones. They won't stick to asking where you got ideas for your designs. Believe it. I make news, whether I want to or not. And because you work for me, they'll put you right on the hot seat."

She'd worried about how she was going to look on the small screen, but he was telling her to expect something much worse. Her background lay just under the surface, and exposure was a constant fear. What if the interviewer decided to dig that deeply? After all, one fashion writer had seen right through her. What if she were exposed on national television!

CHAPTER
ELEVEN

IVORY stared at Curry with eyes that didn't even see him. The faintly hunted look on her face made him curious.

"What's wrong?" he asked.

"I didn't realize," she began. "About their digging for confidential information, I mean."

He nodded. "I didn't think you would. That's why I want you to work with our public relations people before you even get on camera. This show is live, not taped. You'll be totally on your own when you get on stage. We can't help you."

"I can't talk to public relations people about what to say if I'm asked about sleeping with you!"

"Then ask me," he said softly.

She bit her lower lip until it hurt. "Okay. What do I say?"

"Tell them that you love me," he said with a smile.

"I will not!"

"You do, don't you?" he persisted softly. "Despite everything?"

She stared at him but she didn't deny it. How could she?

His arrogant face lifted and he smiled at her again. "So tell them. And tell them that I love you back," he added in a tone that told her nothing, not even if he really meant it.

She flushed. "That won't stop them."

"Yes, it will. Then they'll start pumping you for wedding plans, and you can mention our new line of couture wedding gowns."

She gaped at him.

"Manipulation," he said in a wicked voice. "They use us, we use them. Play the game."

Her fists clenched in her lap. "It's dishonest."

"Everything is," he replied. He shot back his cuff, glanced at his watch, and scowled. "I've got to get down to the Regency Room. They're holding a showing of those new holiday gowns for the press. I'm taking Belle."

She thought she camouflaged her disquiet well, but he saw it.

"I take Belle to a lot of events. She wears our clothes," he said, without coming close to her as he spoke. "I do nothing else with her," he added. "Or with any other woman. Not since that night. I couldn't."

Her legs felt wobbly. She couldn't look at him. "You

don't come around at all," she said, betraying her pain for the first time.

"When do I have time, Ivory? When do you have time? We're both caught up in situations we can't resolve overnight. And my mother's dying. I have to share the responsibility for her care with my sister. I can't let Audrey do it all alone. We want to do all we can for her, while she's still here. And," he added heavily, "it won't be for much longer. She's going downhill more every day." His voice sounded tormented, but when she looked at him, his face was as calm and impassive as ever.

"I know. I'm sorry." She drew in a soft breath as she rose to her feet. "It all seems like a dream sometimes," she said absently, "the time we spent together. Now it's all business and money."

"We all have to adjust to situations," he said. "Besides, you've got your career to advance. You won't make it if you don't hustle right now while your designs are hot. I think you know that."

"I know it." She smoothed her skirt. "I suppose I should thank you for letting me give my whole attention to designing."

"Yes, you should," he said shortly. "But I can't claim credit for it."

"Does your mother know about me?" she asked.

He nodded. Then he laughed. "At first she was obsessed with protecting me from you. She thought you were a gold digger."

Her eyes shot to his face. "And do you?"

"Of course not."

But he didn't sound convinced. She stared at him with misgivings. She'd said that her career came first, that she wanted success and money. Had those assertions undermined the impression he'd had of her and poisoned his mind against her? He loved his mother. A few words from her could do untold damage. Apparently it already had.

"I've got to go," he said reluctantly. "I'll be in touch. Pay attention when the publicity people talk, will you?"

"Yes, I'll do that," she said, her tone only a little strained.

He nodded, and dismissed her with a faint smile. But after she left, he couldn't help wondering if her single-track mind on the subject of her career hadn't prompted her into playing up to him. She felt something for him, that was obvious. But behind it, there was always that competitive leap for glory and fame. She hadn't seemed to mind when his visits to her apartment stopped, or when he'd stopped seeing so much of her. Once Ivory made it to the top—and she almost had—would she still want a man so much older than she?

Ivory went back to her office feeling torn between glory and despair. Curry might care for her, but he was becoming a stranger. He hadn't sounded convincing at all when he'd said he didn't believe she was using him for her career's sake. She wanted a career, yes, but not without Curry. All the money and glory on earth weren't going to make up for the lack of him in her life, even if they protected her from her mother and made everyone in Harmon, Texas, take a second look at her.

She was coached for two days on how to handle the media without flinching or giving away anything she didn't want to. She learned to push aside probing questions with other questions or with artful pauses and hedging. She was nervous at first and suffered from lack of confidence, but she was assured that she would learn as she went along.

Tim was excited to hear that she was going to be on television. He was the same boy he had been, but there were rough edges to him that she hadn't seen before. He was having a bad time of it at school. People knew he was HIV-positive; some were kind, others cautiously friendly as long as it didn't require being too close to him. Others were callous and unfeeling, with no reservations about voicing their fear.

She put an arm around him as they sat on the shelter's steps and looked up through the haze of pollution to the clear summer skies above.

"One day they'll find a cure," she assured the boy. "And you'll be whole and healthy again."

He shrugged, staring down at his shoes. "Think so?"

"Yes. You have to think so, too."

"I hate school," he said. "I'm glad it's out for the

summer. But it won't be long until we start again now, and I don't want to go back.''

"Tim, you have to," she said gently. "You want to get a good education, don't you?"

"What for? I'm gonna die!"

"No!" She hugged him closer. "You listen to me, young man, you're a long way from dying! You can't die. I don't have so many friends that I can afford to lose one, especially my favorite one!"

He looked up at her cautiously. "Am I really your favorite one?"

She nodded.

He grinned. "That's nice."

"Isn't it, though?" She ruffled his curly hair. "So let's have no more talk about dying. I'm going to be on television!"

"We don't have a television."

"I have one, and a VCR," she said, naming her new purchases. "I'll tape it and you can come to my place one Saturday and watch it with me."

"All right! I never knew anybody who was on television before, except for that guy who was almost killed down at the shelter."

Her heart skipped. "At the shelter?"

"Yep. Don't you remember? I told you about him, that man from Haiti who had AIDS. These big boys said he'd give it to somebody, and they shot him." He grimaced. "He had to go to the hospital. My mama got real scared and said maybe we'd have to leave and live somewhere else, you know, where people don't know about me." He looked up worriedly. "Ivory, those boys don't even live at the shelter, but they're always around. I don't want anybody to hurt my mama and my sisters."

She drew in a sharp breath. "Oh, Tim, I don't want any of you to be hurt." She felt the worry right down to her soul. She couldn't protect Tim. Neither could anyone else. "Oh, damn the stupid virus!"

"That's what I say all the time."

She rested her face in her hands propped on her knees and stared at the street. "If I get rich, I'll give money to research," she said. "We'll find a cure, Tim."

"That would be wonderful. Ivory?"

"Hmmm?" she asked absently.

He grinned. "Got any gingerbread?"

She chuckled. "As a matter of fact, I asked Mrs. Horst to teach me how to make it all by myself, and yes, I have. It's in the bag I left with your mother. Come on. We'll have a slice."

He followed her up the stairs to the shelter. None of her neighbors knew about Tim's condition, which she supposed was a godsend. Not that it would have made any difference. She wasn't going to stop bringing him home with her on occasion, regardless of any minuscule risk. And if her neighbors had a problem with that, she'd just move. She could afford to do that. She just hoped that Marlene didn't find out how famous she was

becoming and how much money she was making. Her
mother would demand so much, Ivory would have nothing left to help kids like Tim.

Unfortunately for Ivory, Marlene had found out. Ivory
was featured in one of the major fashion magazines,
and an issue of it showed up in Harmony, Texas, in a
beauty salon where Marlene was having her hair cut
and colored.

One of the customers who knew Marlene casually
had spotted it and was enthusing not only about the
new collection Ivory had created, but about the woman
herself.

"But your name isn't Keene, Marlene," the woman,
a catty sort, said loudly enough for everyone to hear.
"It's Costello."

Marlene laughed a little loudly. "Now it is," she
said quickly. "My mother's maiden name was Keene."

"Well, isn't it odd that Ivory uses that name instead
of her father's?"

"Surely everyone knows that Ivory wants nothing to
do with me," Marlene said with assumed anguish. "She
hasn't even written to tell me about her success in New
York. I had to find it out in a magazine! How ungrateful
she is," she added huskily. "And after all the sacrifices
I've made for her. Children these days just don't care
about anything except themselves."

"That's the truth," a middle-aged woman nearby

agreed. "My son lives in Canada and can't even be bothered to write to me!"

"I thought Ivory sent you a check every month, dear," the catty woman reminded Marlene.

Marlene pushed her colored hair back from her still-pretty face. "Yes, she does," she replied. "For appearances, you know, to make everyone think she hasn't forgotten about me. That's all it is."

"She's never been much of a daughter to Marlene," the middle-aged woman told the catty one. "Everyone knows how much trouble she was when she was a girl, always causing heartache for her poor mother. She ran off to school without even a word, and never came back once to see Marlene."

"I don't remember Marlene ever going to see her," the catty woman murmured.

"Well, of course not, I was never invited," Marlene said huffily. She glared at the woman. "She's washed her hands of me, hasn't she?"

"If it was me, I wouldn't let her get away with it, now that she's a success," the middle-aged woman said vehemently. "By gosh, I'd get on a plane and go up there and make her share that money. God knows, you deserve more than a puny little check once a month from that girl, after all you've done for her, Marlene."

Marlene was considering the angles. The woman was right. She did deserve more than she was getting. If her daughter was famous enough to get in major magazines, then she must be worth big bucks. Ivory had been sending her that pittance when she was probably able to afford diamonds and furs for herself. Well, that wasn't going to continue. A little prodding, Marlene decided, and she could get what she was entitled to and more. Yes. Much more!

Unaware of her mother's plotting, Ivory was making the most of her talents as she worked feverishly on her fall and winter collection. It was hard to feel comfortable working with wool when the city was smoldering hot outside. The air conditioner wasn't doing its usual job, either, and she was irritable from the heat.

"Sushi and hot tea for lunch?" Dee suggested.

She looked up from her drafting table. "Ice cubes and ice cream?" she countered with a grin.

"Done! Let's try that new place . . ."

The opening of the door cut her off in mid-sentence as Curry walked in. He looked unapproachable somehow, and his face was unreadable as well.

"Excuse us for a minute, would you, Dee?" he asked. "I need to talk to Ivory."

"Sure." She went out, closing the door behind her.

He stood just inside the doorway, his hands in his pockets, his narrow gaze encompassing the harried young woman at the table. Her golden hair was collar length now, wavy and clean, framing a face with a complexion any cosmetics company would have loved. Clear gray eyes stared at him from it.

"What's wrong?" she asked gently.

He shrugged and a faint smile touched his hard mouth. "The time is growing shorter," he said. "I want to see the new designs."

She grinned. "I've outdone myself," she said impishly. She pulled out her sketches and displayed them for him, watching his face to see how they registered.

He picked up the black crepe evening suit with its distinctive black onyx butterfly and the smile grew.

"Nice."

"Thank you. It's another variation on Dee's suggestion, remember?"

"Yes. I'll give her a raise. Let's see the rest." He perched himself on the edge of her desk and looked through the sketches one by one. Some he liked, some he didn't. The rejects went onto the floor, and all Ivory's protests didn't faze him. Cost of production had to be considered, he reminded her, and the company was far from out of the woods yet.

While he was looking through the designs, the boy from the mailroom stuck his head in the door.

"Special delivery," he told Ivory, handing her an envelope. "You have to sign."

He produced a clipboard. She scribbled her name without looking at the return address, and he thanked her and left. But when she saw the return address, she gasped audibly and Curry immediately turned his head to look at her and then the envelope.

She put her thumb over the return name and address, so that he wouldn't see it: M. Costello, Harmon, Texas. "Who's it from?" he asked casually.

"A . . . cousin," she lied quickly. "Back home."

He searched her flushed, anguished face. "Now it's my turn to ask you what's wrong. Why has this letter upset you when you haven't even opened it yet?"

"It's from my cousin Jane. Her husband, my cousin Claude, has been very sick," she invented.

"Is this Jane the poor relation you've been sending money to?" he asked gently.

Her face felt on fire with the lies she was rattling off. "Yes! That is, it's really for Cousin Claude. For his medical care. They don't have much insurance."

He wasn't suspicious. He smiled at her gently. "You really are as sweet as you look," he said softly. "Dee says they love you at the homeless shelter. And then here you are sending money to relatives in need."

"You do the same thing," she accused gently. "You take wonderful care of your mother."

He chuckled. "She's the only mother I have." He nodded toward the letter clutched in her fingers. "Aren't you going to open it?"

"Not just yet," she said, slipping it into her pocket while all sorts of nightmarish thoughts revolved in her mind. "I'd rather wait until I get home, so that it doesn't start me worrying if it's bad news."

"Odd woman," he chided. He touched her hair lightly and his face became solemn. "We've become two people with problems instead of two people looking for solutions together, haven't we?'' he asked quietly. ''Both of us have backed away, Ivory.''

She touched his hand where it rested on her shoulder and the eyes that met his were sad. ''As you said, we both have responsibilities.''

He nodded and searched her expression. ''I want you to meet my mother.''

Her heart jumped. ''What?''

''She asked me to bring you when I visit her tonight.'' His hand contracted on hers. ''Do this thing for me,'' he said quietly. ''It will give her peace, to meet you. I want her to see your eyes, Ivory.''

''My . . . eyes.''

He nodded. ''The windows of the soul,'' he murmured as he looked into them. ''I see shadows there, but among them, I see tenderness and compassion and love.''

She flushed. ''You shouldn't . . . !''

He bent and brushed his mouth softly over hers, teasing her lips until they parted. ''Say the words,'' he whispered.

The tender, aching tone brought back the most exquisite memories of one long night together. Her breath caught delicately in her throat. Marlene's letter, Marlene's threat, was momentarily forgotten.

''I love you,'' she whispered huskily.

He smiled against her parted lips. ''And I love you. Too much.'' He kissed her softly, lifting his head before she could savor the warm pressure. "This isn't the place, *querida*," he whispered, indicating the glass walls that enclosed the office.

"You own it," she pointed out. "If you can't kiss the employees, who can?"

He chuckled as he got to his feet. "I have to set a good example. We wouldn't want anyone to think I'm practicing sexual harassment."

"Is it harassment if both people want it?"

He cocked an eyebrow. "We'll discuss it later." His eye narrowed on her face. "I bought a bolt of red satin," he said suggestively. "Suppose we go to my apartment after we see Mama, and we'll create a dress together."

Her whole body burned at the way he looked at her. "Tonight?"

He nodded. His gaze slid over her and back up to her face. "It's been a long time."

She shifted restlessly. "And you've been out on the town every night," she accused.

"You know better," he replied simply. "I told you at the very beginning that if I had you, I wouldn't have another woman. I meant it."

Her face cleared. Her eyes widened as they searched his hard, solemn face.

"You're hesitating." He moved closer. He seemed so much taller when they were standing toe to toe, she thought as she looked up into his face.

"Am I?" she asked absently.

He touched her lips with the tip of his forefinger.

"You were a virgin until me. Were you chaste because you think of lovemaking as a sin?"

She touched his shirtfront, frowning. "My mother . . . had to get married," she said. "You know, wealthy socialite families don't like scandal," she added quickly.

"Ah. And you didn't want to be forced into marriage by your family because of a mistake."

Her nails bit into his skin through the shirt. "It wouldn't be a mistake," she whispered without looking up.

He stiffened. She felt it and lifted her eyes to his face. There was a hesitation and she wondered why.

"But you're careful," she said, coloring a little as she recalled how careful.

"Too careful, perhaps." He caught her fingers in his with a long sigh. "I married when I was twenty-four," he said. "My wife died in childbirth. So did the baby. It was a long time ago, and I know it isn't so dangerous these days. But it has left scars." His fingers tightened. "She was a long time dying. She blamed me every second of it. Sometimes I can still hear her voice."

Suddenly she understood more than she had before— so much more. She nuzzled her face against his chin. "I'm sorry," she said. "You haven't had an easy life, Curry."

"Not like yours, certainly," he mused, feeling the faint start of her body where it touched his. "I was nobody's cherished child. My upbringing was harsh, brutal. It shaped me, I suppose. My father was forever promising things that he never did. He lied, always lied. Even love doesn't forgive so many lies. I suppose I haven't really lost my suspicion of people, my distrust. Except with you.'' He kissed her forehead. ''You've restored my faith in the world.''

She felt panic growing inside her. She managed a laugh. ''I'm not perfect,'' she began.

''You are to me.'' He moved back with a gentle smile. ''What do you think about a baby?''

Her heart stopped beating. ''Wh . . . what?''

''Not right now,'' he emphasized. ''But a little way down the road, would you like one with me? I think I could face the risk now, with medicine so much improved. And you look healthy enough. Are you?''

''Yes, of course. I . . .'' She laughed nervously. ''I never thought of you as a man who'd want a wife and family. Or, did you mean . . . marriage?''

''I'm Catholic,'' he said. ''Not a very good Catholic, but I don't believe in divorce, so I'm careful. Maybe not so careful, now.'' He searched her eyes. ''We love each other. It isn't just physical with us. Do you like children?''

Her head felt as light as her feet. She smiled slowly. ''Yes.''

He smiled tenderly at her. ''So do I. When we've had time to get to know each other, we might consider making some plans.''

She knew she was barely breathing. "Oh, I'd like that," she said huskily.

"So would I. I like the way your eyes look when you're happy." He checked his thin gold watch. "I have to go. I'll pick you up at six. We'll go by to see Mama. Then we'll go home."

Home. It felt like home when she was with him. But she was worried about the letter. Maybe it wasn't anything upsetting. Maybe . . .!

She didn't open Marlene's letter until she was in her apartment. It was the letter she'd hoped she'd never receive. Marlene knew everything. She'd seen the article in the magazine. She wanted more money, as Ivory had suspected, a lot more. And she'd like to come to visit, she added as a threat. She'd like to do some real shopping. Surely her only child would like to have Mama visit for a few days. After all, Ivory wouldn't want Marlene to talk to reporters. Or anything like that.

Ivory felt as if cold sweat was running down her back. It was blackmail, of course, but how could she possibly refuse? She was just on the threshold of fame. If she didn't do what Marlene wanted her to do, she was going to be destroyed in the press. She knew without a verbal threat that Marlene would hash up the past and make it something totally sordid. She recalled an incident that would make her look as if she had no morals at all, an incident that Marlene had instigated, that still gave Ivory nightmares.

No, it wouldn't be a pretty story, and Marlene was an expert at concocting believable lies. She had a true gift for it. Ivory would have to send more money back home. And if she could steer Marlene through a small shopping spree and out of the city before Curry met her . . . that would be the easiest way to handle things. After all, there was no reason for him to have to see her mother, or even know that Marlene was visiting. If Ivory were careful, she could cope.

Now, of all times, when she and Curry were thinking of a future together, she couldn't let the threat of her mother destroy it all. She had to clear her mind of panic. She could work it out. All she had to do was remember that she was a grown woman now, not a child. She had no reason to fear Marlene any more. She could manage the older woman, if she just didn't panic. One day at a time, she thought. One hour at a time. And right now, she was going to meet Curry's mother. She had to let tomorrow wait and not try to anticipate it. First things first.

Having settled that in her mind, she went to dress for her evening with Curry. She chose one of her own designs, one of the black crepe suits with the black onyx butterfly surrounded by tiny Austrian crystal jewels in ruby, sapphire, and emerald hues. She let her hair fall softly around her face and smiled at her reflection. She hoped Curry's mother would be pleased, that she wouldn't take an instant dislike to her. Curry wouldn't let that stop him, but it would strain things between him and his mother; and, under the circumstances, that would never do. Ivory couldn't bear to have him hurt any more than he was being hurt by the prospect of his mother's imminent death.

C H A P T E R
TWELVE

CURRY was prompt. He called for Ivory at her apartment exactly at six. He hesitated in the doorway when she opened the door, stunned by the picture she made.

"It's the model I made for the new evening collection of suits," she said breathlessly. "Do you mind? If you'd rather I wore something else . . ."

"Wear it," he said huskily. "You take my breath away!"

She beamed. "Thank you."

"I won't have to tell my mother why you were hired," he added as he waited for her to get her purse and the new black silk jacket she'd splurged on at Saks Fifth Avenue. "She'll see for herself."

"I'm glad you like it. It did make up well, didn't it?" she asked, checking her seams.

"The fit is perfect."

She locked the door and turned to him with her silk

jacket on her arm. He took it from her and slowly, gently, draped it around her. His face was solemn as he looked down at her, his gaze lingering on the deep vee-neck of the jacket where the soft rise of her breasts was just visible.

"What are you thinking?" she ventured. "Or should I ask?"

His expression was complex as he looked into her eyes. His fingers stroked on the coat. "You're very young."

She smiled. "Is that all?"

"We're almost a generation apart."

"And what a gorgeous old man you are," she teased breathlessly, going on tiptoe to brush her lips against his chin. "Tall and sexy and beautiful to look at."

His fingers tightened on her shoulders over the coat. "I'm serious."

"I won't let you be serious," she countered. "I love you. Love doesn't count gray hairs or wrinkles or imperfections. It doesn't even see them!"

"That isn't realistic."

"Have you noticed that my nose is crooked and that one of my earlobes is lower than the other?" she challenged.

He lifted an eyebrow. "No."

"See?" she replied, satisfied.

"And what does that mean?"

Her eyes adored him. "That you love me, of course."

"Ah, is that it!"

She slid under one of his long arms and pressed close. "I'm nervous about meeting your mother. Maybe she won't like me. You said she thought I might be a gold digger."

He held her closer as they walked toward the staircase. "I calmed her fears about that. She'll adore you," he promised.

Mrs. Kells was lying in a hospital bed in her luxurious bedroom. She resembled Curry, but she was drawn and thin and pale, and her thin hair had gone almost completely gray from the devastation of her illness. A tube ran from her nostrils to an oxygen tank. It was a stark reminder of the reality of her condition.

Her black eyes were alive in her face, though, when Curry presented Ivory to her. They were curious eyes, sharp and hard and perceptive. They didn't miss a thing. Ivory felt her heart stop at their keen appraisal. But after Teresa Kells had given the younger woman a long, hard scrutiny, those dark eyes softened as if by magic.

"No," she said in a strong, if hoarse, voice. "No, you're not what I thought." She held out her hand, and Ivory took it, holding it firmly. "You're Ivory, yes?"

"Yes. And you're Mama."

Teresa Kells laughed hoarsely, pausing to cough with a jerky, racking motion that manifested itself as pain in her drawn face. She waved away the nurse and lay back against her pillows, adjusting the oxygen back into place while still clutching Ivory's hand in hers.

"It's part of the illness, this cough," she said. "I don't breathe so well these days. So we can't talk long."

"I know," Ivory said gently. She sat down on the bed beside the older woman. Probably the nurse wouldn't like it, but she didn't care. She knew about Mama Kells from Curry. This woman had given all she had, all she was, to the comfort of others. It inspired Ivory to know that such women existed. Her own mother had been nothing but a torment, a cross to bear, since Ivory's earliest memories.

"This suit, you designed it?" Teresa asked, touching the crepe material of the skirt lightly.

"Yes. Do you like it?"

"It's lovely. I'd like one of my own."

"Done!" Ivory said, smiling. "When would you like it?"

Mama Kells searched the young, kind face. "Oh, my dear," she said gently, "if only I'd known you sooner." She patted the hand resting on the cover. Her eyes closed. "So many things in life come too late." There was a painful shallow breath and then another before her eyes opened again. "You love my son?"

Ivory glanced at Curry. He wore the smile of a man who knows how deeply he is loved. "Oh, yes," she said huskily. "With all my heart. And then some."

Teresa nodded. "Then explain to him that it's not dangerous to make babies," she whispered. "He's afraid of it, because his first wife died in labor."

"I know. He told me. But he's not afraid of it anymore," she added with a smile.

"He told you?" Teresa looked at her son and they exchanged quiet glances. "Then he must truly love you," she said. "Because this he has never talked about."

"I like children," Ivory told the older woman. "I was an only child."

"Curry told me," Teresa said heavily. "And that you were a rich girl. You do not mind that we come from such poor stock?" she added with great pride.

"Of course not!" Ivory felt ashamed. She wanted to blurt out the truth to Curry's mother, to bare all her hurts and anguish to this loving woman. Teresa was the sort of person who would embrace a broken world without censure or complaint. Ivory was hungry for that kind of unconditional love. She'd never known it. Quick tears sprang to her eyes, and she ducked her head to hide them.

"Ah, you feel sorry for us," Teresa assumed, patting the slender hand again. "There is no need. See what my son has done with his Latin pride. And my daughter, another success. Poverty is not always a handicap, my girl. Sometimes it is the thorn that causes the foot to lift higher on the ladder."

"Why, what a unique way to put it," Ivory said, impressed.

"Mama is full of these expressions," Curry teased. "She always has the last word."

"And with you, I needed to have it!" She waved a finger at him. "He was always impetuous, impulsive, mercurial. Jumping to conclusions, losing his temper, and always regretting his outbursts when it was too late to recall them. You be careful," she warned him. "That quick temper may be a liability to you one day."

"Who did I get it from, huh?" he tossed back at her.

"No fighting," Ivory said, looking from one to the other. "Time out."

"A peacemaker you bring me!" Mama groaned. Then she smiled. "I have what I wished for. Now I can see what she is. Take her away to someplace more cheerful than this and buy her a nice supper," she told her son as she slid down to a more comfortable position amid the pillows that had propped her up. "I will sleep now."

The nurse came forward to check her vital signs.

Curry frowned, but the nurse nodded. "She drifts off more easily now, because of the narcotic," she explained. "It keeps her comfortable. There's very little pain right now."

"But that will change," Curry said flatly.

The nurse grimaced. "It's best not to think ahead."

"Has my sister been here yet?"

"She couldn't come right away because she and her husband had to attend a banquet. She said that she'd check on your mother after dinner, that she was sorry to have missed meeting Ivory and that she'll see you Saturday night."

He nodded. "Thank you. You know how to reach me if you need to?"

"Yes. Have a nice evening."

"You, too."

He took Ivory's hand and led her through the luxurious penthouse apartment to the elevator. He was quiet all the way down, remote and thoughtful.

"You could take me home, if you'd rather be alone," she offered when they reached the bottom floor.

He turned and looked at her, slowly and covetously. "She's dying."

"Yes. I know. I'm sorry."

He moved a step closer. The doors were still closed and he pushed the button that held them that way. He didn't touch her, but he came close enough that she could feel the warm threat of his body, catch the clean scent of it as she breathed quickly.

"Stay with me tonight," he said quietly. He held up a hand when she started to speak, and shook his head. "No. It isn't sex I want." He hesitated. "I want you in my arms all night."

She reached out and caught his lean hand in hers. "I think I can manage that."

He searched her soft eyes. "You liked my mama."

She smiled. "Yes. She's one of those special people who give more than they take." Her face tightened. "Do you know how very rare they are?" she added, thinking about her own background.

His hand closed around hers. "I have some idea.

You had everything, all the advantages; but I don't think you had a lot of love, did you?''

She grimaced. "Not a lot, no. But, then, you can't miss what you've never had, can you?''

He drew her closer. "You have it now, don't you?''

She breathed in the warm, clean scent of him and felt life surging through her. She nodded. "And so do you.''

He smiled back. "And so do I.''

They were both tired. The demand of the week had been powerful, and Curry had the added trauma of his mother's deteriorating condition. They had one drink and then he undressed her lazily, tenderly, and put her to bed. He turned off the lights and joined her, drawing her into the curve of his body with no sexual message at all. She felt the sadness in him and wrapped him up tight in her arms.

"I'm sorry," she said against his hair-roughened chest. "I'm so sorry.''

He drew a long breath. "Oh, *querida*, what a hard thing it is to have to let go of people we love.''

She held him tighter. "I'll be here. You won't be alone.''

He groaned softly and smoothed her hair. "Neither will you," he said solemnly. "As long as I'm alive, I'll love you.''

The red satin of the sheets was soft against her bare skin as she awoke to unfamiliar sounds and smells.

Her pale eyes opened and when she saw the satin she laughed.

He saw her exploring glance and smiled wickedly. He was fully dressed, wearing a pin-striped suit and a tie. His glance slid over her body where her breasts and part of one long leg peered out from the lush red of the fabric.

"I was going to have a bolt of that to drape you in," he murmured sensuously. "But I thought the sheets would be better. Like them?"

"Yes," she murmured. "But they're wicked."

"So they are. White the first time, red the second," he chuckled. "Next time, I'll buy sapphire."

"Why?"

"Because I love the way you look nude against those colors," he said quietly. "And I love the way satin feels next to your skin when I make love to you."

She stretched luxuriously, enjoying the way he watched her. She lifted one leg and eased the satin away. Her eyes made him a blatant invitation.

"No," he whispered, bending to kiss her parted lips gently. "Not this morning."

"Why?" she whispered back.

He loosened her clinging arms. "Because I don't have anything to use, and I don't want to make you pregnant just yet."

She searched his face slowly. "It's all right, you know. I'm on the pill."

He scowled. "Why?"

She grinned. "You look jealous."

He hesitated. Then he laughed self-consciously. "Why?"

"Because I kept hoping that you'd come back after that night," she said honestly. "But you didn't." She drew the satin across her waist and looked up at him. "You were so adamant about not making me pregnant, and I didn't want you to have to use something," she murmured.

He sat down beside her on the bed, propping his weight on his hand beside her head. "Why?"

She looked up into his dark eye and blushed.

"So," he mused, reading the look accurately. "You wanted to get closer to me than you could that night, yes?"

"Yes," she whispered huskily. "So close that you could feel me in every cell . . . !"

His mouth ground into hers. He groaned hoarsely as she lifted to him. His hands clamped onto her hips and he rolled with her, so that she was under him, feeling an arousal that was sudden enough to take his breath away.

He nibbled ardently at her mouth while he fought buttons and zippers, cursing until he managed to free himself enough to join his body to hers.

She whimpered at the unexpected intimacy, but she welcomed it ardently, hungry for him, oblivious to everything except the quick, hard thrust of his body.

She cried out even as he did, frantic minutes later, feeling his powerful body ripple convulsively over her.

They clung to each other as they waited for the madness to drain out of them. He was still wearing his suit and shoes, having only rearranged his clothing instead of removing it.

"Why, you lecher," she whispered into his mouth. "You ravished me!"

"It was mutual," he whispered back. "No, you don't," he protested when she started to move. "Stay right there."

"But we're . . ." she began.

"Ummm. Yes. Aren't we?" He lifted his head and looked into her eyes and deliberately shifted his hips. She shivered. He did it again. She felt the slow, sweet change of his body with fascination that was reflected in her eyes.

"You can't do that," she said. "I read it in a book."

"Change authors." He rolled onto his back, taking her with him. "Now," he said huskily. "You do it this time."

She flushed. "I don't know how," she faltered.

"It's easy. Here. Like this." He taught her, laughing at her first attempts until she was able to master her inhibitions and the awkwardness of her own body. "You still make love like a virgin," he teased.

"Well, I don't feel like one," she said, amazed that they could talk with such intimacy, that they could laugh and play like this.

He smiled sensuously. His hands moved her hips against his and he groaned. "Like that, *querida*. Yes. That's it."

"You aren't even undressed," she said unsteadily. It was even more erotic because he wasn't. He was almost fully dressed, and she was nude. The feel of the fabric of his suit against her skin was arousing.

His gaze went from her belly to her high, firm breasts with their hard pink tips, to the frantic pulse in her throat and farther up, to her swollen lips and flushed face and passion-glazed eyes. Against the soft flesh of her hips, his lean, dark hands looked exotic as he helped her achieve the necessary rhythm for satisfaction.

He whispered something rough as his body lifted under her. He was breathing like a distance runner, his powerful hands gripping her bruisingly. "Oh . . . God . . . do it . . . now! Now!" he groaned in anguish. "*Querida*, help me . . . !" Through taut lips, he told her how, told her when.

She obeyed him and then hung on the edge of ecstasy watching his proud head go back and his neck arch as he cried out. She laughed with delight at his momentary submission to her, but before she could enjoy it entirely, the culmination bit into her own body and she cried out.

"You laughed," he accused as he whipped her onto her back and increased the waves of pleasure almost to unconsciousness. "Laugh now," he dared through his own satisfaction. "Laugh. Are you laughing? Can you laugh?'' He moved like a sorcerer, draining the last tiny breath of pleasure from her in minutes that seemed unending. She felt his gaze on her, but she was as helpless now as he had been, powerless, his object, his toy. She arched her body to him in submission, accepting his invasion of it, his conquest, his mastery with little gasps that took her last strength and left her exhausted.

When her eyes opened again, she was trembling faintly from the exertion and he was standing over her, fully dressed again, with an expression on his dark face that made her heart almost burst with feeling.

''Arrogant beast!'' she managed.

He smiled with pure satanic pleasure. ''You'd make a stone statue arrogant. God, I love to watch you! You make me feel like a conqueror, as if you could die of the pleasure I give you.''

She swallowed with difficulty. Her body felt like one long ache. ''I thought I had, for a minute. It wasn't like that before.''

''For me, either,'' he confessed solemnly, letting his eye search over her. There were faint marks on her breasts and her belly, even on her thighs, and his chin lifted with a pride he couldn't help feeling. Badges of honor. She'd gone with him every step of the way. He knew that if he'd been as nude as she, there would have been matching marks on his back, on his hips and thighs. They were violent together in passion. She was more than his match.

"I'm sorry," she whispered huskily.

He frowned. "For what?"

"That I'm taking the pill," she said, meeting his gaze. "You would have made me pregnant if I hadn't been."

His jaw grew firm. "I know."

Her lips parted. "I want a baby," she whispered.

"I do, too, with you; never with anyone else, not since the first one that cost me my wife." He traced her with quiet possession. "I'm not afraid of it anymore. But you want a career first, remember?" he said, disoriented by the way she looked at him, even by his own response to her. Their first loving had been nothing like this maelstrom of emotion and satiation.

"A career," she echoed blankly. Then reality began to come back. Marlene. She had to send Marlene more money. Marlene wanted to come to New York and shop with her. Marlene.

She levered up on her elbow, wincing at the discomfort.

"Did I hurt you?" he asked quickly, when he saw her expression.

"Yes." She looked up at him wickedly. "You hurt me all over."

The look made him smile. "Did I?"

"It's like pain, at the last, isn't it?" she added huskily. "It hurts in the sweetest way, and throbs and makes you want to cry because it's so good."

His chest rose and fell. "Yes."

"Is it like that for a man all the time?" she asked curiously.

"Not like what we just did together," he said quietly. "Perhaps because I never loved like this before."

She smiled gently. "I never loved at all, before you."

His eyebrow lifted. "Do you mind if I gloat about that?"

She made a face at him. "Yes."

"I will anyway." He checked his watch. "One of us has to go to work. You might consider doing the same thing," he added with a grin. "The boss might fire you."

"Heaven forbid!" She got to her feet slowly and was drawn to him to be kissed softly, tenderly. "I'll have to go to work in the model," she groaned.

"No, you won't. I'll go with you to your apartment."

She bit her lower lip. "The driver will know . . ."

"What driver? I'm taking the Jaguar."

She knew he was doing that for her sake. She looked up into his face. "I don't mind if people know we've been lovers," she said quietly. "I love you. I'm not ashamed."

His breath caught. He touched her cheek. "You're full of surprises, sweetheart," he said. "For what it's worth, I'm not ashamed, either. But, if we don't get to work, we may lose the company years before we have children to inherit it!"

CHAPTER
THIRTEEN

"**D**O you mean it?" she asked solemnly.

He nodded. "I mean it, all right. And while we're at it, how do you feel about becoming a Catholic?"

She lowered her eyes to his chest. "I used to go to a Catholic church, once," she said, without revealing when or where. "I could do it again."

He relaxed. He tipped her eyes up to his. "I want to marry you."

Her heart felt as if it could fly. "I want to marry you, too," she whispered. "And live with you always."

He drew her to his heart and held her there, wrapped up hungrily in his lean arms. His eye closed. "I've never had anyone of my own, except Mama. Now I've got you."

"And I've got you." She clung closer. Her eyes closed. God protect me from my own mother, she prayed silently. Make her go away, just for a little while,

so that I can have just a taste of happiness and peace
and love.

But Marlene didn't go away. The letter was followed
by another, later in the week. And even the delight of
knowing that she and Curry had a future together didn't
soothe the wound of having Marlene back in her life
again. Marlene wanted to come to New York, despite
the increased amount of the check Ivory had sent by
express mail. She wanted Ivory to pay for the ticket,
too. And there were more veiled threats.

Ivory put her head in her hands. She'd just been
interviewed for another magazine article. They were
calling her the "crystal sensation." She'd been invited
to a famous couture house in Paris, to an exclusive
showing. She was scheduled to do one of the best talk
shows. Her designs were selling out in the stores. And
just now, just when Curry wanted to marry her, just
when she had it all . . . she could lose it all in a heartbeat. Because of Marlene.

"What will I do?" she asked aloud.

The answer was obvious; she'd do what she had to
do. She'd pay for a round-trip ticket for Marlene, send
her shopping, and then send her home. Some luxuries
might satisfy the woman for a time. At least, until she
could plan against any future upsets.

The tricky part would be keeping Marlene from meeting Curry. But she should be able to manage that. She'd
find reasons why he couldn't come to her apartment,

why she couldn't go out with him. He was spending more and more time with his mother, anyway. Perhaps she wouldn't even have to make excuses.

She sent Marlene the ticket. Then she waited anxiously, and with obvious trepidation, for her mother to make the trip up from Texas. All the while, she worried. Her apprehension was so great that it was noticed by everyone, especially by Curry.

"What's bothering you?" he asked her at lunch, the very day her mother was scheduled to fly in to La Guardia.

She managed a wan smile. "Oh, I'm just nervous about that new talk show they want me to go on," she lied. "It's controversial, you know. They like to dig for dirt."

"What could they dig up about you?" he scoffed, touching her hand lightly. His dark eye looked warmly into hers. "You're a crystal-clear pool. No dirt. No ugly secrets."

She felt guilty and lowered her eyes before he could see what she was feeling. "No ugly secrets," she echoed. In her mind were flashing pictures of herself as a ragged, dirty little sharecropper's daughter playing in the freshly picked cotton with the black kids in the autumn fields back in Texas. And there, screaming drunken abuse at her, was Marlene in her red lipstick, with a drink in one hand and a lighted cigarette in the other. Marlene, haranguing her, laughing at her, telling lies about her to anyone who would listen. Back home,

everybody believed those lies. Everybody thought that
Ivory Costello was a petty criminal. Marlene had told
them so.

"Come back," Curry chided. "Where were you?"

In a nightmare, she could have said. One that might
never end. She looked into his face and ached to tell
him the truth, before it was too late. But he thought she
was the product of a privileged upbringing. He thought
she had a mother who loved her, a fine family name.
What was he going to feel about her when he knew that
she came from poverty even worse than he'd endured,
and that she had an unwarranted but black reputation
in the small town where she'd grown up? What if Marlene told him?

"I was just . . . thinking. About my mother," she
added, which wasn't really a lie.

"When am I going to meet her?" he teased. "You've
met mine. I want to get to know my future mother-in-
law."

She caught her breath. It was a natural enough question, but it gave her the shock of her life. She couldn't
ever introduce him to Marlene. It wouldn't take more
than a few minutes with Marlene to give the show away.
Despite her traces of remaining beauty, Marlene had a
Texas drawl and she dressed like a tramp. Her idea of
haute couture was a dress cut to the navel with tassels;
she smoked like a furnace, drank like a fish, and her
conversation could make a sailor blush.

"Well, she's in Europe right now," she began.

He scowled faintly. "Does she live there? Every time you mention her, she's overseas."

"We have relatives there. She stays with them."

It sounded weak, and he looked suspicious.

Her fingers curled around his. "Will you take me to the opera?" she asked. "I've always wanted to go."

He relaxed and began to smile. "There's something we have in common. I love opera."

The comment led to a lengthy discussion about composers and tenors that lasted until lunch was over.

Marlene's plane was due to arrive at three-forty-five, and it was impossible for Ivory to get away to meet her. She sent a limousine, with instructions to take Marlene straight to the apartment. She'd already phoned the apartment manager and arranged for Marlene to be let in.

But her plans went awry in the most extraordinary fashion. She became tied up in a business meeting. The car was late getting to the airport and didn't arrive in time to meet the plane. Marlene, as usual, grew impatient and refused to wait. She hailed a cab and had it take her to the offices of Kells-Meredith.

Just after a viciously angry Marlene strode into the building and demanded to see her daughter, Curry Kells came in the front door. He and Marlene arrived at Ivory's office at the same time.

"Allow me," he said politely, and opened the door, wondering who the woman was. She looked vaguely like one of the street people. She was wearing a tight, cheap suit, shoes with run-down heels, and a green silk jacket. Her long hair, worn in a French twist, was fastened with a rhinestone clip, and she was coated with enough makeup to furnish a drama department. She reeked of cheap perfume. He couldn't imagine what such a woman would want with Ivory, unless this was one of the women from the shelter where Ivory and Dee volunteered. He was about to ask her when Ivory's head lifted from some sketches she was showing to two of the salesmen.

"M . . . mother!" she stammered.

Curry had never been lost for words in his life. He was now. In one word, Ivory had made a liar of herself. If this was her mother—and now he did see a resemblance—then everything she'd told him about her background was false. This woman was no Louisiana socialite, nor was she from any impeccable European background.

He looked at Ivory and saw her face go as pale as the paper in her shaking hands.

"So there you are," Marlene said, containing her temper. It had occurred to her that the man standing next to her in that expensive suit was some important person in the company. She couldn't afford to rage at Ivory. "You forgot me, didn't you, dear?" she asked plaintively, and looked up at Curry with sad, resigned eyes. "She doesn't like her friends to know about me.

She's ashamed of her poor old mama, aren't you, honey?''

Curry, whose own mother was second best to a saint, couldn't conceive of any other sort. He stood stiffly beside Marlene, with his unbelieving eyes on Ivory.

"I sent a car, Mother," Ivory said uncomfortably.

"Did you, honey? It wasn't there." She shifted her purse in her hands. Every finger except the thumb wore a cheap costume ring. "It's all right. I got a cab. It's waiting downstairs. Could you let me have some money to pay the driver, and get my bags out?" she asked sweetly.

"I'll attend to it," Curry said. He took another look at Marlene, and then at Ivory, and walked out without another word.

Ivory felt sick. The salesmen and even Dee were giving her covert looks. She'd planned so meticulously to prevent her mother from coming here. But her plans had backfired. Curry's face had said everything. He knew she was a liar. He'd think she was ashamed of her mother, and he'd hold her in contempt for it, because he knew nothing about Marlene. All he knew was that he'd been lied to, by the woman he loved.

"Why don't you go home with your mother, Ivory?" Dee asked gently. "I'll carry on here. I'm sure you want to visit."

Ivory glanced at her, but there were doubts in her friend's face, too. It was the past all over again. Marlene was framing her.

"Yes, dear, we have so much to talk about," Marlene said, smiling at everyone. "So, this is where you work! How exciting. I didn't know . . . she never writes or phones me," she explained gently to Dee. "I had to beg her to let me come, so I could see where she lives, and make sure she's all right. She's the only family I got, you know."

Ivory flushed. Lay it on with a trowel, Marlene, she was thinking.

Marlene looked at her tall daughter and smiled. It was a smug, cold smile, but the others couldn't see Marlene's eyes.

"Let's go home, then, Mother."

"Aren't you going to introduce me to these nice people, Ivory?" Marlene asked, rubbing it in.

"Of course." She made the introductions, and Marlene charmed the whole group. By the time she left with her daughter, Ivory felt two inches high.

When they were in the hall on the way to the front door, Marlene gave her a cold glare.

"You got what you asked for, leaving me standing at that airport like a country hick!" she raged. "You didn't send a car!"

"I did," Ivory said through her teeth. "It's probably still there waiting for you. He was to hold up a sign with your name on it. Did you even look for one?"

Marlene's chin lifted. "There was a sign with 'Keene' on it," she said with a sarcastic smile. "My name is Costello. So was yours, until you decided to change it and start everyone talking.''

Ivory stepped back at the revolving door to let her mother go through. She wondered how she was going to manage to get through the visit without screaming. In the back of her mind was the fear of what Curry would think of her now, and what he might do. She'd lied to him. He knew it. How could she ever explain it away?

She took Marlene to the apartment in a cab, because that was now an affordable expense. As they entered the small but tidy rooms, Marlene gave her surroundings a cold appraisal.

''Well, it ain't the Ritz,'' she drawled. ''But I guess it could be worse.''

''There's a bedroom,'' Ivory said. ''You can sleep there. I'll sleep in the living room.''

Marlene turned and looked at her, her eyes lingering on the pale blue suit with a patterned blue scoop-necked blouse that Ivory was wearing. ''Don't you look elegant,'' she said. ''In that fancy suit, using that polished accent. Who was the one-eyed man in your office?''

''Curry Kells,'' she said. ''My boss.''

''He looked shocked when he realized who I was. What did you tell him about me, Ivory?'' she demanded.

She put her purse on the end table. ''I told him my people were a well-to-do Louisiana family, and that my mother was visiting in Europe,'' she said flatly, glaring at Marlene. "Not that he'll believe it anymore. Not after he's seen you."

Marlene's eyebrows rose. "Backtalk? I'm amazed. You never talked back at home."

"What good would it have done?" Ivory asked wearily. "You'd tell a lie even when the truth would suit better. Why did you have to come here and ruin everything for me?" she demanded. "Why couldn't you have taken the money I sent and stayed home?!"

"I saw your picture in that magazine and read that article," Marlene said, shaking with anger. "You didn't even tell them your real name. You put on airs and made yourself out to be some rich socialite, didn't you? Well, it was a lie, and your boss knows it now, doesn't he?"

"Yes, thanks to you. What if he fires me?" she continued, facing her parent with cold contempt. "There won't be any money to send you then, will there?"

Marlene scoffed. She reached for a cigarette and lit it, ignoring Ivory's glare. She pulled up a pretty candy dish to catch her ashes. "He won't fire you for lying," Marlene said carelessly. She looked around again. "You've spent a lot of money fixing this place up, haven't you?" She reached out and lifted a silver-framed photo of Curry and laughed mirthlessly. "Well, well, so that's how it is. He's your lover, is he?"

Ivory's face drew in. "What he is doesn't concern you."

"You're my little girl," Marlene taunted. "Of course it concerns me. I want to know what his intentions are."

"He wanted to marry me until an hour ago," Ivory said.

Marlene's eyebrow jerked. "If he loves you, he still will."

Ivory wrapped her arms around her chest and laughed. "Oh, sure," she said. "He'll be rabid to marry me when he finds out what I really am: the daughter of a sharecropper and the town drunk!"

Marlene's hand shot out and caught Ivory's cheek viciously. "Don't you ever call me that again!" she spat, her pale blue eyes blazing. "Don't you talk that way! I'm no drunk!"

Ivory touched her cheek, amazed that the violence didn't affect her as it always had before. She looked at her mother and really saw her for the first time. Why, Marlene was all bluff. It was an act, that maniacal rage. She knew exactly what she was doing, but she was pretending to be out of control, to make Ivory afraid.

The younger woman pulled herself to her full height and dropped her hand to her side. "Feel better now?" she asked with deceptive softness. "Try that again and see what happens."

Marlene's instincts bristled. She restrained the hand that wanted to deliver a second blow, because Ivory's eyes were telling her that it would be returned, with interest.

"You've changed," she said.

Ivory's eyes narrowed. "I've had to," she said. "You made me into the town joke. I was laughed at and taunted and ridiculed and held in contempt because of the lies you told. I got out. Nobody laughs at me here, and nobody thinks I'm lower than dirt."

"Yet," Marlene said, making a veiled threat of it.

"Oh, you did a little damage today," Ivory conceded. "But nothing irreversible."

"Think so?" The older woman finished her cigarette and ground it out viciously, her long red fingernails curled around the stub in a death grip. "Wait and see." She looked up. "You're going to make me over," she said. "I want new clothes, a stylish haircut, a manicure and some things for my face. I want a new coat, too; a mink, maybe."

"Where will you wear a mink in Texas?" Ivory asked coldly.

"In department stores," Marlene replied. "It's your fault I never got anything. When your papa knocked me up, his folks and mine made me marry him," she said with pure venom. "I gave up all my dreams to look after you."

"You never looked after me!" Ivory shot back. Her fists were clenched by her side as years of anguish tumbled past her lips. "You never cared what I did! After papa died, you had one boyfriend after another until your last rich man took you on. And they made my life hell!"

"You asked for it," Marlene said haughtily. "Parading around in tight jeans and low-cut blouses!"

"They were all I had! Your cast-offs!" she choked. "You let them handle me . . . !"

Marlene let out an angry breath. "Don't carry on so," she snapped. "You weren't raped or anything."

"I was handled!" Her lower lip trembled as she stared with wounded eyes at her mother. "You can't imagine how repulsive men were to me because of that. And you laughed about it, so drunk you could hardly sit up at all, you and your lecherous boyfriends!"

"You're exaggerating, as usual." Marlene refused to argue. She lit another cigarette. "I want to go shopping tomorrow," she said. "Then we can go out to eat, somewhere fancy." Her pale eyes lit up. "Twenty-one, maybe, or Sardi's."

"Wrong decade," Ivory said tersely. "Try The Four Seasons."

Marlene shrugged. "Whatever." She turned on the television and moved the dial to the shopping channel, grinning as she saw the merchandise being offered. "Look, isn't that pretty!"

She sat down, captivated by the screen, while Ivory stood beside her and watched her watch television. Marlene wasn't a conversationalist. She liked soap operas and talk shows, and not much else. When she wasn't glued to the television screen or having her hair done at the beauty parlor, she was reading pulp magazines or drinking. She had no intellectual life and very little social life because her looks no longer attracted men.

Ivory could have wept as she studied the other woman and compared her to Curry's fiercely loving mother who would have sacrificed anything for her children. Marlene wouldn't have given up a bottle of nail varnish to buy a carton of milk for a hungry infant.

"Didn't you ever want me?" Ivory asked aloud in a hushed tone.

"What?" Marlene wasn't listening. "Look at this watch, Ivory. I sure would love to have one like that. I'll look when we're out shopping. Get me a drink."

"I don't have anything alcoholic."

"Then go out and buy me a bottle!" Marlene snapped. "I'm not going without my gin."

Ivory grabbed her purse and went out the door, blind and deaf as she stalked down the hall with cold resignation. Neighbors called to her but she didn't answer. Her mind, like her spirit, was tied in knots.

She tried to phone Curry but he wouldn't talk to her. His secretary at work, and then his valet at the apartment, gave her the same message over and over until she finally accepted defeat and stopped trying.

"Won't the big boss talk to you?" Marlene asked, hefting another slug of gin to her mouth. "Poor baby!"

"Why don't you get help?" Ivory asked as she looked

down at the woman who had borne her. "Don't you even realize that you have a drinking problem?"

"This isn't a problem! It's the solution." Marlene toasted her before she swallowed, smiling dizzily. "It feels good. I can't do without it, and I don't have to. I've got you to take care of me." She lay back in the chair with a satisfied sigh. "You don't want me to tell your friends that you neglect me."

"Why not?" Ivory said heavily. "You've been telling people that all my life."

"All your fault," Marlene said heavily. "Never wanted to get married, never wanted to get pregnant. You made me get married. You ruined my life!"

"You let it happen!" she shot back, sick of being accused for something she hadn't done. "You did! You could have said no, couldn't you?!"

Marlene blinked. It wasn't like Ivory to talk back. This was an odd situation. She frowned. "He said he'd buy me a new dress if I let him," she explained. "A pretty one, with embroidery on the hem."

Ivory folded her arms over her breasts. "That's why I'm here? Because you wanted a new dress?"

"More or less."

"Didn't you love Dad?"

"For about ten minutes, I did," Marlene said, laughing at her little joke. "But he was always in a hurry. I never even had any fun doing it with him." She sprawled her arms. "Now Larry could make love!" she said, recalling her rich boyfriend. "And he bought me pretty things. But he died." She lifted her head and looked at Ivory. "So now, you can take care of me."

"Why can't you take care of yourself?" Ivory asked her.

Marlene's eyes widened as if this were some foreign language. "What?"

"Get a job," Ivory said. "Go to work."

"What would I do? Pick cotton?" she chided.

"Why not? You made me do it," Ivory returned coldly. "You put me to work on your boyfriend's place with the day laborers and took off for Corpus Christi with him on a fishing trip!"

"Hard work never hurt anybody."

"You'd know all about that!" Ivory could hardly breathe through her anger. "But what you didn't know was that I felt like part of a family with those people. The Gonzalezes taught me how to speak Spanish like a native, and the Joneses treated me like one of their own kids."

"Don't I know it!" Marlene said with contempt. "You didn't even think of yourself as white when you started to high school. Always sitting with the colored children and the Mexican kids instead of your own kind!"

"Careful, mother dear," Ivory said coolly. "These days, it's not politically correct to spew racial hatred. In fact, it can get you into a lot of trouble in New York City."

Marlene made a sound in her throat. "Naturally!" She sat up. "Tell me, honey, do you mix with that sort up here? Or do you play the rich society girl to the hilt, right down to avoiding everybody who doesn't belong to a country club?"

Ivory thought about the shelter and Tim and his mother and sisters, and Mrs. Payne, and the other people who lived there. She didn't even bother to answer Marlene. It didn't matter. The woman was three sheets to the wind already and getting stiffer by the minute. Eventually she'd start falling down and then she'd be sick, and then she'd sleep. It was the old pattern, all over again. Ivory had never felt so alone or so frightened, despite the fact that she was coping better than ever before. She wanted Curry in her most desperate hour, but Curry wouldn't even speak to her.

CHAPTER
FOURTEEN

IVORY had an unexpected telephone call from Curry early on Monday morning. She was worn out after spending the weekend escorting her mother from one side of New York to the other and buying her things that she couldn't really afford. But the alternative to the spending was too dreadful to contemplate. That was, if her mother could do any more damage than she already had.

"How did your weekend go?" Curry asked, when she answered her phone. "Is your mother enjoying her visit?"

"I took her shopping," she said in a toneless voice. She resented his assumption that her mother was the victim. It was the old story, but she'd never expected Curry to be taken in. If his own mother had been less compassionate, perhaps he wouldn't have been fooled by Marlene. She had to remember that people who'd known Ivory all her life believed Marlene's lies. That made it a little easier to bear Curry's contempt.

"I'm sure she enjoyed it. If you take some time to get to know her, you may discover that her life hasn't been a bed of roses either. Sometimes we take our parents for granted. We shouldn't. Mothers make tremendous sacrifices for their children."

She wondered how anyone could have taken Marlene for granted, and Marlene had never made any sacrifices that weren't to her advantage. But she didn't say that. She didn't say anything.

"I thought you might like Friday off, since it will be her last day in town," he added. "We're rushed, but I won't begrudge you some free time."

"That's very thoughtful of you," she said stiffly. "Thank you."

"Don't forget the talk show next Monday night."

"I won't. I'll be fine," she said through her teeth. He was ice cold, but she had to try to reach him. "Curry, I want to explain . . ."

"What is there to explain?" he asked in a silky-smooth tone. "I knew everything the minute I realized who your mother was. You played me for a fool, Ivory."

"I didn't mean to," she began. "I only wanted . . . !"

"You were looking for a boot up the ladder. After all, fame is all you really wanted, isn't it? You've got it. You'll get even more as you go along. By the way, you don't have to worry about your job, if that was concerning you," he added. "You're worth a lot to the company. Although I hope you realize that your value to me personally has taken a nose-dive, 'rich little girl from Louisiana.' "

The tone cut. "I wanted to be somebody!"

"And you will be," he said. "This television appearance almost guarantees it. You told me that you wanted to be rich and famous, Ivory. But you never told me why. I didn't know you came from poverty."

"You still don't know everything," she challenged.

"I know that you're ashamed of your background, and of your mother, and that you lied about both to me," he said icily. "That's what I hold against you most. How could you be callous enough to turn your back on her when you became a success? She deserves to share in your good fortune. But you took her for granted, Ivory."

"That will be the day," she murmured.

"Don't joke about it. You're not the woman I thought you were. All of it was an act, wasn't it? Your concern for me, the lovemaking, your work at the shelter—none of it was from the heart. You were playing a part to get you what you wanted. Well, you've got it. I hope it was worth the price you had to pay."

What I wanted, she corrected silently, was you. Maybe I wanted protection against Marlene, too. But she didn't say it. He wasn't in a listening mood. He was wounded and he was going to withdraw like a wounded animal.

"I'm sorry you won't listen," she said quietly.

"I've listened once too often already," he said coldly. He hung up, and she went back to her designs; but her heart wasn't in her work. Her dreams of success had been nebulous, but they had included being with Curry and sharing it all with him. They also had included being able to use the money she earned to do things other than buy her greedy mother luxuries.

Mr. Johnson's wheelchair was wearing out and she knew that the elderly couple couldn't afford to replace it. That was one of her projects. She had other small projects going in the neighborhood shelter, such as organizing a small cooperative among the people at the shelter who could do crafts. Curry knew nothing about that. But he knew nothing about her, either, she decided angrily.

"Don't forget you're taking the buyer from the Chic Boutiques chain out to lunch," Dee reminded her.

She caught her breath. "But I've got my mother . . ."

"Take her with you; Curry won't mind. Use the company's corporate card. You have yours, surely?"

"Yes, but . . ."

"He won't mind. Trust me." Dee paused by her desk. "You really are afraid of your mother, aren't you?"

She looked down at the cost estimates on her desk. "Everyone believed her, the minute she opened her mouth. It's been like that all my life. Back home, she convinced everyone that I was a tramp, a cheat, a liar."

She looked up into her friend's concerned face. "I changed my name, I changed my voice, I changed my address . . . but I'm still me, Dee," she said heavily. "I can't change me."

Dee laid a gentle hand on her shoulder. "Why should you want to? You're a warm, kind, sharing person. I like you."

"You believed her," she accused tartly.

Dee chuckled. "Did I? Oh, Ivory, I saw right through her. She smirked when she told us you never wrote or called. I've known people like her before. She's a good actress; she should have gone on the stage. But she didn't fool me."

"She fooled Curry."

"He loves his mother," Dee reminded her. "He's got one of the really rare kind, the old-fashioned kind that every child longs for. My mother was a journalist. She never cooked or cleaned; I did. She went looking for new stories, and I took care of my little sister and did the housework. I'd have given my eye teeth for a mother like Curry's."

"So would I," Ivory said fervently. "She's everything I dreamed of when I was little. But my mother isn't like that. He won't listen when I try to explain."

"Give him time. He's hot-tempered; but in the end, he's reasonable."

She remembered his mother saying the same thing. He'd know the truth one day, but it would be too late. Meanwhile, Ivory had to live with her mother's demands and Curry's contempt. She was painted as a gold digger who coveted nothing more than wealth and power. Yet nothing could be farther from the truth.

"I don't know if he'll ever believe me now," Ivory said wearily. "How can I blame him? My mother has fooled plenty of other people over the years. My big mistake was trying to hide my past in the first place. You can't run away, can you?"

"Not really," Dee agreed. "You have to learn from the past and go on from there. We're the sum total of our experiences, good and bad. But steel has to be tempered in fire, remember." She smiled. "Good times never shaped anyone's character."

"I guess not. Mine should be sterling bright in that case, because I don't remember any good times. My mother hated me from the day I was born. I'll never escape her. Never!"

"Don't talk like that. You'll cope. You can do anything you have to. She'll go back home, you know. Everything will be all right when she leaves. Curry will cool down and you can explain it to him."

"No, I can't. His mother loved him and sacrificed for him. He couldn't imagine some of the things my mother did to me. I'm afraid of her," she added, shaking her head. "I know it's cowardly, but I can't help it. She's my worst enemy." She looked up. "She drinks, and when she's had enough, she does irrational things. I'm so afraid that she might try to go to the newspapers."

"You're not *that* well known yet, thank God," Dee chuckled. "Don't borrow things to worry about. Take her out to lunch with you to meet the buyer. It will be an experience for her."

"Okay," she said. "I suppose I might as well."

She gave in. She could just imagine how her mother was going to react to having lunch with one of the top buyers in the country.

Marlene was on her best behavior. She'd downed a goodly portion of her quart of gin in the three nights since she'd been in residence. But either she was able to hold it better than she had when Ivory was a child or she'd grown immune to its effects, because she hadn't been staggering drunk, and she hadn't been sick or hung over.

Marlene waltzed into the exclusive restaurant with her daughter to greet the young, elegant buyer from a chain of upscale boutiques and immediately took over the conversation, knowledgeably and with a sophistication that surprised her daughter. Even her drawl was less pronounced. It could be that she was almost sober, for a change.

"Of course my daughter doesn't give me credit for any intelligence," she told the other woman with a dewy smile. "But I know the clothing industry very well, in fact. I enjoy the fashion magazines."

"You must be very proud of Ivory," the buyer said. "She's come up the ladder quickly at Kells-Meredith, and on the strength of real talent, too."

Ivory thanked the woman politely, and Marlene seethed.

"Oh, you have the creative ability to go far in the industry," the buyer continued. "We're very impressed with your new collection. I understand that Saks and Neiman-Marcus placed large orders."

Ivory nodded. "Yes, they did. I was overwhelmed."

Marlene made a noise, distracting the conversation to herself. "I think I'd like a cocktail."

Ivory caught the eye of a waiter and ordered coffee for herself, leaving the drinks to the other two women.

"Don't you drink, Ivory?" the buyer asked with a smile.

"No." The word was flat and unapologetic. Marlene gave her a hard look, but she refrained from making any comments.

The conversation revolved, naturally, around high fashion, and Ivory managed to hold her ground despite her mother's interference. Marlene gave the corporate credit card a hard look when Ivory brought it out to pay for their meal, but the comment about her status that Ivory expected was never made.

"If I'd had your chances when I was your age, I'd certainly have made more of them than you have," Marlene said when they were on their way back to the apartment in the limousine Ivory had hired. That, too, was Curry's idea.

"I make the most of my chances," Ivory said. "I'm doing very well."

Marlene sprawled back against the soft leather with a hard laugh. "And living in Queens?" she chided.

"Queens is the best place to live," Ivory replied stiffly. "I have good neighbors and I feel safe where I am."

"No men, of course."

Ivory looked at her mother coldly. "You had enough for both of us."

Marlene's face hardened, and Ivory knew that if it hadn't been for the driver's glance in the rear-view mirror, she'd probably have been slapped for the comment. It occurred to her, however, that this time she was willing to hit back. That reaction was as new as the self-confidence even Marlene hadn't been able to shake.

"Brave, aren't you?" her mother asked icily.

"Well, I don't see much to be afraid of," Ivory replied evenly with a look that clearly expressed her opinion of the older woman.

There was a sharply in-drawn breath. "You little tramp!"

Ivory managed a cool smile. "Temper, temper."

"You'll pay for that, my girl," Marlene said under her breath. "Oh, but you will!"

"I've been paying all my life," came the reply. "Emotionally and then financially."

Marlene looked away. "You owe me!"

"No, I don't," Ivory said quietly. "It's the other way around. Someday, the truth will come out, you know. And not everybody believes the lies you've told about me. What will you do if they ever dig deep enough to find out what sort of childhood I had? Or about that last night when your boyfriend came to the house and I ran screaming out the back door?''

Marlene actually went pale. She pushed back her hair nervously. ''You asked for that!''

''I did not! I never did! You were both too drunk to care about my feelings, and I got away in the nick of time! Wouldn't that be a sweet story to tell back home?''

Marlene glared at her. For a minute, she almost looked ashamed as she averted her eyes.

Ivory had won one battle, for the moment. Marlene had always been her enemy; but for the first time, Ivory had weapons of her own to fight back with. She wasn't the downtrodden child she'd been when she left home.

Ivory went to work half-heartedly for the rest of the week. Marlene was rude to her neighbors, and she complained non-stop about the apartment and the lack of money to spend. Ivory had already gone to the limit of her budget and refused to spend any more on her greedy parent, but Marlene wasn't one to give up easily. Unfortunately for Ivory, she stayed up late one night and dipped into Ivory's purse for the corporate credit card. While Ivory was at work the next day, she practiced until she could forge Ivory's name. Now, if the silly girl just didn't miss the card, Marlene could get the things she really wanted, without her daughter's interference.

Ivory didn't discover that the card was missing. She used it only to entertain buyers, and she wasn't in the habit of checking to make sure it was in her purse—a mistake that was to cost her dearly.

"You haven't brought your mother over to see us again," Dee remarked Thursday afternoon. "Why?"

"You wouldn't enjoy the visit," Ivory replied quietly. She looked up at Dee from her desk, worn and wan-looking. "And I don't think I could stand having to work here if she'd seen my office."

"You have a real phobia about her," Dee said. "Don't you?"

"Yes." She clasped her hands in her lap and looked at her friend levelly. "The truth is, I had a pretty rough childhood. We were poor and I was scarcely literate. My father was a sharecropper. He worked until he dropped, and he finally died of it. After that, Marlene made life hell. She had one man after another, playing them for all she was worth to get things she wanted. She's not pretty enough or young enough to get men anymore, so now she's using me to get what she wants."

"Using you how?"

"We share a dark secret," Ivory laughed coolly. "Doesn't that sound melodramatic? It's true. She could cause me a lot of trouble if she wanted to, and I'm not certain I could get myself out of it unless I was really well-to-do.''

''You mean she's blackmailing you?''

Ivory hesitated. ''In a sense, I suppose she is,'' she replied. ''She's greedy, Dee. I didn't want her to know how successful I was becoming, but she found out anyway. When she came to the office and Curry saw her, he knew that everything I'd told him about my past was a lie. He raked me over the coals for being so ungrateful to my mother. He hasn't the slightest idea what sort of person she really is. It's the old story, I guess. Marlene always could make people believe that she was the victim and I was the villain. She's good at it.''

''I can't believe that Curry could be taken in that easily! Do you want me to talk to him?''

She shook her head. ''He wouldn't believe you any more than he believed me when I tried to explain. It would only make him put more stock in Marlene's lies if you interfered. He'd be sure that I put you up to it, you see.''

Dee grimaced. She folded her arms over her chest and paced. ''There must be some way. How long is your mother staying?''

''She leaves tomorrow, thank God,'' she said. She shivered. ''But I don't think she'll stay away. Now that she knows what a good job I really have, she'll want more and more of my salary. She'll go home and tell everyone that I'm living it up in the big city while I let her starve back home in Texas.''

"That isn't true."

"That's what she'll say, and they'll believe her. They always have, even when I was little. Nobody ever believed I was being ill-treated, except one neighbor, a policewoman. She moved, though, and I have no idea where she went. She's the only person who saw through Marlene."

"Pity you couldn't track her down."

"I hope I never have to," Ivory said. Her insides were clenched tight. "Dee, it's like a nightmare ever since my mother showed up. I thought I was safe from her here."

"I'm sorry."

"Yes, so am I. But that doesn't help me. Even if I give up this job and move, she'll keep coming. I'll never get her off my back until I die . . ."

Dee had her by the arm. "Don't do anything stupid."

Ivory looked hunted, but she composed herself rapidly. "No, I won't do that," she said heavily. "I'm not suicidal. I'm just tired. I'm so tired."

Dee could imagine that she was. Poor Ivory, with a career that was just starting to take off and a blackmailer for a mother. It wasn't fair.

"I've got to get back to work," Ivory said. "When I draw, I can block her out. I used to do it when I was little. It still works, but it's more profitable now."

"Yes, it is, for all of us. The latest sales figures are super. You've put us over the top."

"I'm glad. I hope I can keep doing it."

"Your kind of creativity doesn't wear out," Dee assured her.

But it wasn't creativity that worried Ivory. It was her unpredictable parent.

She got home just after dark. Marlene's bag was packed and she looked a little too pleased with herself for comfort. Still she seemed to be without malice for once as Ivory treated her to supper at a steak house downtown in Manhattan.

It was a restaurant frequented by the executives of Kells-Meredith, and Ivory wasn't sparing her boss's pocket one bit. He'd told her to take Marlene out on the town, and she was doing it—at his expense.

"Isn't this nice," Marlene remarked, looking around. She was wearing a black silk sheath that Ivory didn't remember her mother bringing. It looked expensive, too.

"I don't remember that dress," Ivory began.

"It was under my night things. I've had it for ages," Marlene said dismissively, looking around her. "Do you come here often?"

"No." Ivory started to add to that statement when her eyes caught and held on a familiar tall figure in evening clothes. Curry! And on his arm was one of the new models, a striking brunette named Gaby, dressed in one of Ivory's signature gowns. She felt the pain all the way up and down her body. How could he!

Marlene saw where her daughter was staring and followed the stricken gaze. "It's your boss. Handsome devil, isn't he?"

"Yes," Ivory said through her teeth.

Marlene smiled at him and lifted a hand. He saw her, turning to his companion and leading her over to the table occupied by the two women.

"What a pleasant surprise," Curry said suavely, without mentioning that he'd tricked Dee into telling him about Ivory's plans to bring her mother here tonight. "So we meet again, Mrs. Keene," he said with a gentle smile.

"Mrs. Costello," she corrected. "Ivory was so ashamed of me that she had her last name legally changed when she left home."

Curry was stunned. He glanced at Ivory, who met his eyes bravely and without speaking. It was the truth, but Marlene twisted it.

"Keene is my mother's maiden name," Marlene continued.

Ivory remained quiet, although it cost her some effort.

"Won't you join us?" Marlene added quickly, certain that if she could cajole him into it, Ivory wouldn't miss the corporate card that Marlene still had tucked in her purse. "It's my last night in New York, you know."

Curry glanced at Ivory and then at his companion. "Do you mind, Gaby?" he asked the other woman.

"Not if you don't, Curry, dear," she purred.

He stiffened, but he didn't correct the assumption that they were more than just companions. Ivory seemed frozen in place and, in Curry's view, her mother was very obviously hurting from her daughter's treatment. He was surprised at Ivory's lack of compassion for her mother. It gave his suspicions even more substance.

"Sit down, then," Marlene coaxed again. "The more the merrier."

Curry seated his companion and then himself. "How do you like New York?" he asked pleasantly.

"It's just so exciting," Marlene enthused. "All these lovely stores . . . a little old country girl like me could go crazy. Of course, it's very lonely when you have to spend your holiday by yourself. Ivory's been too busy to come home for years . . ."

She let her voice trail off. Ivory's jaw clenched and Curry glanced at her accusingly.

"I gave her tomorrow off," he volunteered, "so that she'll have some free time to spend with you."

"And I appreciate it, really I do," Marlene said with a sigh, "but I've arranged to change my ticket so that I leave first thing in the morning. I know I'm a burden to Ivory. She'll be so much happier when I'm gone. She doesn't like remembering the past, you see. We were dirt-poor and she hated school, poor child. She could hardly spell her name when she went off to design school, and she talked southern talk, just like her mama! And here she is speaking so well, knowing which of these fancy forks to use. Remember how you tucked your napkin right under your chin the first time we went out to eat?'' she added with just the right touch of motherly affection.

Curry was learning things he didn't want to know about Ivory. Illiterate and unsophisticated and dirt-poor, that was the description her mother gave of her background. He wondered what else she'd kept from him, and if she'd really only used him to get where she was. Everyone from Harry Lambert to his own mother had warned him that she was climbing up his body to fame and fortune, but he hadn't listened. Now he was sorry. He'd been badly hurt to find out the truth about Ivory, just when they seemed destined for a future together. But how could he live with a woman whose whole identity was a lie?

''Please, mother,'' Ivory said under her breath.

''Now, dear, you mustn't worry. I'm sure Curry won't think less of you. After all, he's a man of the world. She had so many boyfriends,'' Marlene added on a laugh. ''Why, after I was widowed, she even stole away some of mine!''

Curry's expression was suddenly explosive. He wasn't thinking straight at all, Ivory saw, and she wondered if he'd think she had pretended to be innocent that first time. But how could he, when all the signs were there for him to see? she thought, panicking.

More sophisticated than Ivory, Curry knew that innocence could be faked, and how. His good eye narrowed as he stared at her, and she could see the wheels turning.

She flushed, lowering her eyes. It looked to the man beside her like an admission of guilt.

"She wouldn't ever get serious about a boy, though," Marlene continued gaily, after the waiter had taken their order and departed. "She said she was going to get rich, no matter what it took or how far she had to go. And it looks as if she has, doesn't it?"

"Yes," Curry said tightly. "It does."

"Fame and glamour, that's all she ever wanted. My goodness, isn't it a long way from the farm, Ivory?" She laughed again. "Can you see Ivory barefooted, slopping hogs? She did hate those pigs!"

Ivory felt her carefully constructed fictions falling around her like paper walls. Marlene was stripping her soul naked and insinuating things that weren't true. There was no defense, though. If she denied it, she'd look even more guilty. And Curry was sitting there, fingering his glass, drinking in every word.

"Well, she won't have to feed the pigs ever again. Now she can ride around in limousines and eat at the best restaurants and afford designer clothes, can't she?"

"Excuse me," Ivory said huskily, getting up. "I have to go to the ladies' room."

"Certainly, dear. Are you ill?" Marlene asked with assumed concern.

"I'll be fine in a minute, mother."

Marlene watched her retreating back with a tiny smile before she turned back to Curry. "Such a kind girl," she said with a sigh. "And so generous! Why, would you look at this dress? She bought it for me at Neiman-Marcus, and these shoes to go with it! And a fur coat . . . oh, I just feel like Cinderella! I had no idea that she was that well-to-do, and I did try to stop her, you know, but she insisted that I have the very best. Isn't she a kind child?''

Curry's brow furrowed. He knew the designer of the dress Marlene was wearing by the lines; it was Chanel. That was a model, and worth thousands. The shoes weren't as expensive, but she'd mentioned a fur. He knew what he paid Ivory, and even with her bonus she couldn't afford such things. He'd have to ask her how she managed it. Perhaps on time. But why would she spend those amounts on a mother she admitted that she didn't like?

Ivory rejoined them a few minutes later, still sick to her stomach but feeling more able to cope. She'd thought she was all grown up, but her mother had a way of making her feel gauche and inferior. It wouldn't have worked, except that Curry was sitting there, weakening her defenses. She looked at him and ached all over for his arms around her, but he wasn't feeling anything similar; she could tell by that thunderous expression. She wouldn't give him the satisfaction of making any sort of defense now. If he wanted to believe Marlene's lies, let him. But it didn't help her feelings when he slid an arm around the back of the chair his companion was occupying and let his long, lean fingers trace her shoulder affectionately.

Ivory ate exquisite cuisine that tasted like wax paper and refused dessert. Marlene held sway, talking about the little town of Harmony where she kept up such a brave front when her daughter never came to visit, never wrote except to send a check. She sounded so pathetic that even Ivory wanted to weep for her. It was useless trying to protest. No one would listen. Marlene even managed two tears. They rolled down her cheeks and she wiped them away quickly, with the precision of a skilled actress.

"You must forgive me," she said huskily, glancing at Ivory, who was sitting like a stone woman. "Sometimes it hurts very badly that my only child doesn't want me in her life."

"I'm sure that's not true," Curry said firmly. He looked at Ivory, too. "And that things will change for the better, very soon."

"I do hope so," she sighed.

Curry glanced at his watch. "I have to leave. I have to be up early to take my mother in for her chemotherapy."

"Is your mother ill?" Marlene asked.

"She has cancer," he replied, glancing curiously at Ivory, whom he would have expected to tell her mother about his circumstances. "They've increased the chemotherapy in one last effort to stop the spread."

"I do hope it's successful. Do give her my best," Marlene said.

"Thank you." He stood up, helping his companion

back into her expensive fur stole. His hands lingered on her shoulders as he looked down at Ivory. "You'll take your mother to the airport, I'm sure."

"Of course," she said. She averted her eyes. It hurt to see him handle the other woman.

He knew it. It gave him a bitter pleasure. She'd kept things from him, deceived him, and she had no feeling at all for her own mother. He was hurting, and he'd convinced himself that she felt nothing for him. Gaby was a very casual date, nothing more, but Ivory wouldn't know that. He despised himself for caring that he was hurting her.

"I'll say goodnight, then. I hope you have a pleasant trip home, Marlene," he added with a smile.

"Thank you, Curry. It was a pleasure to meet you."

"Same here. Don't worry about the check," he added, as Marlene had known he would. "I'll sign for everything before I leave. My treat." He nodded curtly at Ivory and, sliding his hand into the brunette's, led her away. She almost ran to keep up with his long strides, laughing up at him as if she loved him to distraction.

"What a lovely man," Marlene sighed. "You know, I'm sure he was attracted to me. If only I were pretty, like I used to be." She turned her attention back to Ivory. "Well, it's obvious that he has no use for you, isn't it?"

"Thanks to you," she choked.

"I didn't do anything. He had the other woman in tow first, didn't he? I'll bet they're sleeping together. She has that well-loved look. I'll bet he's great in bed . . ."

"Shall we go?" Ivory snapped, rising.

Marlene got up lazily and smoothed down her dress. "If we must. I do want to get an early start tomorrow."

It didn't occur to Ivory to ask why her mother was in such a hurry to go home. She was too preoccupied with remembering how Curry had looked at her, and how easily he'd fallen for all her mother's lies. He'd never believe anything she told him again. He'd made that clear without a single word.

CHAPTER
FIFTEEN

IVORY went with her mother to the airport in the limousine. The other woman still had only the one bag with its matching cosmetic case, but she looked smug somehow. It wasn't anything Ivory could put her finger on, but something wasn't right.

"Have a good trip home," Ivory said stiffly.

"Oh, I will," Marlene said sweetly. Her eyes narrowed on her daughter. "I'll have a very good trip home. You just make sure you keep those checks coming, dear. I'm sure you wouldn't want me to come back again, would you? I mean, your friends obviously believe me more than they trust you."

She turned around and walked into the terminal, leaving her daughter heavy-hearted and bitter.

For the rest of the weekend, Ivory brooded about that smug smile on her mother's face. But she put it into the back of her mind and went to work on Monday, with two days' rest to get her back to normal.

That night, she went on the talk show. Her knees knocked, but she looked very elegant in her oyster-white Crystal Collection suit, and her smile was radiant as she shook hands with the host and sat where she was told.

She answered the first questions about her meteoric rise honestly, spoke very sketchily about her background, and only touched on Curry's part in her success.

"How does Curry Kells treat his designers?" the host probed delicately.

"He's very fair, and he doesn't lock us in the basement in chains to keep us hard at work," she said with a grin. Her eyes lit up at just the mention of his name. She couldn't help that.

"Does he expect favors for promotions?"

"He expects hard work for them," she returned serenely. "He's the sort of boss who makes you feel important. Everyone adores him."

The interviewer's eyebrows rose and he gave the audience a sly glance. "Do tell? There was some gossip about how quickly you rose in the company," he continued, unabashed. "Some people said that you got to the top through your boss's bedroom."

"Did they?" Ivory got to her feet and gestured toward her suit. "I designed this, you know. What do you think?" she asked the audience and she modeled it, to sounds of pleasure from women beyond the lights and cameras.

He chuckled, disarmed. "I think you're very talented. And that this is a good place for a station break."

He signaled to the camera crew, and Ivory gave him a level stare. "Thank you for inviting me," she said, and she didn't sit down again. She smiled and walked offstage.

"Wait! We're not through!" he called.

"You may not be. I am."

She kept walking.

Surprisingly, there was no rude comment about her when he went back on the air. He simply introduced the next guest, a comedian, and Ivory got into the waiting limousine and went home. The next day, she was the talk of the office. Curry sent a memo congratulating her on the interview, but it was terse and contained nothing personal. She hadn't really expected that there would be. Perhaps he'd taken exception to the facetious remark that he didn't lock his designers in the basement. It hurt, just the same.

Ivory didn't see Curry for weeks after her mother left. She assumed that he was keeping busy with his mother's deteriorating condition and Gaby, his new "friend." The grapevine reported that they were seen together at some of the top night spots in the city, and Ivory had seen a photograph of the two of them holding hands in one of the tabloids.

That didn't mean that they were intimate, but it did

mean that they were spending a lot of time together. So much for Curry's assertions about not seeing anyone else, about loving her. He'd believed every lie her mother had told about her, and he hadn't wanted to be part of her life for a long time now. She'd always heard that men would lie when they wanted sex. Perhaps he had, or perhaps he really had thought he loved her. Despite her disappointment at his lack of trust in her, she loved him. It wasn't possible to stop. The only thing she could do was stay out of his way, not let anyone see how hurt she was and hope that her mother's shopping spree had satisfied her.

She threw herself into her work again and managed to think a little less about him as the days passed. He didn't come by the office anymore, or phone. If he needed to tell her anything, he sent memos or messages by other people. Ivory lost weight, but she kept her chin up and no one knew how much pain Curry had caused her. She heard rumors that his mother was worse. She wished she'd had the right to comfort him, but that wasn't what he wanted, apparently. She wondered how he could turn his back on the sweetness of their relationship when just the memory of it kept her going day after day. Although August had given way to the first of September, the days were still long and hot.

Ivory had almost succeeded in putting her mother's visit behind her when a storm broke over her head with the suddenness of a tornado.

It came with no warning at all. She was asked to go to Curry's office, and told that he had something to discuss with her. She thought it might concern her designs or another interview. Or it might be about bills. It was after the first of the month and the charges would come due on her corporate card. However, she'd used it only to take the Chic Boutiques buyer and her mother out to lunch, and even that bill hadn't been exorbitant. So surely it wasn't about the card.

But it was, and he hit her with it the minute she closed the door and sat down in the chair facing his desk. It didn't take a clairvoyant to tell her that he was raging mad. The set of his jaw and the black glitter in his good eye did that for him.

He threw a thick statement at her across the desk. "Explain that," he said in a curiously soft tone for a man so angry. "And you'd better have a damned good excuse for it."

"You told me to take the Chic Boutiques buyer to lunch, and Dee said you wouldn't mind if I let my mother go with us . . ." She was looking at the statement while she spoke, but when she saw page after page of items that had nothing to do with lunch, she stopped dead. There were charges for dresses at Saks Fifth Avenue, for jewelry at Tiffany, for purses at a Gucci store. They went on and on, totaling thousands of dollars. The account number was that of her corporate credit card.

Instinctively, with trembling hands, she dug in her

purse for her wallet. But the card was there, just where it was supposed to be.

She looked at Curry, staggered. It had to have been her mother, and now she understood, too late, what Marlene had meant with her threat that Ivory had better assume the blame.

"Your mother told me that you'd bought a few things for her, but apparently you helped yourself as well. Weren't you getting paid enough?" Curry asked coldly. "Did you have to take it to these extremes? Or," he added with an even colder smile, "did you think your being intimate with me merited perks like this, and that I wouldn't mind kitting you out in the best the city had to offer?"

"I thought no such thing," she defended herself weakly. "I haven't asked you for one single thing!"

"No, you haven't. You took. Well, it's coming out of your salary," he said, leaning back. He named an amount to be deducted weekly. It would leave her enough to eat on, and pay her rent. But she was going to have to be very frugal indeed. The worst of it was knowing that he wouldn't believe the truth now if she swore it on a stack of Bibles.

"Don't you have anything to say to me?" Curry prodded.

She tried one small defense. "Would you believe me if I told you that it was probably my mother who . . ."

"I thought you'd try that tack," he interrupted coldly,

and smiled at her shocked expression. "I had suspicions from the night I saw the two of you together out for dinner. I asked for the statement to be forwarded to me personally instead of to the business office. Marlene told me you bought her some fabulous things and that she tried to stop you, but you insisted. I thought you might have gone into debt charging them for her, but I didn't realize that you'd bought yourself as well as your mother a closet full of things and charged them all to the company. I couldn't accuse you without proof. Well, here it is." He threw the statement at her across the desk.

She had to choke down nausea as she stared at the pages of charges, everything from designer clothes to a mink coat to expensive shoes and hats and perfume. She dropped the thick statement as if it had burned her fingers, and her wide gray eyes stared at him sightlessly. It wasn't true! But he believed Marlene; she could see it in his face. Having spent his life with a loving, self-sacrificing mother, he had no idea that the other kind even existed. He would be gullible because of his own background.

"You don't know how it was at home," she began faintly. "She hates me for just existing, and she hated my father until the day he died for saddling her with a child and being forced to marry him. She's punished me ever since, one way or another. She took me out of school and put me to work on her lover's farm. She

abused me and taunted me, and one night I had to run
away because she was trying to . . . to share me with
her drunken boyfriend!''

He just looked at her. He didn't believe her. If anything, his expression was one of resignation, mixed with
bitterness.

She got to her feet, a little unsteadily. ''You don't
believe me. Of course. How could I expect you to?
Your mother was the exact opposite of mine, and you
love her. You don't even have a frame of reference to
see Marlene as she really is. It's not your fault,'' she
added gently. ''She's convinced everyone at home that
I'm no good, too. She's very good at it.''

His jaw had contracted a little and that one eye had
a faint glitter. ''In other words, I'm convicting you on
circumstantial evidence? How many times have you told
me that money is the most important thing in the world
to you?''

Her slender body stiffened as she stood before him.
''I don't steal. And even if I did, I wouldn't steal from
you.''

''You didn't have to,'' he laughed mirthlessly. ''I
would have given you anything you asked for, don't
you know that? Diamonds, furs, cars . . . you could
have asked me for anything!''

''I didn't want those things,'' she said slowly. ''You
don't understand. I thought that if I got rich, I could
give Marlene enough to make her leave me alone. And
there are so many other things I could do with money,''

she continued, thinking of Tim's care when the time came.

But Curry, with his experience of young women, didn't think about unselfish reasons for an obsession with wealth. He thought that despite her protests Ivory, like the others, wanted expensive presents and luxury. Didn't that charge statement prove it?

"Money is the most important thing on earth when you don't have any," she said fervently. "It's the difference between life and death."

"My God, you are obsessed, aren't you?"

"Obsessed." She looked at him with longing and disillusionment. "I should have realized . . . it's a matter of trust, you see. If you love people, it's instinctive to trust them."

She was babbling, but her nerves were in shreds. She took a deep breath. She didn't look at him. "Am I fired?"

He hardly heard her. His mind was on what she'd said, about trust. He felt guilty somehow, although God only knew why he should.

"No, you're not fired," he said tersely. "You're too valuable to us. But you'll repay the company. And I want that card, right now."

She pulled it out and placed it on the desk, careful not to touch his long fingers as he reached for it.

She looked so vulnerable and hurt that he had to clench his teeth not to get up and reach for her, even in the circumstances.

"May I go now?" she asked huskily.

His eye smoldered as he stared at her. "By all means," he said with gentle contempt. He noticed belatedly that she was wearing the same suit she'd worn to work several days recently, the gray one with the pink silk blouse that matched it. The only jewelry she had on—that she ever wore, in fact—was the pink pearl necklace and earrings he'd given her last Christmas. Her fingers were ringless. Her shoes were new, but hardly designer quality. He scowled suddenly. If she'd spent all that money on designer clothes and jewelry for her mother and for herself, why wasn't she wearing any of them?

She'd gone by the time his mind stopped inquiring. His eyes were back on the list of purchases, and he became more intent on it. He wanted to go to her apartment and have a look around. If she'd bought the things, they'd be there. It irritated him that even now, after her mother's damning remarks, he couldn't bring himself to believe that she was basically dishonest. He wanted to see for himself what she had in her closet.

But those plans came to nothing. He had a telephone call before he left the office, and he had to go straight to his mother's apartment. The nurse was with her, pampering her while she got over the aftereffects of her latest radiation treatment.

Teresa Kells' hair was painfully sparse now, and her face was thin and drawn from pain and sickness.

She looked up at her son with a weary smile. "It's

not good for you to spend so much time here. Who called you?"

"Audrey. She had a meeting and couldn't get here. She worries." He sat down on the bed and kissed her thin cheek gently. "We both worry."

"It won't do any good, my boy," she said heavily, closing her eyes. "I don't have much time left, you know."

"Don't talk like that!"

She opened her eyes and managed a weary smile. "You'd talk like that, too, in my place. I'm tired. So tired. I feel bad all the time, the treatments make me sick. I get transfusions twice a week. I can't go on much longer. Listen. You need to marry and have a family. A nice, good girl to love you." She glowered up at him. "You're taking out some new model. Audrey tries to hide the tabloids from me, but the housekeeper brings them. I saw this new girl. Who is she?"

"She's just one of the models from work, Mama," he said tersely. "I take her out to show off pieces from our new collection, that's all."

She studied him curiously. He was fine-drawn, too, and he wasn't happy. He hadn't been happy for a long time now, and she wondered why she hadn't noticed. She reached up to him and he took her wrinkled hand in his and held it tight.

"What happened to Ivory?" she asked huskily. "You never brought her to see me again."

"You were right about her the first time," he said

coldly, ignoring the voice at the back of his head that denied it. "She ran up some high bills on the company card. Jewels and furs and designer clothes. I'm docking her salary to get it all back."

She saw the pain he couldn't quite hide. "You loved her."

He shrugged and put her hand back down. "I was infatuated. She wasn't what I thought she was."

"It hurts when people we love betray us. I was hurt when your father left. He wasn't a bad man, but he was irresponsible. I missed him, all the same. You don't stop loving people because they're flawed." She hesitated. "My mind, it seems to come and go. I don't want you to be unhappy. I'm sorry about Ivory."

"Yes, I know, Mama."

She touched his sleeve. "Audrey and I watched that girl when she was on the talk show. She's pretty. That man was unkind to her, but she held her own. She's got class."

"Class! She lied about her background," he said icily. "She's the daughter of a Texas sharecropper. She was dirt-poor, and now she won't even have anything to do with her own mother!"

"She didn't seem that sort of woman," Teresa murmured. "Maybe she thought you wouldn't want her if you knew about her background."

"She knew about mine," he countered. "She knew I wouldn't hold it against her. Poverty is no shame."

"Of course not. But if she came up poor, maybe she

thinks money is the answer to everything. When the man mentioned you, she blushed. She loves you. Remember, I asked, and she said she did.''

His face was harder than ever. ''That was before she made it to the top of the design ladder.''

Her fingers smoothed over the fabric of his jacket sleeve. ''But you loved her, too.'' She closed her eyes. ''I'm sorry it didn't work out for you. It will be harder for you, if you don't have somebody to hold onto, when I go.''

''Stop talking like that!'' He laughed uncomfortably and patted her cheek. ''You're going to be fine!''

Her dark eyes opened, full of pain. ''We both know that is not so, my son. You must let me go.''

His face contorted. He lifted her hand to his mouth and kissed it fervently. ''All my life you sacrificed for me, for Audrey. And now, when you need it most, I can do nothing for you.''

''Oh, but you have,'' she replied gently. ''It is such a great gift for any mother to have the unconditional love of her children. You have been all I could have asked of my son.''

''And you, all I could have asked of my mother.''

She drew his head to her shoulder and smoothed over his dark hair. Her eyes closed with a weary smile.

She died that night. Ivory heard about it, as did the rest of the office staff, and she contributed money to send flowers. She phoned Curry's apartment, but there was no answer. He was at Audrey's house, apparently, and Ivory didn't know the number or the address there. It was painfully significant to her that he hadn't called her for comfort or support. He was too angry still, she supposed, but he was grief-stricken and she wanted to comfort him.

She didn't go to the funeral, even though she knew her absence would raise eyebrows. Curry quite obviously didn't want her there, or he'd have been in touch with her. She didn't want to impose on him at such a time. She was sorry about Teresa Kells, whom she'd liked very much.

CHAPTER
SIXTEEN

CURRY went to the Bahamas for a few days afterward, and when he returned, he was as icy cold as death itself. He spoke to no one except on business. Ivory caught a glimpse of him in the hall one day, but he looked at her as though he didn't even recognize her.

He did, of course. He regretted bitterly the way they'd parted, because he'd wanted her with him through the anguish of his mother's funeral. But he hadn't telephoned her, and she'd had the intuition to know that he wanted to be left alone. He respected her for that. It would have been easier if he could hate her. But he couldn't. In spite of everything, he was still vulnerable, and he didn't dare let her close enough to see it. If she was the amoral person his imagination had carved from Marlene Costello's remarks, then she'd use his love as a weapon against him. Perhaps that was why he took

Gaby to a cocktail party the week he returned from
Nassau.

Not that it was a romantic date. Gaby looked lovely
in one of the evening crepe suits that Ivory had concocted, this one with Ivory's signature butterfly in onyx
and crystal. It reminded him of the suit Ivory had worn
the night he'd taken her to meet his mother. Although
the outfit brought back painful memories he told himself
that it was smart to show the new design off at such a
gala event as this evening charity trunk show. Some
of the most influential people in the city would be in
attendance. Still all the while that he was doing the
rounds with Gaby after the show, his mind was on Ivory.
People, especially women, commented with delight on
the suit Gaby was wearing, and that fanned the flames
even more.

"I saw your designer on television when she went
on that talk show," one of the buyers from Saks remarked as she paused to speak to Curry. "She held her
own quite well, I thought!"

"Yes," he said noncommittally, smiling.

"Ivory Keene. She's very young, isn't she?" she
added.

The manager of an exclusive boutique in Trump
Tower overheard the remark and turned. "Ivory Keene?
She may be well-preserved, but she isn't young," she
laughed. "Her hair is colored, you can tell, and much
too black to be natural."

"Black?" The buyer was stunned. "Why, she's blond."

The manager's eyebrows went straight up. "She was in my store not more than a few weeks ago, and I could hardly forget her. She went on and on about her job and how successful she was. That's why she bought those two Dior gowns, to wear to showings."

"Why would she want to wear a Dior gown to a showing of her own collection?" the buyer demanded.

Curry held up a hand. He felt uneasy. "Describe the woman you sold the gowns to," he asked politely.

The manager of the boutique described a middle-aged woman with a coarse, drawling voice, slender and with dyed dark hair. It was a perfect description of Marlene.

Curry muttered something under his breath. He'd been had. He'd been royally had!

He searched the room until he found the woman he'd brought with him.

He drew her to one side. "Gaby, get a cab home when this is over, will you?" he asked, pressing some bills into her hand. "I have to leave. An unexpected emergency."

"Sure," she said.

It took him an hour to get to Ivory's apartment, with the traffic so heavy at that time of night. He left the limousine and its driver at the curb and took the steps two at a time. He buzzed Ivory's apartment and waited impatiently for her to answer.

"Yes?" she said, expecting to hear Miriam's voice, because it was just at the end of Miriam's shift, and Ivory had Tim and the girls with her. Tim's mother was always punctual, and she'd been lucky enough to get on second shift, from four in the afternoon until midnight. It was almost midnight now.

Ivory had slipped into the habit of keeping Tim and the little girls with her at night because their mother couldn't afford a baby-sitter. Miriam was doing her very best to get off welfare, but child care costs were too high for her small salary. Really, Ivory thought irritably, with so many single working mothers in the country, it was absurd that there was no government provision for that expensive and most necessary service! Not that Ivory minded having the children. They were a constant delight to her. She pulled the cover closer over the little girls, who were asleep on her bed. Tim was still half-awake on the couch.

But the voice that replied to her question wasn't the one she expected. It was deep and terse. "I want to come up," Curry said curtly.

There was a pause and then a breath. "I'm sorry," she said in a wobbly tone. "It isn't convenient." She hesitated. "I have someone with me," she added defiantly. Let him stew on that!

It was the truth, but Curry didn't know about Tim. The insinuation hit him right in the gut and made him want to double over. He couldn't have described in a million years the feelings that ran through him at her admission. Naturally, his first thought was that she had a man in her apartment. Perhaps he'd given her reason to find someone else, but the disloyalty of it made him furious.

"So you couldn't wait," he said in an icy tone. "Is he young?"

"Yes," she said harshly. "He's very young, in fact!"

That added to his doubts about Ivory finding him too old. "Why am I surprised?" he asked heavily. "It was what I should have expected, wasn't it?"

"What did you want?" Ivory asked with wounded pride.

"Nothing at all. A business matter," he prevaricated. "I'll talk to you at work. Goodnight."

He turned and went back out into the night, climbed into the limousine, and went home.

Ivory traced the pattern on the intercom without feeling it. Odd, that he'd come over at midnight to talk about work. She hadn't even said that she was sorry about his mother, because his cutting tone had made her lose her temper. She shook her head. Just when she thought she was getting over him, he bounced back into her life in the most disturbing way.

"Was that somebody to see you, Ivory?" Tim asked sleepily from the couch.

"No. It was a stranger asking directions," she lied. She touched his curly hair. "Go back to sleep, little man,'' she said gently and with a sad smile. ''It was nothing at all.''

Work took on a nightmarish aspect from that day forward. She was sent to showings all over the East in the days that followed, and often she felt that it was only because Curry wanted to inconvenience her. Her presence wasn't even necessary at the shows, but she had all the exposure she could have once asked for, and more. Her name had already been on the fashion pages of most major newspapers, on television fashion shows, on the news, in magazines. She was already well known in the industry.

Of Curry, she saw nothing at all. And her mother hadn't called or written. Ivory hoped desperately that Marlene had enough pretty things to last her for several years. In the interim, Ivory would have the chance to get a promotion, to make more money, to be able to protect herself if the time ever came when she needed to.

But that wasn't to be the case. When she returned to New York the following week, from a trunk show at a Philadelphia department store that had gone very well indeed, there was a message for her that Curry wanted to see her.

She went to his office and sat in the waiting room— probably by his design, she thought—for a half hour before he asked for her to be shown in.

He'd kept her waiting, still smarting from their last meeting. But when he saw her, he was sorry about it.

She was living on her nerves, and it showed. Her gray eyes were huge in her thin face, and her shoulders were drooping under her suit—that same damned gray suit she'd worn for two seasons. He remembered why he'd sent for her and his conscience stabbed at him.

"Sit down," he said tersely.

She dropped into a chair and perched on its very edge. Her hair had grown to collar length. It fell onto her forehead when she leaned forward to straighten her skirt, and she pushed it back with an indifferent hand.

"You look worn," he commented, leaning back in the chair. "Is your boyfriend exhausting you?" he asked with a mocking smile.

She crossed her legs. "I don't have a boyfriend."

"No? Then who was at your apartment the night I came around?" he asked, because the things he'd found out made him certain that Ivory wasn't the kind of woman to two-time him.

She gave him a resentful look. "Tim."

"Tim?"

"He's eight," she said irritably, looking away from the soft delight that curved his mouth. "He has AIDS," she added with faint belligerence.

He didn't bat an eyelash. "Is he the boy from the shelter?"

She was surprised. "Why, yes."

"Dee told me about him. About Miriam, too, and how you've helped the family." He shrugged. "I haven't been much of a judge of character. I've learned, however, to dig deeper when I think I have all the facts." He smiled tenderly. "So Tim has AIDS. And he doesn't scare you, does he?"

"No, he doesn't."

He stretched lazily. "He doesn't scare me, either. I like kids." His eye smoothed over her body. "You've lost weight, *querida*. I'm sorry. I feel responsible."

"You needn't. You didn't send for me to see how I looked," she added firmly, ignoring his tender term of address. Since he'd come to her apartment that night and thought she was with another man, he'd scarcely spoken to her at all. It was nice to have the air cleared, but she was apprehensive about why he'd sent for her.

He hated the look on her face. She was a far cry from the happy, caring young woman who'd approached him so long ago on the steps of the cathedral to make sure he was all right.

"I sent for you because I found out where all those clothes went," he said, hating himself for not having checked sooner, before those buyers at the gallery showing had piqued his curiosity. "It took a while to run it down, and I had to get over my grief for Mama, first. But after I talked to Dee and a couple of saleswomen, I got the picture. Those clothes were shipped to Harmony, Texas."

"To my mother's house," she said without surprise.

"Why the hell didn't you tell me?!" he demanded, letting out his frustration.

She didn't remind him that she'd tried to. It made no

difference. She was famous and becoming more so; she had a good salary. But she wasn't obsessed with fame anymore. It wasn't what she'd expected. After the first thrill of seeing her name in print, she slowly became self-conscious when it appeared in magazines and when she heard it on television. Even though she'd achieved status, some of the old-line fashion writers and designers had ridiculed her crystal collection as a fad. Fame was a double-edged sword, but she hadn't known that until she'd earned her small share.

Curry sighed heavily. "She said you wanted her to have some pretty things. She said you were ashamed of her and neglected her. What else did she lie about?" he asked gruffly, because he knew certainly that it had been all lies on Marlene's part.

She traced around the unvarnished nail on her forefinger. She couldn't quite find the right words to answer him.

His fist hit the desk and she jumped, gasping.

He looked murderous. She'd never seen such rage in a man's face. His black eye glittered dangerously. "You're afraid of her, aren't you? Why?"

"You believed everything she said about me, the first time you saw her, in my office. You told me to my face that I was no better than a gold digger. You believed that I was greedy and shrewd enough to spend thousands of dollars on designer clothing for my mother and myself, and you dare to question me?" she replied quietly.

His broad shoulders seemed to relax as he sighed.

He pushed back his hair, and for a minute, he looked even older than she knew he was. "Come on," he said after a minute. "Tell me the truth."

"Do you think your stomach is strong enough?" she asked in that assumed cultured voice. She smiled bitterly. "Very well, then. My father got my mother pregnant when she was in her early teens and they were forced to marry. He was a sharecropper, illiterate, with nothing to give her except hardship. She hated him because she couldn't have pretty things, and she blamed it all on me. After he died, she let her rich lover put me to work on his farm with the blacks and Mexicans who slaved in the fields."

The memories made her face draw in and he frowned. "That's where you learned such fluent Spanish," he said slowly.

"That isn't all I learned," she returned. "I learned prejudice. I was one of them, a ragged, dirty little girl who couldn't speak proper English, who didn't even have table manners. My mother drank and she had sticky fingers. She made sure everyone in town thought I was the thief, so she could do what she pleased. If you ask anyone in Harmony, Texas, they'll tell you that I steal and lie and that I'm an ungrateful, heartless brat, because that's the identity Marlene gave me." She clasped her hands tightly in her lap. "I tried to change those opinions, but Marlene was too convincing. At least, she was convincing when she was sober. More often than not, after my father died, she drank. One night, shortly before I left for Houston, she and her boyfriend held me down on the couch so that he could enjoy me. I managed to get away before he raped me, but it left me with scars. I guess Marlene realized that she'd crossed the line, because she never had him over to the house at night again,'' she added, averting her eyes from the look on Curry's lean, dark face. ''That was when I was desperate enough to enter the design scholarship contest, and lucky enough to win it.'' She closed her eyes. ''I got away from her. I learned how to walk and talk and dress and act, and I left it all behind me. Or I thought I had.''

She looked at her hands. She'd left marks on one palm with the grip of her nails. ''When I started making money, she wanted more and more. She insisted that I let her come up here and shop, and give her a good time. I was afraid . . . but I was more afraid that she'd do something, go to the newspapers maybe.'' She lifted her sad gray eyes to his. ''I never wanted you to meet her at all. But everything went wrong when she got to the airport. She came to the office and in no time, my co-workers were looking at me just as people back home used to when I was small.'' She laughed dully. ''And so were you.''

He lifted one hand and let it fall. There really was no excuse, he thought. None at all.

''Your mother was exceptional,'' she continued. ''A real paragon, and I don't mean that sarcastically. I'm very sorry that you lost her. But my mother would have sold me to the highest bidder without a glimmer of conscience. She never felt anything for me except resentment. Even now, my only worth to her is monetary.''

He didn't reply to the remark about his mother. His loss was too new, too raw, to be talked about just yet. ''Had you no family at all?'' he asked.

She shook her head. ''She was an only child. My father had a brother, but he was killed in Vietnam. Both sets of grandparents died before I was grown. And I had no friends. Marlene didn't like people coming to the house. It wouldn't have done, to let anyone see what my home life was like.'' She shook her head. ''Not that I'd have wanted anyone to see it,'' she added, wincing. ''We lived in a shack. That's a better description than it even deserves. Her rich boyfriend gave her nothing except cheap costume jewelry and gin. He knew exactly what she was, you see.'' She met his eyes proudly. ''I came from nothing. My people were all sharecroppers and all of them were illiterate. I was the first one to get a high school education, much less a specialty education.'' She smiled coldly. ''And if you'd known that at the outset, you'd have been sure that I played up to you to get a better job, or more recognition, or publicity.''

He studied his hand without really seeing it. ''I've been used ever since I grew up and got rich, in one way or another.''

"And you would have expected it from a poor Texas sharecropper's daughter."

He looked up. "Yes," he said bluntly.

"At least you're honest." She uncrossed her legs. "So what do we do now, Mr. Kells?" she asked politely. "Do you kick me out? Do you demote me? Do I start knocking on other doors?"

"Why didn't you tell me the truth?" he asked quietly.

"Because you liked me when you thought I had all those advantages that you never had," she replied cynically. "You have money but you don't have a monied, social background. You liked my accent and what you thought was my status."

He laughed without humor. "Did I? Perhaps so. But after a time, it was you, not your background, that held me in thrall."

"Only physically," she reminded him. "I discovered a part of myself that I'd never known when I was with you." Her eyes grew sad. "I never dreamed that I could submit to a man, after what had happened to me. But you were everything I could have wanted in that way. You said you loved me." She laughed a little self-consciously. "Even if you didn't mean it, no one else ever said that he did," she added curtly. "Even my father only tolerated me. I reminded him too much of Marlene."

He hadn't dreamed that she was so delicate emotionally, that there was this vulnerable side to her independent personality. He leaned forward. "But you have talent," he said gently. "And grace and elegance. You charm buyers and even the most vicious fashion writers."

"One of them saw right through me immediately," she recalled. "She was kind enough not to give me away."

"She saw it. And I didn't."

"You're proud of your disadvantages. Even your mother was proud of them, because you came so far from sheer determination and faith in yourself." She shook her head. "I hated my past. I wanted to conceal it, to hide it, to run away from it. But I didn't run far enough or fast enough. Marlene caught me anyway. She always will. I'll never be rid of her, or the voices taunting me, demeaning me."

"That's ridiculous," he said shortly. He stood up, towering over her. "Your shortcomings are all right here," he said, tapping her head, "in your own mind. You are what you think you are. If you believe in yourself, if you like yourself, so will other people. To hell with what people back home thought! If you know the truth, what does it matter?"

She gave him a hard glare. "It matters! You can't imagine how much it matters to me!"

"You're still in bondage," he commented, thrusting his hands into his pockets. "You won't let yourself be free of the old image."

She crossed her legs again. "Marlene won't let me."

"Think so?" He sat on the edge of his desk. "She forged your name on credit card charges. She impersonated you to get expensive merchandise. That's theft and it's a felony, and you can prove it. Here's the evidence." He tossed her a packet of papers, which contained the forged charge slips and affidavits from two saleswomen who gave vivid descriptions of the purchaser—Marlene.

She lifted her eyes slowly to his. Her heart skipped a beat. "A felony?" she echoed.

"Yes. She may have rushed back to Texas in a blaze of glory, but the law has long arms." He smiled at her. "You think she's invincible. She's not. You've got enough rope in your hands to hang her."

"It's your company," she began.

"It's your mother." He folded his arms over his chest. "There'll never be a better opportunity to pry her fingers loose from your life. Go get her."

She saw possibilities that had never existed before. He was right. She had a weapon, and Marlene had put it in her hands. It was the first time she'd ever been in a position of power over her mother in her entire life. The elation was consuming. Her whole expression changed as she looked again at the documents and then began to smile.

She stood up. "I'm going to Texas!"

"I thought you might. When do you want to leave?"

"Tomorrow morning on the earliest flight out."

He lifted the receiver and buzzed his secretary. "Get

Miss Keene a round-trip, first-class ticket on the first morning plane to . . . ?''

" . . . San Antonio, it's closest to Harmony,'' she answered his unvoiced query.

" . . . San Antonio. Arrange for a car to meet her coming and going. Get the biggest, newest stretch limo you can hire. Black. And make sure there's a male driver. A big, ugly one. Yes, that's right. I'll tell her.'' He hung up. "She'll phone your office when it's arranged and you can pick up your tickets at the airport.''

She straightened her jacket. "Thanks,'' she said stiffly.

"When you get back, I want to know who you are.''

Her eyebrows lifted.

"You've fed me a steady diet of glitzy lies,'' he explained. "Now I want the truth. I want to know what you did as a child, where you went, whom you played with, what you felt about life and the world. I want to know how you started drawing and how you ended up in design school.''

"It's all ugly,'' she said uneasily. "Ugly!''

He slid off the edge of the desk and caught her by the waist, holding her gently in front of him. "There were good moments,'' he said. "You've buried them under the bad things, but they're there. The Mexican family . . . you loved them, yes?''

"Yes,'' she agreed slowly. "How did you know?''

"You speak Spanish with such tenderness, *querida*. Didn't you know?''

"You make love in Spanish," she said, lowering her eyes shyly to his throat.

"Only to you." He kissed her forehead tenderly and let her go. "I've been lonely without you. Gaby was just window-dressing. There hasn't been anyone else. You see, it was no lie when I said I loved you. I haven't stopped. I'll never stop. And when you come home, I'll ask you to forgive me in the sweetest way I know."

The world became full of color again as she looked up at him with her heart in her eyes. "You don't need to ask me to forgive you. It's the other way around."

"We're going to start over again, together," he told her gently. "No lies, ever again, Ivory."

She touched his tie, loving the silky feel of it. Pain washed over her face at the sound of her own name. "She named me for a brand of soap," she said huskily.

He lifted her chin and searched her wounded eyes. "Did she?" He smiled tenderly. "But when I hear your name, I think of the way you look against white satin, and the purity of your character, and the light you bring into my life."

Tears stung her eyes at the interpretation. She stared at him without speaking.

He chuckled. "You see? It's all subjective." He bent and bit her lower lip delicately and then kissed it tenderly. "Now, would you like to get out of here before my staff starts gossiping about us?"

"Would they dare?" she asked.

"My dear," he drawled, "have you ever noticed

some of the more innovative uses people have discovered for desks on late-night television?''

She glanced at the gleaming dark wood of his desk and she grinned. ''I'm leaving,'' she said.

''That might be a good idea. While there's still time. I'm quite impressionable, you know. It's my Latin nature.''

She peered up at him mischeviously. ''You rake.''

''You'll have your work cut out for you after we become parents,'' he said easily. ''I expect our sons will all take after me.''

Her eyes adored him, and all her heartaches seemed to be fading. ''I hope so,'' she said softly.

And that easily, they became engaged.

CHAPTER
SEVENTEEN

CURRY'S secretary was a magician when it came to easing the path of a harried traveler. Ivory made it to San Antonio without a hitch, arriving at mid-morning to find a huge black stretch limousine and an immaculately dressed driver in a dark suit waiting for her when she got off the plane.

He opened the door for her and she got in. He was a big man, not at all ugly, but formidable looking. Ivory had to hide her amusement at the order that Curry's secretary had apparently followed to the letter.

She gave him directions and then sat back in the leather luxury of the interior and watched out the window as they drove the short distance to Harmony.

People watched them from the small downtown area as they passed through, awed by the limousine. Ivory could see fingers pointed in her direction, and she smiled. Probably they thought the passenger behind the smoked glass windows was some rock star or wealthy oil man. She was fascinated by the way people stared. She wondered how they would feel if they knew little Ivory Keene Costello rode in the back.

She'd taken a chance in coming without checking to find out where her mother was, but she knew the woman would be at home or at the beauty parlor because those were the two places she'd frequented most often in Ivory's youth. Even groceries took second place to Marlene's hair.

She looked closely along the sidewalk as they passed the beauty parlor, the only one in town. Ivory's quick eyes spotted a woman just going inside. She was wearing a mink coat despite the heat, and Ivory didn't have to guess twice about her identity.

"Pull up to the curb over there, please," Ivory told the driver.

He nodded, sliding easily to the side of the road. He parked the limousine, attracting attention from all sides. Then he got out and opened the door.

Her heart was beating in double time. There was a measure of fear in her slender body as she got out; but she had a thick envelope in her hand, and it was going to change her life.

She was wearing one of her own suits, with her signature crystal butterfly, in an oyster wool blend. It was really too hot in Texas for the wool, but it had felt just right back in New York City. She wore expensive designer pumps and carried a purse of equal quality. Her blond hair was perfectly groomed, her face made up delicately. She looked far more expensively turned out than Marlene in her mink coat. And she smiled at the unexpected opportunity to show the evidence she had to Marlene in a very public place. It gave the confrontation a special edge when she remembered that the woman who owned the beauty salon had accused her of stealing things when she was a child.

When she walked into the salon, the owner, who had known Ivory from childhood, didn't recognize her.

"May I help you, madam?" she asked respectfully.

Ivory raised an eyebrow. She looked around the salon until she saw Marlene, with the mink in her lap, sitting at one of the stations.

"No. I came to speak with my mother," she replied, and turned to walk slowly down the aisle toward a shocked, speechless and pale Marlene.

"Why . . . Ivory!" the proprietor gasped.

Ivory didn't reply but strode through the shop until she was standing face-to-face with Marlene. The salon was filled with secretaries and girls from the nearby factory using their lunch hours to have their hair done.

"Hello, mother," Ivory said. "Nice mink. Did you tell everyone where you got it?"

"What?" Marlene croaked, visibly staggered to see her daughter here.

Ivory pulled out photocopies of the credit slips Marlene had forged, along with affidavits from the store clerks who described the woman who'd forged them. She dumped them in Marlene's lap.

"Why, what are these?" Marlene asked faintly, shocked by her daughter's unexpected appearance and the proof of her deceit.

"Enough evidence to put you in jail for forgery," Ivory said pleasantly. She looked around the beauty shop, particularly at the proprietor, who was obviously shocked speechless. "My mother came to New York to visit me. While she was there, she went on a shopping spree and forged my name to some sales slips, using our corporate credit card. My boss was, to put it mildly, upset."

Marlene had gone very pale. She put a hand to her throat. "Well . . . well, I deserved something! You left me down here without a dime and never sent me a penny . . .!"

Ivory pulled out canceled checks and dumped those in her mother's lap as well. "Canceled checks in an amount totaling more than ten thousand dollars, written out to you, cashed by you." She looked around. "If any of you would like to see them, feel free. I believe my mother has spent most of her life telling everyone in town that I neglected her. What she failed to tell you was that she deserved to be neglected. Why don't you tell them about your boyfriend, Marlene, and how the two of you got drunk and held me down while he tried to have me, right on the living room couch? Or how you drank like a fish and slapped me around, and then lied and told everyone that I'd attacked you? Or how you pilfered things from every store in town and told people I was a thief so that you wouldn't be prosecuted?''

Marlene's face was drawn like cord. ''She's lying!'' she cried.

''If I'm lying,'' Ivory said carefully, ''then why are you about to be arrested for forgery and theft?''

''A . . . arrested?!''

''Arrested. You know, when men in uniforms come and take you to jail for stealing things . . .?''

''Marlene said you stole from her, and from other people,'' the proprietor of the beauty shop spoke up. ''In fact, you stole nail polish from me . . .'',

Ivory held up her nails, nicely manicured, but never polished. ''And it never occurred to you that I didn't use nail polish, ever?'' she queried, nodding toward Marlene's thickly red fingernails.

The woman's mouth clamped shut.

''She stole,'' Ivory replied calmly, turning back to her pale mother, ''and blamed me for it. Most people in small towns don't like to prosecute children, you see.''

There were murmured comments and Marlene bit her lower lip, getting red lipstick all over her teeth in the process.

''Ivory, it's all a mistake,'' Marlene burst out.

''You tell these people the truth, right now,'' Ivory demanded, gray eyes blazing, ''or I'll not say one word when Curry Kells sends the police here to arrest you! That's what he wants to do, I promise you! He's already been in touch with his attorneys.''

Marlene caved in. She knew when she was beaten. ''All right, I wanted a few pretty things! It's your fault,'' she added icily. ''If I hadn't gotten pregnant with you, I would have had nice things! I could have married a man who had something, instead of your stupid father, with his dirty clothes and rotten teeth!''

All her life, Ivory had been intimidated by the woman who sat in the chair before her. Perhaps in a way, she always would be. Despite the small crowd in the beauty salon, there were plenty of other people who would believe every lie Marlene told. But as she saw, really saw, her mother for the first time, it no longer mattered.

The ugliness inside Marlene was quite visible, along with her narrow view of life, her selfishness, her immoral character, her callous disregard for everyone's happiness except her own.

''I always despised you,'' Marlene spat the words at Ivory. ''You went on television and told lies about your past.''

''Yes, I did,'' Ivory said carelessly. ''I thought people would reject me if they knew I'd been poor. Now, I don't care what they think. I'm famous and rich, and I'm going to be even more so in the years ahead. I'll have a husband who loves me and children. And you, mother . . . well,'' she looked around the salon, ''you'll have all this.''

Marlene understood exactly what her daughter was saying to her. She turned an ugly green. "Damn you," she whispered, shaking with rage. "I'll go to the tabloids!"

Ivory smiled. "Help yourself." She picked up the checks and the affidavits very deliberately. "I believe you're allowed one phone call," she added meaningfully.

Marlene drew in a sharp breath. The implication was quite clear: go to the tabloids and Ivory would go to the police. She shifted violently in the chair. "Well, just don't expect to come back here! I don't want to see you again," Marlene said spitefully.

"A mutual feeling. I have a plane to catch, and someone is waiting for me in New York." She put the evidence back in her pocketbook and gave a pitying look to the woman who had borne her. "How different your life and my life might have been if you'd wanted me."

There was a cruel burst of laughter. "What woman in her right mind would ever want kids?" Marlene countered.

"Oh, I do," Ivory said, thinking of Curry and tall sons who would look like him. "I want them very much."

She turned and walked out of the salon to the waiting limousine, and she didn't look back. The past was truly behind her now, but it had become a basis for her future. She'd accepted it, and put it in perspective. She no longer had to be afraid of it, or of her mother.

Marlene would surely bounce back, and she would always pose a threat in some way. But never again would Ivory be ruled by fear or intimidation. Those days were over. She had a lifetime ahead of her, and a future she'd given up for lost. She'd grown into someone new, someone different. She could hardly wait to get back and tell Curry about it.

CHAPTER
EIGHTEEN

IVORY spent the night at Curry's apartment, in his arms, and the next morning she woke to the delight of never having to leave him again.

He was leaning over her. His expression would have told her he loved her even if he hadn't said it over and over again all night long.

"Do you remember that I gave this to you last night?" he asked, lifting a gift-wrapped box from the bedside table.

"Yes, but you kissed me before I could open it and afterward I forgot all about it."

He chuckled at her blush. "Well, open it now."

She tore off the wrapping and uncovered the box. Within it was another box, a small square velvet one. She fumbled it open.

There, nestled inside, were two rings: a diamond in a plain Tiffany setting, and beside it a simple gold band. She had no words.

"I can wear one, too, if you want me to," he offered.

"Of course, you'll wear one, too," she said immediately, finding her voice. "A great big one, so that Belle and Gaby can see it . . ."

He kissed her, laughing with explosive delight.

She pushed him over on his back and loomed over him. "Did you sleep with them?" she demanded.

He stretched and sighed, moving lazily under the delightful pleasure of her hands on his chest. "No."

"Not ever?"

The smile grew. "You made me impotent when I wasn't with you," he explained. "I couldn't make love with anyone else. It would have felt like adultery."

"Impotent? I don't know about that, but you certainly lost weight."

Her eyes lingered on his lean face. "You have to eat more, now. You don't look healthy."

"You're pretty thin yourself," he replied tenderly. He reached up and caught a lock of her hair, smiling at her. "We can be married Wednesday."

She didn't feel inclined to argue.

He took the diamond out of the case and slid it onto her finger, then lifted her hand to his mouth and kissed it hungrily.

"When did you buy it?" she asked.

"Two days after New Year's Eve."

"It isn't New Year's yet. It isn't even Christmas . . ."

She stopped dead. Her lips parted. "Last . . . *Last* New Year's Eve?!"

"Yes."

She stared at him, uncomprehending.

"So if you think that wanting to marry you is something new with me, think again. I wanted it the first day I saw you, when I was sitting on the cathedral steps. I'd been praying and I looked up, and there was an angel standing looking at me."

"Oh, Curry." She kissed his closed eyelid. She slid her arm over his chest and nuzzled closer with soft contentment. "Do we have to go to work?"

"Not today. I'll call in sick for both of us."

"Everyone will know."

"Of course they will. I'll tell them when I call in that we're getting married." He chuckled softly. "The tabloids will have a field day with us."

That worried her. She raised herself up and looked at his dark face. "What about my mother, if she sees that?"

He pursed his lips. "We still have enough evidence to hang her, remember?"

She relaxed. "I'm paranoid about her."

"I can understand that. But she's only a threat if you let her become one. Remember that."

She searched his beloved face. After a minute, she sank down against him with a sigh and closed her eyes. It was the end of the rainbow to be with him this way, to know that she loved and was loved. "All right," she whispered at last.

Audrey came to the wedding, along with Dee and Tim and his mother and sisters and the rest of the K-M staff. Of course, Ivory designed her own wedding gown, another in the growing Crystal Butterfly Collection, and swanned down the aisle with six of Kells-Meredith's best models—*not* including Gaby—as bridesmaids, all dressed in pale pink gowns and big floppy hats. It was a show-stopper; the bridesmaids carried crystal baskets to hold their flowers, and Ivory carried crystal roses tied with white satin bows, for a bouquet. The whole theme of the wedding was crystal,and it didn't lack for press coverage. Curry said later that he'd noticed half the New York media in the cathedral.

After the ceremony, a reception was held at the Wald-orf-Astoria Hotel, and Ivory stood close to her handsome husband with her hand locked firmly in his. When he looked down at her, she felt as if she owned the whole world and everything in it. She loved, and she was loved.

They flew to the Caribbean for their honeymoon and returned to Manhattan after two glorious weeks in a secluded resort in Montego Bay, Jamaica, getting to know each other as they'd never had time to do before.

Shortly after their return, the Crystal Collection won them one of the highest fashion awards and put Kells-Meredith on the cutting edge of couture competition.

Ivory's keen insight into the market had made her as valuable an executive as a designer, and in short order, she was promoted to vice president of design.

She had everything in the world, and on Christmas Eve she gave her husband the most wonderful present of his life: the news that they would be partners in a new enterprise: bringing up their baby.

Epilogue

FIVE years and two children later, Ivory and Curry Kells stood outside the boardroom of Kells-Meredith with expansion proposals for the design office tucked into their respective briefcases. It had been a beautifully successful partnership. Ivory had taken over from Harry Lambert when he was promoted into the hierarchy of Curry's financial empire, and she now had charge of the entire design firm. She still designed occasionally, but the business end of the concern was the most exciting to her. Even more exciting than that was the joy of being able to work from their home in upstate New York, by using the fax and computer hookup via a modem with the office. She needed to spend only two or three days in Manhattan every week. The rest of the time she devoted to her children.

Marlene still lived in Harmony, Texas. She'd married a local man and surprisingly seemed to be changing for the better since her new husband had insisted that she

get treatment for her drinking problem. Sober, Marlene
was somewhat different, but Ivory found it more comfortable to keep her distance. Belittling her daughter
was a way of life for Marlene, even if she was kinder to
her grandchildren. But, like the old axiom, few leopards
ever change their spots.

Ivory and Curry had a relationship that was the envy
of all their friends. Even Audrey had started thinking
about delegating more so that she and her husband could
have a child. It was the influence of her brother and
sister-in-law, she joked. Being a corporate giant was
beginning to pall next to the wonder of playing with
Ivory's children.

Curry just drank it all in, glorying in his intelligent,
loving wife and his two sons. This forthcoming addition
to the family had to be a girl, though, he informed his
wife. He wanted an excuse to go into production of a
line of couture dresses for little girls.

They stood hand-in-hand outside the boardroom,
pausing before they went inside.

"Think we'll win?" Ivory asked her handsome husband.

"Why wouldn't we?" he returned with a chuckle.
"When have we ever lost?"

"There's always a first time. They look formidable."

He pursed his lips and studied her. She was carrying
their third child, and she looked like a dream wearing
a cream-colored silk maternity suit with her logo—the
crystal butterfly—on its pocket. "They'll melt when

they see you," he remarked lovingly. "They always do."

She glowered up at him. "I'm beginning to catch on, you know."

His eyebrows lifted. "Catch on to what?"

"You needn't pretend to be so innocent," she chided. "I have noticed that you wait to call board meetings on major issues like expansion projects until I'm visibly pregnant. This is the third time," she reminded him.

"Well, we need all the edge we can get," he defended himself. He grinned. "Besides, I like showing off the new line. Don't you?"

She laughed. "Yes. But . . ."

The boardroom doors opened. "But, nothing," he said, taking her arm. "Let's go in there and persuade them."

"Cross your fingers."

He smiled with pure delight as he led her toward the waiting board of directors. All it took was one look at their faces to tell him they wouldn't need to count on luck. Ivory saw that expression on his dark face and smiled softly to herself. As usual, he had the advantage.

She walked beside him with her eyes twinkling, remembering other meetings, other victories. Her hand tightened in his as she counted her blessings. He'd said once that all that glittered was not gold, and he was right. The real gold was the joy and wonder of loving and being loved. And it grew brighter and richer by the day.